A Fly in the
Ointment

A Fly in the Ointment

Nathan Leslie

2/19/23

Naomi —
So great to have
you in the
Reston Readings
— gang !!
Keep up the
great writing!

Apprentice House Press

Loyola University Maryland

First Edition

Library of Congress Control Number: 2022950343

Hardcover ISBN: 978-1-62720-465-1
Paperback ISBN: 978-1-62720-466-8
Ebook ISBN: 978-1-62720-467-5

Design by Kamryn Spezzano
Editorial Development by Cat Cusma
Promotional Development by Rachel Brooks

Published by Apprentice House Press

Apprentice
House Press
Loyola University Maryland

Loyola University Maryland
4501 N. Charles Street, Baltimore, MD 21210
410.617.5265
www.ApprenticeHouse.com
info@ApprenticeHouse.com

Acknowledgements

Some of the stories in this collection were previously published in the following journals:

Cimarron Review: "Cucumber Sandwiches"; *Corium Magazine*: "Rocks"; *Mud Season Review*: "A Fly in the Ointment"; *Little Patuxent Review*: "A Concrete Slab"; *The Meadow*: "New Slots"; *Foliate Oak*: "A Straight Arrow"; *Pidgeon Holes*: "Five Visitations"; *JMWW*: "The Caretaker"; *Swamp Ape Review*: "Glory Be to Those Who Choose the Light; *This is What America Looks Like*: "The Hill."

Contents

Leftovers of Leftovers of Leftovers 1

Sticks 15

Rocks 27

Fly in the Ointment 33

I'm Not Finished Yet 45

Concrete Slab 53

New Slots 59

A Straight Arrow 69

A Compelling Interest 79

Cucumber Sandwiches 87

Five Visitations 99

Glory Be to Those Who Choose the Light 107

Good Filth 117

A Little Blood Company 131

July in the Sticks 143

A Fresh Launch 155

The Hill 167

Cascade Falls 175

Scarfers 183

Queen Bee 191

Shards 203

The Caretaker...207

The Lone Caucasian male 215

The Looser...223

The Room of Sun...235

One Toe In 241

Go Ahead...253

A Sordid Boon..259

Acknowledgments...271

About the Author...273

Leftovers of Leftovers of Leftovers

Austin and Carissa didn't know any better. They grew up with the feet of strangers shuffling in their front yard, musty boxes stacked in the kitchen, the odor of dust and ink and cardboard and mothballs. Carissa never thought of herself as sad or downtrodden. She knew that, come weekends, their father would want them up-and-at-em same time as always: 5:30. Three years older, Austin had a bit more perspective. He remembered a time before. It was a hazy, dissolute memory, but a memory nevertheless. He remembered Mom taking him on "strolls"—at least that's what she called them. They would take the path following the creek down to the river, whiffs of skunk cabbage and yellow rod. He wished he could play on a soccer team or go camping with the boy scouts as some of his friends did. His father would never have it.

Austin and Carissa wanted to please their father, Gary, especially since their mother up and "moved on to greener pastures," as he described it. The way his tongue ticked over "pastures" made it sound so alluring. He excelled at shining turds.

So for years Austin and Carissa lugged the tubs of coins and stamps and knives and guns and beat-up baseball cards and paper currency and whatever "special items" their father may have accrued at the dump since the weekend prior. In cold weather they would watch their breath and bundle up and gasp at the weight they carried as their feet crunched through the stiff grass; in summer they'd sweat. That walk out to the street—they carried those tubs alone. For him. Daddy was drinking his coffee, eye-balling them from the window. It was an estate sale! Vintage collectibles! Every weekend. It was never a question of if; they accepted Saturdays as sale day. It was just something they did.

Austin made the mistake of asking if he couldn't be excused from the sale "just this one time." He suffered from a heavy fever and his stomach churned something terrible. Austin explained his reasoning, but his father simply told him to drink a Diet Coke. "You'll be fine." When his father wasn't looking, Austin snuck off to the bathroom—another prohibition. He wanted them front and center. Carissa wondered if he would return them to the days of the bathroom pass. In the bathroom Austin mucked around to bide time.

"We sell more if the whole family is front and center," Daddy said. "Such as it is currently constituted."

"But why?" Austin said this in his feverish state.

"We are a family. People like children and families. It makes them feel positive and encouraging. Families represent the future. All of these are helpful in inducing purchase of collectibles. Which are not *necessary*. Which is what I dally in, so lucky me."

As stated, their father believed Austin and Carissa to be primarily symbolic in function. They were there to help set up and break down, but mostly he wanted his children there to bolster appearances, or so he said.

"Love you," Carissa said, before she drifted off.

Gary nodded and clacked his tongue and picked some gristle from his teeth with his pinky fingernail.

• • •

Spring and autumn Gary was in good temper. Summer was different. He was not equipped physically or mentally for the ravages of ninety-six and humid. On the day when things changed, this was exactly the weather report: ninety-six and humid with late afternoon thunderstorms. The thunderstorms didn't concern Gary. The heat and humidity did because aside from his comfort level, the hot days saw less of a turnout. Much less. On the real scorchers he was left to smolder alone. In addition, if buyers did come out when it was especially hot, they were early birds—which set a frenetic pace that pressured Gary's nerves and forced his hand early and stripped any relaxation and enjoyment from the overall experience.

He rang the bell at 5:30, as usual. Austin popped up and tugged on tube socks. Carissa resisted the time, but ultimately scuffed into the kitchen once she heard the clink of cereal bowls. Then it was time to set up the tables. Then it was time to lay out the glass cases and arrange the goods and set up the change box and erect the umbrellas (key on a day of this sort).

Carissa wondered. Why can't they leave the knives and paper currency and coins *in* the cases all the time? That would be easier, more efficient. Carissa wondered why they couldn't leave the tables propped up all the time. She knew the ready-made answer to that would be: It's bad for the yard. Dead grass, all that. But they didn't have a lawn, they had dirt. Nobody would care. Carissa wondered why they couldn't wake up an hour later. They always had too much time after the initial burst of preparation and then he'd make them do something pointless and asinine like sweep the rug or vacuum the lawn or fold plastic bags and count quarters.

She was only eight, but her eyes were open. She knew

what was what.

Then nobody turned out for the wares. Their father plastered Estate Sale! signs all over 246 and Williams Drive and all the way down 152, as usual. People would know. But nobody was there. One lousy grandma who was looking for *Hooked on Phonics* for her grandson. That was it. Gary was patient (he considered himself a patient man), but by 10:30 and ninety-two degrees he was ready for some payback for his time wasted.

"Let's pack this shit up," he said.

Austin knew nothing good happened when the profanity started whizzing around.

Austin and Carissa did what they were told.

"Hurry the fuck up," their father barked. "Lazies."

When Carissa dropped the box of stamps her father swatted her on the back of the head. She bent over, picking stamps out of the dusty yard. She felt it coming.

"And blow the dust off those, fuckwad."

They did what he said. When they were done, they hunkered into their room, lights off. Carissa read by flashlight and Austin watched her. He knew something had to change and fast.

● ● ●

The next weekend it was cooler and more people came out.

"You need to *entice* them," Daddy said. Carissa didn't know what that meant, but Austin explained that he wanted them to *greet* the customers, not sulk in the shadows. "You look too sullen," he said. "Nobody likes a frown."

Carissa thought, Can I help how I look? I look how I feel. Carissa and her brother were genetically gifted with widely spaced eyes. In Austin's view, this gave them the resemblance to hammer head sharks. Austin was tall for his age and lanky. This caused his teachers concern, but Austin never questioned his diet of Kraft Mac and Cheese and Granny Smith apples. An apple a day….

Carissa thought she looked weird. Her pale freckles, dirty-blonde hair, and thin lips made her think of an alien species. She felt other-worldly, as if she barely belonged in her body. Perhaps this is what drove their mother away?

The customers mostly approached Gary, but when he was busy, they would ask Carissa or Austin about pricing or condition, or what they might have in the back somewhere.

"Did someone pass away?" an older man in a suit and tie asked. "Forgive me for prying."

"No, it's an estate sale," Austin said.

"Yes, I understand. That usually means someone has passed on. Doesn't it? Did someone die?"

"You can ask my father," Austin said. That was a line Austin and Carissa repeated frequently.

Never, ever say more than you need to, their father demanded.

• • •

When Mom was still with them, she used to head out early with the pickup truck each Saturday. Add to inventory. She'd list all the garage sales, yard sales, estate sales, and rummage sales in the area, buy up anything she thought they could resell. Collectibles did well. Some books. Some clothes. Their mother "had the eye," as Gary called it, and she rarely overspent. Their father wanted Austin and Carissa to develop "the eye," also. He was grooming them for down the road.

Back in those days their father would take the family to

Denny's for dinner if they had a good Saturday. Austin and Carissa haven't been to Denny's since their mother left, except for once on Carissa's 7th birthday. Since Mom left, if they had a good day their father splurged for a Hershey's bar down at the gas station and they split it three ways with their father getting the largest chunk.

Austin knew his father worked harder now. This was a large part of it. His father went out with the pickup truck, just like his mother did before. However, his father couldn't catch the best sales because he held his own at the same time. He could hit the Sunday sales, which he did, but often these were leftovers. On bad days his father's tables felt like the leftovers of leftovers. Daddy would never admit that in a million years though. He believed his house was a treasure trove and that anyone blessed enough to view his valuables was a lucky egg.

One day Austin knew he would have to man the sale with Carissa while their father scoured for more supply. He knew this was training, that his father was grooming him.

Austin couldn't wait to be an adult. He'd leave the state and never come back.

• • •

Austin and Carissa shared a room, always had. It was a small room—a bunk bed, a small desk (which they shared) and a small dresser for each. Austin and Carissa would often recline in their respective bunk beds after lights out and talk.

"I pocketed eight quarters yesterday," Carissa said.

"Really?"

"I wasn't going to but he slapped my head. I didn't do anything."

"You could've gotten more."

"Not without him noticing," Carissa said. "Are you nuts?"

She thought it disconcerting that her brother got the top bunk because what if he was too heavy and it collapsed? She should be up top, if anything.

They sprawled there on their respective bunks, listening to the fan. Austin wondered if she should tell her, if this was the right moment. Timing was everything.

"Know of a place," Austin said. "I think we can get there pretty easily."

Carissa got it. She was with him, always was. Carissa just wasn't sure about the particulars.

"How long?"

"Half a day." He told her there were a few keys: the bikes, making sure they got up early and didn't wake him, packing food early.

"We'll need some dough," Carissa said. "We'll need it for food."

"Okay, but not a lot. If he catches us…I don't want to end up in a ditch."

They knew he would be breakneck and feverish.

They agreed to snag about ten silver coins—enough to last a while, but not enough to provoke continual wrath if they were caught.

"I'm worried, Aus," Carissa said. "I can't pedal that fast yet."

That's why we leave early, Austin suggested--when he's sleeping. His Sunday mornings.

They planned on a week later.

• • •

The day before was a "big success." Daddy was in a good mood and sales were brisk. In the afternoon he napped on the sofa in front of the race and when he was out they began packing: tuna fish and crackers and pears and cheese and bottles of water. Carissa unlocked the case and grabbed the silver coins she didn't think he'd readily notice—the Franklin half dollars and Jefferson quarters especially. He wouldn't do a full count of those.

Austin hardly slept that night, but Carissa did, dark birds swooping down on them in her dreams as they pedaled the open road. Birds merged with shadows and seeped upwards, back into the sky.

"Let's go," Austin said. "It's 5:30." The same time their father had them rise and shine on Saturdays. Austin didn't want to help him a whit more. Still, a dark spot lingered in his gut. He was nervous.

They pedaled as fast as they could north on 216. Luckily, the road was flat and empty, and after five miles of this Austin and Carissa took the bike path that lead down to the river and along it for eighty miles up to Gillard and Festown and beyond. It was still dark, only a smudge of sun below the horizon. Austin carried the food and water on his back and pedaled in front. Carissa looked behind her shoulder every five minutes.

Dank water lapped against the shore as they passed and sunbeams leaked through the canopy. A box turtle lounged in the grass. Carissa watched a heron lift off from the shore over the water, startled by their squeaky wheels. Sticks and clusters of leaves littered the path from previous thunderstorms.

They paddled for miles—past farms and the trailers in the low lying parts and over trestles and wooden plank bridges.

"Are we close?"

"Yes, we are. It's over past the next trestle."

And they pedaled past, old couples taking their morning

walks and saw deer leap into the woods from the trail. They pedaled past tall grasses and all manner of raggedy wildflowers and skunk cabbage stinking sweetly.

Austin led them off the trail and down the gravel incline past a "No Trespassing" sign and to the barn. The barn sat ten feet from the river and the door was open.

They leaned their bikes down.

"Isn't this somebody's barn?"

"I don't think so," Austin said. "I've been by here a thousand times with Ken and we've never seen anybody." Ken was their older cousin on their mother's side.

They ate crackers and cheese and drank water and fell asleep in the cool places in the straw.

• • •

Two days later and nobody had found their way to the barn.

"See, it *is* abandoned."

They heard motorboats on the river, lawn mowers off in the distance and a few bikers churning up on the trail, but otherwise they didn't see a soul.

Mostly, Austin and Carissa rested. They felt wrung out and relieved both. But Carissa felt too paranoid to be utterly relaxed.

They were almost out of food already. Austin said he knew there was a store five miles back up the road, but it meant leaving the safety of the bike trail and sticking their necks out just a bit, but just for a bit. Carissa handed him the money.

"I'll go. This way if he's out there looking for us, he won't know where you are."

But Carissa wanted to go with him. She was eight and the thought of being alone in a barn ten miles from home felt terrifying.

They biked up the path and then the road itself towards the store. They passed raspberries and honeysuckle and birch trees leaning over the path and dangling limpid branches over them. They biked over the gravel and mud and alone the flat passages leading from the trestles downriver.

On the road Austin felt a sense of menace and dread and he wondered if he made a mistake. Perhaps they should have stayed in the barn, let the hunger burn in their bellies. Perhaps they should have biked further away. These thoughts seeped into his consciousness.

A mile down 201 Carissa saw the red Ford Pickup. It rose over the hill and barrelled in their direction.

"The truck!"

"Crap," Austin shouted.

They hit the brakes and leapt from their bikes. However, at this juncture of the road the foliage was thick and knotted and by the time they found a point of entry into the brush and away from the road, their father was already on them.

"You little fucks," he shouted, snagging Austin first, pushing him face down, then hog-tying him and dropping him in the grass. Carissa clawed at Gary's back.

"Aus!" Carissa shouted. "Get off him!"

Gary grabbed her by the arm and tossed her into the cab first. He led Austin by the hair.

"Right in you go now."

Locked the door.

Carissa was screaming, but Austin knew it was helpless. The more they struggled the worse it would get later.

Daddy ran over their bikes on the shoulder, then backed up over them again for safe measure. The frames were crushed.

Austin watched with horror.

• • •

It was difficult being a single parent. Gary never asked for this. When he and Kara tied the knot, it was "for better or worse." It was "till death do us part." What happened to those vows? She wasn't a woman of her word is what happened, Gary thought. It was good at one time, not as much later. That's not a vow. This was a pattern. People constantly abandoned him, cutting out on the world to appease their own best needs. Mom, Kara, all assortments of friends and neighbors. People were an eternal disappointment.

Yes, he wasn't always the most faithful person in the world. There were a few skanks he got to know in one form or another, but it was devoid of meaning. Why should that count?

That's what Kara couldn't seem to wrap her head around. What made him mad was the high moral standard. He didn't expect her to be perfect, just duty-bound. Why did she expect him to be so?

In the years since she left, she called only a hand-full of times—each with a request—not a demand—to speak to her children.

"I know I gave that up by what I did, but I still miss them. They're mine, also."

"Don't ask again," he said.

Inevitably they'd squabble and she'd hang up on him or vice versa. He knew she loathed him.

He never asked to raise two kids by himself. It was too much to ask and he wasn't equipped.

When he called his mom over to help out, Austin and Carissa would complain and say all she wanted to do is watch television and eat donut holes.

"You don't get a say," Gary would shout. "Not no more." He had to be forceful or they'd run the house. Somebody had to be in charge. It wasn't going to be them, he knew that.

• • •

Austin knew he wouldn't kill him. He trusted in the blood connection, at some base level. Plus, he knew he didn't mess up that bad. Austin was sure his father was disappointed and angry, both—and filled with righteous indignation and vengeance. But he knew he wouldn't actually *kill* him. It would end soon though, in some other way. Had to.

Carissa just wanted to sleep. Really that's all she wanted. She couldn't listen to her brother moan in agony any longer. She couldn't listen to the slap of fist to skin. Instead, Carissa curled beneath her blanket and retreated. What else could she do?

They were tied down to their respective mattresses— Austin in the top bunk, Carissa on the bottom bunk. He left them each a filthy Big Gulp of water with a long straw. Austin spilled his attempting to reach it and the water seeped into the mattress. Carissa could reach hers, but she drank most of the water in two hours and then had to pee something fierce.

Gary felt no pity, no remorse. He wanted them to suffer. Then he wanted them to remember. Ungrateful wretches.

Austin wanted the pain to end. He wet himself. Carissa did the same—twice. Austin realized this was just more work for him. No matter what, he'd have to clean it up.

• • •

"I'm going to untie both of you. Then I'm going to feed you."

"We don't care," Austin said. "You're the world's worst

father. The *world's worst*."

"This is nothing. You two run off again, I'll smash your stupid heads in. How's that? I don't care."

Carissa and Austin looked at each other, watched him. Gary untied them. Carissa and Austin embraced, stayed that way, coiled into each other.

• • •

Austin and Carissa ate hamburgers and salad and banana pudding. It was Friday and their father said he needed them for Saturday. He said he had some new product and that he received a spate of interest from online postings.

"We need to get organized."

Gary had Carissa consolidating the stamps into small baggies, sorting books (classics) alphabetically, and polishing the silver to catch and retain eyes. He had Austin collating the wrinkled and stained baseball cards from the 70's, polishing knives and guns.

"See, I trust you with these, even after."

Austin did what he was told.

"Our mattresses smell like pee," Austin said. "Can you do something? I might mention the whole thing to my teacher when I go back. Then you will see what happens."

Gary eyed him and Austin looked off. He listened to his father trudge back through the living room and back into their room. This was a sign. He mumbled something about never going back to school if he could help it, but Austin couldn't make out the particulars.

In the morning, Austin and Carissa had to wear sunglasses. Their father said that he didn't want any questions and if anybody asked, just tell them: "I have a condition."

He was right. The "estate sale" was the busiest ever. Austin hunched in a lawn chair for most of it, unless someone needed help. Mostly his father fielded the questions, sold the collectibles. By noon he made $300. Austin and Carissa could have felt better if he took them to Denny's. It was Chef Boyardee and frozen spinach and entertain yourself with cartoons until I'm ready. Goddamnit. Then I'll take you for a Hershey bar. Just a regular one too, nothing special. That's what you earned, nothing special.

Austin slept hard that night, and so did Carissa. But before that, they whispered.

"What now?"

"I don't know," Austin said.

They listened to the crickets. They listened to the cicadas. Austin swore he could even hear the mosquitoes whine. It reminded Austin of the two days of peace.

"Can we find new wheels somewhere?"

"I don't know," Austin said.

"We might have to wait."

They listened to each other breathe. They were alive. Things could be worse. Carissa heard the faintest smile, which told her all she needed to know. They would have another shot. It might take some doing, but this would end. She had to believe this.

"I don't know," Austin said. "It's tough."

"Yeah, it's tough."

Sticks

Nobody liked Moo-nica, but the Quadrant found her particularly Moo-ey. The Quadrant was me (Katy), Teresa, Sylvia, and Todd. We lived at Harvest Basket that summer, situated deep in the brambles, upstate. My memory is moss. The woods were dark and spectral and they made me think of Hansel and Gretel or Red Riding Hood—breadcrumbs and capes. Perhaps this sounds melodramatic, but our 'rents weren't visiting until August, so that was par for the course.

Harvest Basket was a stick camp; our parents decided we had one brand of food malady or another (pica, anorex, allergies, whatev) and they wanted us to *fall in love* with food all over again. Or at least they wanted us to consume food. We were "sticks" they said. They knew nothing.

Teresa came from Nebraska and she had an ashen complexion, almost-white blonde hair, but she could peel your head off with her acid tongue. She picked at her arms and the resulting little bloody scabs made it appear as if she was a heroin addict or had a run-in with a mosquito farm. Sylvia said her parents told her she was anorex, even though Sylvia didn't think she was. She was normal and easy to like, though she had bony jutting shoulders and ears a bit too droopy and large for her head. Todd was a twit and we didn't care for him—nobody did—but he mostly ate dirt and bark, and his father had given up on him, so we felt a kind of foot-dragging pity. I watched Todd's father shake his head and hang back in the shadows on "meet and greet day." Todd was the only boy in camp—though he was an object of odd affection and curiosity. I just didn't like food—it grossed me out and I didn't like putting it in my mouth. Nothing in my mouth. Except water or juice. And I especially hated listening to the sound of other people (my sister especially) chewing. That revolted me. It was a "phase," my mother said. It would've helped if she wasn't always dieting herself. The nuts and figs diet—that does not work.

Moo-nica was new to Harvest Basket, having just arrived two weeks after the rest of us. That was one obvious strike against her. Another was the fact that she wasn't skinny at all—at least not to me. Not like the rest of us and nobody but nobody in the Quadrant thought she was sick. "She's no farking stick," Teresa barked. "And I heard she had two pounds of candy in her luggage. Isn't that farked up? Isn't that grounds for *instant* kick-in-the-ass dismissal?" Teresa was on a "fark" kick. "Sex-ay," was the word of the week prior. "Sex-ay!"

"I want to shake her fatty belly fat off," Todd said. "Fatty Moo-nica."

But she wasn't fat really—she was normal looking in all respects—brown hair, puffy little groundhog cheeks, missing two teeth up top. What were her parents *thinking*?

So we hatched a plan.

But the problem was we rarely had a chance to talk as a full Quadrant. They kept us busy with so many small group doings, we were constantly separated and in motion—kayaking, volleyball, capture the flag, wallyball, rope obstacle course, climbing the tree, canoeing, archery. They were trying to create the need in us for food by sheer nutritional depletion. After all that work, we'd eat *anything*!

Plus, when we weren't engaged in sporty-nature stuff

they had us watching films (which we suspected contained subliminal "EAT" messages), plays, campfire BS sing-alongs. Everything "food positive." Friendly brainwashing measures. Aren't all brainwashing measures friendly, on the surface?

There was no such thing as an unplanned minute.

In the meantime Moo-nica was always there, just there, making us feel like bigger freaks than we already were.

It was Teresa who came up with the wristband strategy. We all had tons of these things—they were trendy and we could easily get a baggie of new ones from pretty much any other girl in camp whenever we wanted (well, except for Briana, who liked to chomp on synthetics—plastic, rubber, pleather—so you had to evil-eye her). Plus, we could vary the wristbands to mean any number of things. So the Quadrant were all garnished with multiple bands up and down our arms—so much so we looked like Incan soldiers from some old textbook. Orange, red, blue, red, orange, yellow, green—up and down both arms. It was delightfully confusing.

Our plan was to take Moo-nica out on a canoe ride during a "relaxation ceremony" (Wednesdays, after dinner). We would befriend her with jokes and niceties, paddle her out to the interior of the lake, near Mount Island—really just a little boulder in the middle of the lapping water that jutted up about fifteen feet. Then we'd push her out of the farking canoe. She'd swim to Mount Island for safety and we'd paddle back, laughing at the poor, poor plight of the normal girl—welcome to stick-hood, Moo-nica. It would all be fine. They would see her or hear her and go fetch her with their little fancy power boat and we'd snarf in our cereal in the morning and move on. And she wouldn't say a thing because she'd be quaking in her normal (non-stick) boots.

We used our wristbands to communicate the hows, whens, wheres—who would get the boat ready, where we would divert attention, where we'd rendezvous, how we'd split off afterwards. Yes, we were mean and barbaric, but also organized—for kids our age. There was a reason we stuck together. Yellow, red, blue, red, yellow, green, blue, red. In that order and all was peachy.

So, just as we finished eating, Todd started chatting up Moo-nica, per the strategy. He pretended to carry a heavy crush on her (part of me thinks it wasn't all make-believe, knowing his wiles) and then, with a deliberate-but-meaningful pause, Todd told Moo-nica that he has some friends that he'd like her to meet. In talking her up, he discovered her hobbies and interests and would play on these, as well as her sympathies, to suss out what, to her, might seem interesting/worthwhile. If she liked houses, he'd tell her there was a gorgeous mansion on the island. If she was into gymnastics, he'd tell her there's a ton of old equipment on the island left there by a former Olympian. If she liked the circus, he'd tell her escaped clowns and trapeze artists are hiding out on the island (that would be an obvious stretch and might result in a credibility cave-in). Once we rendezvoused, he'd throw out the code word then spell out the hobby/interest by adjusting his bands appropriately and obviously, but without calling attention to himself. Fine line.

I was waiting with Teresa and Sylvia at the boat launch paranoid as fark. Ms. Kitty or Mrs. Bob would be on guard, neon green flashlights in hand and glow-in-the-dark baseball caps tipped jauntily askew (as if they weren't taking it too seriously—they were). Luckily for us, everyone was at the fire pit in full relaxation ceremony mode. It was all very self-conscious, fey and completely artificial. We hated these sessions as if they were demonic fire ants crawling around our nether regions.

We could hear the sluuuush sound of rain sticks and then the light bongo drumming that followed from where we crouched under the magnolia tree.

Here's the thing though: I liked Moo-nica. When she showed up, Todd trolling along behind her, I immediately realized that if I had to pick one of the two to ostracize from the Quadrant it would be Todd, not Moo-nica. She was far prettier up close and in person. She also asked soft, polite questions about each of us and cocked her head gently, as if she really cared—she seemed interested and concerned and filled with positivity and feeling and not the fake kind promoted by the counselors, but rather the real kind that emanates from the generosity of spirit of a true-to-the-core good person. I could almost look beyond her normalcy.

I hated *myself* at that moment. She was too nice and I realized I had to block that out quickly.

"How do you like it here?" I asked. I expected full-bore complaints and excuses and perhaps even some weepy, homesick nostalgia (common as crabgrass). Instead, she said: "Oh, it's fun. Everyone has been so kind to me and they don't have to be. I mean, I know I'm not perfect. We are all here for a reason. I heard horror stories about sleep-over campus, but it's a delight. Really."

They weren't pangs, they were bolts of guilt. I just tried to remember the Quadrant. The purity thereof.

"Do we have an anchor?" Todd said anchor was the "code word." Then he started arranging his bands in such a way that it was signified "art." She was into art also. I knew, but then I was supposed to make-believe to not know. I didn't give it away.

All five of us were in the canoe—far too many and the canoe seemed overly wobbly and extremely unstable from the outset, as if we were floating on rocks, not water. But regardless, we pushed off into the darkness. The obscurity was all encompassing, especially with only a thin sliver of moon up above on a cloudy night.

Todd did most of the talking—elaborating on the massive carved statue on the other side, not visible from our side of the mainland.

"Sarah Vanderbilt Vaughn was a famous early twentieth century artist—somewhat forgotten today." Sylvia and Teresa rowed. Teresa scowled at me—at least I think it was a scowl. I wasn't sure why and I started manipulating my bands to find out—yellow, blue, purple, black. Nobody could see them anyway. Why didn't we think of this? The night.

"Was she related to the other Vanderbilts?"

"I'm not sure what you mean."

"It's a very famous family—"

"Oh, yes—of course. She was, but only slightly. She was a cousin—distant, on one side."

"Cousin of-----?"

"I forget. Anyway, what matters is the work, isn't it? Vaughan constructed these amazing statues out of natural materials, right on the spot—she rarely took material out of its natural setting. 'The culture of artificiality,' she called it."

"Fascinating," Moo-nica said. "Really, really fascinating." Sylvia looked as if she might yack at any minute. For a moment I wasn't sure if the canoe ride was our dire purpose, or the other thing.

So we headed towards the dumping point—not too close

to the island (the lake was so shallow there, we guessed she could jump right back into the boat) but not too far off to put her in real danger. As we got closer Todd mentioned the second code word "mosquitoes" and we braced the sides of the canoe on either side, readying ourselves for the push-off. I had my fingers crossed at this point, that it would fail. I wanted to warn Moo-nica. But I didn't. Instead, I provided the diversion.

"Would you look at that, Monica!" In my mind I imagined a flying purple mongoose.

I kneeled forward. Moo-nica did too. "Look over there," I said, pointing.

At this Todd gave her a quick little shove and over she went, straight onto her belly—she slapped the water. But her shoes caught the lip of the canoe as she was tumbling over, almost taking all of us with her.

"Let's go!" Todd said. Sylvia and Teresa reluctantly picked up their oars and pushed us off back towards the mainland.

"Katy," Moo-nica said from the water. "I can't believe you'd go along with this."

She was treading water, which made me feel somewhat better, knowing she could survive. Otherwise, I would throw myself off a farking bridge, I know that. We pivoted the canoe away from her.

"Just swim to the island," I said. "Somebody will come and get you."

"That's right, starve for a while, fat ass," Todd said. "You've been got. 'Stick,' my ass." He was laughing into his hand.

Even Teresa said that was over-the-top, like some kind of silly villain from the old *Batman*.

She asked if they shouldn't just let her back into the canoe, point being made.

But we had already paddled off, leaving Moo-nica bobbing in the water. I could hear her crying.

"But I can't swim," she said. At least that's what I thought her say. Then again perhaps it was the water slapping the boat. My mind plays tricks on me, I know it.

Then we were out of range in the dark, paddling through the still, dark water. My stomach was jelly and I felt it curdling with stomach acid. I dipped my hand into the water. It felt thicker and colder on the way back.

We didn't say anything for a while.

"You think she'll be okay?" I asked. "Right? She'll be fine?"

"Jesus, what are you her mother? Yes, she'll be fine," Todd said. "The water isn't deep." You know Miss Kitty will be out there lickity-split."

"How will she know where Moo-nica is? We can't rat ourselves out."

"Trust me. Take it on faith. She's fine, Katy.

I wasn't so sure. I felt like I was going to farking pee my pants.

• • •

That night was rough. I barely slept and when I did (if I did) I was three quarters of a mind to race off to the boat launch and go rescue Moo-nica. But I was a coward—I simply didn't want to get caught.

I kept imagining her drowning, crying and babbling about how disappointed she is in me as she went under.

I nervously played with my wristbands.

I could hear the counselors shuffling around the B lodge, trying to find Moo-nica—calling out. Then they were inside— flashlights and whispers. I laid frozen, my arms pinned under the scratchy blanket, trying not to give myself away, trying not to breathe. I lay there sweating.

In the morning the missing camper bells were ringing and Todd shot us the evil eye—don't you dare say a word. He flashed orange, black, red, orange on his wrists: split up, don't be seen together. I didn't care about getting caught any more. I just wanted Moo-nica back safe. Otherwise, I'd never eat another bite for the rest of my life. I was sorry—five seconds from blurting out the truth when Sylvia beat me to it. That always happened to me.

"She's on the island!" Sylvia said.

"Idiot," Todd hissed.

The counselors ran to the boats. Their power boats in particular.

We were twisting our wrist bands like nobody's business—signs flashing like nobody's business. We were toast.

The other kids were screaming at us and a few threw sticks at Todd, and he got into it with the girls—he wasn't afraid to push and shove and pull hair, but Miss Marcie broke it up and took Todd by the ear to the kitchen.

He ratted all of us out—Sylvia, Teresa and me. He even told Miss Marcie I was the ringleader, though I'm not sure she believed that. The counselors called our parents. It was a scene.

Luckily Moo-nica *was* okay. She didn't drown, somehow. Otherwise I'd be relating this tale from prison, and that, surely, wouldn't cure my food issues. The counselors found her on the islands sitting there with her chin in her hands, as if she were routinely waiting for a school bus. She was dripping wet, of course, and shivering.

"I never found the statue," she said—this according to Ms.

Kitty, who liked me despite it all.

Moo-nica made me feel even worse, however, by handling it with grace. She didn't say anything to me when she returned, but she also wasn't hateful about it—which pissed me off. If I were in her shoes I would've been on a mission. She nodded to me and smiled and breezed on past me as if nothing happened. As if I wasn't an accomplice to a near drowning. *Her* near drowning.

Our parents were forced to take us home right away— which for the Quadrant was actually a quasi-reward on one level (we wanted out of there big-time, anyway). But the wrath of our parents was deep and wide—and seemingly never-ending. I was not to speak to any of the Quadrant members; I had to work off all the money my parents lost; I had to write a long letter of apology to Moo-nica (which I didn't mind doing, frankly, and we even exchanged a few more letters after that, though they petered out when we returned to school), but worst of all, I had to cook dinner every night—for what seemed to be a year.

• • •

In an odd way this last punishment may have "cured" me of my aversion to food—I had to make food seem enticing for someone else: I may have even bought into it myself.

Later that summer I cut up all of my wristbands into little pieces. I dropped the pieces in a grocery bag and buried it in the backyard when my parents were off seeing a matinée. The Quadrant never spilled the beans about the wristbands, but I could never wear them again.

Oddly, it took weeks for the skin tone on my lower arms to catch up to the rest of my body. Even today, many years later, I can't bring myself to wear bracelets or bangles and I distrust anyone who wears them—as morally loose and malevolent. I am married. I am seemingly "well-adjusted" with a bevy of friends, a hobby (biking), and two boys. Strangely, I eat like a "normal" person now though and actually I could use a month or two of dieting. It would do me good.

Rocks

We're in the scrub. That's what McGhee calls it. McGhee's prosthetic clicks on the stibnite, the orthoclase. We're manning the booth. If you can call it a booth.

Druids come and go, children of flower children. In the scrub everything is hybridized—cars, tents, contact lenses. It will rain someday, and when it does, it won't be purple.

We foster belief.

We sell hope to hopers.

They come, buy our Brazilianite and morganite and typed instructions for healing. This before or after the reiki sessions. This before or after the happy pills. We're only there for one reason. Don't go inside, I tell myself. I'm my own guru. My shit life has me kicked. I have about zero confidence at this point. Want to straighten the ship.

They come, they buy. Shaved heads, loose puce gowns, pot-belly pigs in cribs, rolling their own dope. They are inside a state of being.

At night we roll down the windows, listen to the bongo sessions. Even in the air-tight cabana-on-wheels we can smell the pinyon and mesquite burning. And the more fragrant smoke. We can hear the chanting. Jasmine sleeps with her fingers in her ear holes. If she had her way she'd be out there amongst them.

· · ·

These Gotham children won't question. It goes against the

whole spirit. McGhee closed his eyes. He does this to think, like a computer's whirring. Tapped a cold finger against his forehead twice.

"I've never been so far from the ocean," he said.

McGhee has a sea fetish. Says it's the only thing which can rejuvenate. What we'll do is take the way you see the salt water, transfer that to rock—make a buck.

We were twenty large in the red. House foreclosed. Running out of ways to shuffle dough from one piece of plastic to the other. American way.

The cabana was our way of consolidating. Still is.

• • •

At the rock pit. We lug milk crates. We lug burlap sacks. We lug shoe boxes. All quartz, all quartz McGhee said. He should know—he took the introduction to geology class at the community college. He's the smart one. He's got the pedal to the metal. I'm just along for the ride.

Which is why I call him fingers.

It's not about his prosthetic.

He's got his paw in the maw. Me—I'm trying to see the maw. Get past my cloudiness.

• • •

But back to the quartz. It was a find. Different colors, stripes. Who would know? Who would care? We were in Clarke County. Tuesday morning. The park officials were sleeping in, fishing, drinking their morning Joe. Whatever it is they do.

Victimless, I said.

McGhee clicked. We gathered, even Jasmine. She drove us off, quartz clacking behind us.

• • •

The extra drag mileage-wise would be worth it, I told him. "You think too much," I said.

He didn't like it when I judged. McGhee said judgment is the essence of despair. He may or may not be right about that.

He raised his eyebrows. Problem was McGhee never held a real job. Laundromat operator stock boy. Bus boy. Garden center "associate." How we ever owned a house in the first place is a miracle. Beyond me.

Well, I was assistant manager at Great Reads. Used books. Then they went under.

Fingers was always coming in, using my quarter-off discount. Never graduated high school, but somehow he manages to read Santayana. *Finite and Infinite Games*. *The Critique of Pure Reason*.

He doesn't talk about his best years. On the water. Living on the dinghy was "by choice," he says. His skin still tastes of salt and brine.

Living on the dinghy was his way of being homeless, I think. The uncounted homeless. Boat people.

Jasmine is his. Boat people include boat women, apparently. Or mermaids. She has long, bushy eyebrows. I count her as mine anyway. Sweet thing.

• • •

McGhee's conscience is bothering him, he says. Which is why he's up and thumping around. Nursing a plastic cup of skim milk. Chewing on pretzels. Wakes me up, too. Jasmine sleeps in the cab, so she's probably okay.

"I don't know," he says. "What if somebody calls us on it?"

He's not looking at me. He's folding up the pretzel bag. Sourdough.

"We've already unloaded how many?"

"Maybe a third," he says.

"We're on the way," I say.

He mumbles something about no harm in calling it quits. Giving the rest away. No skin off our backs.

This would be fine if it weren't for the bloodsuckers, I tell him. We can't be so choosy now. He shrugs and pulls at his hair. Says it's an anti-baldness preventative. Sounds equally suspect about that.

● ● ●

Rocks. His bag of rocks is opaque. He can likely relate to the festival-goers in search of their inner-dharma. I don't even know how old he is for sure. Not 100%. I see flecks of gray in his stubble, though. I'm not blind.

We have them labeled. Uranimite. Nickeline. Purpurite. Diaspore. They're in boxes. We've typed up "healing powers" on small slips of paper. Used a Kinkos back in Louistown.

We sell a bunch of them. For days the hippies snap them up, juggling rocks in their hands.

Two mornings later I'm drinking guava juice, nibbling on wheat toast. Jasmine is just rubbing her eyes. A guy in a leather jacket thumbs through our selection. After ten seconds he snorts.

"Who are we fooling here?" he says. "You all should be locked up is what I think."

"What?" I say.

"Yeah," he says. He picks up a rock in the sanidine box. He holds it out flat in his palm.

"I teach science in a middle school. I don't know much about geology. I do know, however, that this is quartz. All of this is," he says. "It's pretty basic."

I'm looking out over the scrub. It's ugly land really. Grey and brown. No mountains. No real vegetation. No color. So much for the serene beauty of the desert.

I'm glad McGhee is inside. If I'm going to eat crow, might as well do it without embarrassment.

"You don't want to do that," I say.

The man is shouting that we're "crooks," "scam-artists," "not even scam-artists, just scammers." He's going tent to tent. He's waking them up. Jasmine and me, we look at each other. We don't even pack up the rocks. We just fold up the canopy and peel off. Play it safe.

• • •

Jasmine's driving. I'm in the passenger seat, chin in hand. Watching the brown scrub turn scrubbier.

I'm wondering how I arrived at this point.

I'm watching dry lightning flash some fifty miles off.

When Bill left me, I understood. It wasn't working out. Or that's the story we agreed on. I wonder where Katherine might be at this point. What became of the split-level under the maples. The oak bedframe. The photo albums. All of it.

McGhee claps his prosthetic on the vinyl seat, pulls himself up front. He sits in the middle. He'll never gloat. He knows. There's nothing to say. We're all picking up our own pieces.

"Where are we headed?"

Jasmine hits the spray then the wipers. The windshield is gummy with dust.

"South and West," she says. He closes his eyes. He's probably thinking of the gulf. I don't know. We won't make it that far south, I think. Hope not.

Fly in the Ointment

Happiness is a place called Fawn Lake. Happiness is the rose-laden trellis by the pool, the gentle burbling of the hot tub; the pool dangles over the lake improbably. The sun glows delightfully—neither too hot nor too distant. Perfect sailboats dot the lake, their sails blowing in the ever-so-slightly wafting wind that blows through the leaves of the old-growth forest remnants we have preserved just for the visual delight of the Fawn Lake community. I don't know sailboats, but they are always there. Sailing. I am there still.

We live for the perfect choreography of elements. We live for the amenable amenities, for the smiling children, teeth sheening in the honey-glazed sun.

A slowly idling motorboat on Fawn Lake churns by me as I sit in the hot tub. I dangle my toes into the cascade of bubbles. I feel the warmth of jets on my tender Achilles (I can relate to the nomenclature). It is early still. Coffee steams next to me on the shelf made just for this purpose. Black and perfect. I am alone.

I have my checklist on hand, ten feet away. My mental list is even more extensive. If I complete it on any given day, I cycle back through and begin at the top. These are rare days. Frequently my checklists—mental and otherwise—exceed my physical ability at this point. I wish this were not so. I overshoot because I care. I am on the downward slope.

• • •

Abigail is my friend. We had known each other for years, since her family lived a block up on Crestview Circle. She had wisdom and maturity beyond her years, and she made it patently known that she understood this to be true. She also referred to me as Big Daddy. Her own father passed on a decade ago—tragic beach drowning. Made the papers.

I received a message from Mr. Smythe. He is Chair of the Board (COB), a rotating position.

"Grover—please come see me at your earliest convenience. No urgency."

"No urgency" coming from Mr. Smythe usually *did* mean urgency. One did not receive messages from Mr. Smythe if they were not urgent. Urgent was his milieu.

Abigail was my friend. A friend for life.

• • •

I enjoy order. I suppose I have always enjoyed order. I am orderly. I appreciate a clean row of bricks, a well-painted wall, a crisply ironed white shirt.

Seventeen years ago I began this journey into caretaking. Seventeen years ago Fawn Lake was all old-growth forest, but I was elsewhere. I was a previous incarnation. Early on I was positioned at a place in the sky—a place with space, a place where I needed to maintain a certain decorum. I handled the refreshments. I made sure everyone was hunky-dory. There is nothing wrong with a male airline attendant. It is a valued and worthy position in society. Nothing to be ashamed about.

However, did I desire a life of constant maneuvering? Did I desire a life of continental breakfasts and priceless beds and constant time adjustments? Not particularly.

Instead, I found myself at home—unemployed, sacked, laid-off. The great airliner went under. I was adrift.

· · ·

Abigail was a good help. When I did Sweeping the Green, she'd pick the pine needles up one at a time. When I did Deadheading the Rose Garden, she'd bring her own pair of scissors. When I did Rolling the Courts, she got the lines. She especially liked to help me with Polishing the Knobs and Cleaning the White and Pocked.

There were other Fawn Lakers, of course. I was one of many. Abigail, if I could speak for her, liked the way I jested and told stories and she admired the care I took with each step of the job, with each task. When she was eleven or twelve, she'd follow me around and her parents didn't mind. They trusted me. They knew where I lived (behind the retaining wall which separated the tennis courts from the woods).

"Come over for supper," her parents would tell me. "We have pork loin and grilled zucchini. There's no way we can eat it all."

"Oh, you should see what I have in the fridge! My wife is going to town for me tonight."

If only it wasn't a fib—the dinner and the wife. I was all too married. Bethany had her room; I had mine. We were comfortable together. We spoke often enough.

· · ·

The board liked "The Code," a way of being as much as anything else. The Code was the Ten Commandments of Fawn Lake. One had to follow its ethical strictures.

Since I had been employed at Fawn Lake for years I was "grandfathered in." I had to "pass," but didn't need to suffer the indignity of affirmation or reaffirmation. I was a fortunate man.

The Code was everything.

It governed our lives. Each house had a plaque affixed to a foyer wall.

The plaques shined and dazzled the eye. The golden cursive, the marbled wood (how did they do that?). One could barely look away.

To live on Fawn Lake was to live the Code.

To live on Fawn Lake was to accept the premises of the Code and all it entailed.

• • •

My mother loved me in her own way. My mother's way was not the usual way. My mother's way was the way of tending to orchids and photographing hummingbirds. We had a greenhouse. We had a planetarium on the top floor. My father wanted to make her happy and we were all happy, but my mother was happiest of all.

She dusted with fury. Each morning she dusted. We saw her fluffing the house in this way, applying feather to wood and plaster. In this way the house remained museum-clean.

When my mother put me to bed as a child, she used to tell me stories from her childhood. There was the one where she learned to speak with cardinals—they recited their dreams to her. There was the one where she climbed the town Christmas tree from the inside to affix herself as the ornament. There was the one where she ate frogs for a week on a dare. There was the one where she created a dictionary of smells for her classmates, going so far as to invent new smells, and new words and utterances to describe those smells.

My friends found my mother odd, beyond description.

I loved her despite this, because of this, perhaps.

• • •

Abigail swam in the lake. She dove in from the wall which separated the lake from the pool. As I tended to the coleus and begonias, which I carefully planted along the edge of the wall, she waved up at me and announced which stroke she was in the midst of performing (I was expected to clap and offer copious praise for each). She was particularly interested in learning the butterfly. After attempting it for several minutes, slashing the water, she'd stop and shout: "Mr. Grover, how was *that*?"

"An excellent butterfly," I said. "You can do it even better though."

This added fuel to the fire.

"Okay, I'll try again," she'd say. "This time it's the moth."

Then she'd say she was trying the dragonfly, making up strokes as she went along.

• • •

In the early days I didn't live on Fawn Lake, as they wouldn't permit it. The board drained the lake, as it was, for a time, unseemly. Difficult to believe in retrospect.

I lived on a cabin by the Rust Creek, forty minutes away up in the hills. The cabin was a shack. It had a single bedroom, a room to eat and another to bathe and shit. The stove had two burners and would flicker out on occasion (so would the power). The walls smelled of squirrels. They ran through the rafters at night.

On the drive to and from Fawn Lake, I would watch the trees. They became so familiar I knew the patterns. I knew the gulches, the places where billboards popped up, where telephone wiring crisscrossed the road.

I'd see a woman sometimes. She sat on a stump by the

gravel road that lead to her cabin. She'd sit there slouching in the dark waiting for me to drive by. If I saw her, I'd turn in. I'd seek my refuge. If I didn't see her, I'd drive on home.

Then she died. A tree fell on her cabin and crushed her in her sleep, or so the story goes. She always said she heard voices in the trees. They were poplars, a wicked species. She said the arboreal voices contained evil in them. I try not to think of her any longer, though sometimes I relapse.

• • •

I seek perfection in everything. Certain rug makers, I am told, bury small imperfections in their work as an honor to God. I strive for perfection only.

Some days I would tend to the fly fishing pond. I would rake the outlying edges of the pond until they struck me as the way in which they should look. I would rake and cut the reeds and sticks and leaves so that if someone happened to take a photograph of that exact spot it would capture the image of beauty itself. If it were possible, I would rake the water. I would rake the sky. When I did rake the Parking Lot, Abigail would help.

• • •

Abigail grew. When her family first bought in Fawn Lake, she was six. Then she was no longer six. She was eight. She was twelve. She was fifteen. This began a new pattern—it was a pattern of growing. This began a new Abigail, a new Grover. I was suddenly suspect.

Men and teenage girls are not to be friends. Men and teenage girls are not to associate, outside of limited exchanged. This is just the modern restriction, the barrier. I was expected perhaps to cease contact with Abigail once she developed her womanly parts. Once she developed her womanly parts, she became a precious object. She became glass. I was supposed to look away. But we were friends for life. She saw my soul, made me whole.

• • •

I maintained friendships with members of the board. When I say "friendship" I mean something above and beyond acquaintanceship, which is clearly different. I mean something better. They seemingly offered their respect to me, and I believe I reciprocated. Appearances are always themselves fragile, however.

In particular, I was friendly with Glena and Harvey and a woman by the unlikely name of Silvia Gold (I chastised her parents in my mind, though Silvia said it was a fictional surname—I wondered if she was on the lam). They saw me waxing the trash receptacles or pulling dead leaves from the red maples and they offered glad tidings. Glad tidings were always received with open arms by me.

"How are you, Grover?"

"Mr. Grover, the grounds look divine"

"Our most valuable of all members of our community. You are such a help."

They never said I "worked" for them. I "helped" them. I "assisted" them. I was a member of the Fawn Lake "team."

• • •

By the time she could drive, Abigail had a steady. His name was Rick. On occasion I would, accidently or not, call him "Rich." It was not a conscious decision. He detested "Rich." Abigail seemed to find it funny.

"He's just saying you have money," she'd say.

She was precious and perfect.

"It's not my name," he'd say.

Rick had a head of spikey hair he kept hard and gelled. His face was chiseled and smirky, as if he knew something about me. He liked to arch his eyebrows, to talk quickly. He had six brothers, of which he was the oldest. Rick must have borne the brunt of expectation.

They walked by the road, hands swinging. They glommed by the pool. He kissed her neck by the boxwood I trimmed the day before. I could see them.

"Rich is good," I said. "Nothing wrong with that name."

"I don't like it," he said, stepping toward me. He lifted his shoulders, as if attempting to appear taller.

Live your vacation. Life is your playground.

• • •

If I had a spare minute, I might glance at a book in the lending library. The lending library was inside the clubhouse. The clubhouse was above the pool, above the gym. In the clubhouse everything was polished wood and brass.

We had bestsellers, serious nonfiction, romance. I was never much of a reader, having not finished school myself. Who had the time? But I knew what made sense to me. I could speak.

In one book I read about a man detailing how to dissect a conundrum. First, you identify the problem, he said. This takes the power of observation. Then you confront the problem, which takes courage. Then you break the problem down to its root causes, which takes brains. Then you attempt to piece the problem back together, which takes know-how.

It was something like this.

I remember the book had a bright blue cover, with clouds

and a man standing in the forefront, dressed in a maroon suit. I wish I had that book now.

• • •

I found her in the pool parking lot. She reclined on the hood of her car. It was dark around Fawn Lake. The night was humid and moths thumped against the parking lot lamps. I watched the Wellingtons just walk home from the restaurant. Vickie needed me to help fill a gap in the kitchen, which I was happy to do. I did that sometimes.

Abigail wasn't exactly crying, but her face showed that she had been.

"Mr. Grover," she said. She waved me over. She smelled of Merlot and goat cheese.

I sat on the hood next to her.

I know exactly what had happened. She didn't need to tell me the gory details. She knew I didn't need to hear them, also.

Her breathing was quick and short. Her head was loopy. She sighed and breathed.

I kissed her on the cheek and patted her thigh. That is all. She was a girl. She would be a woman.

"Goodnight," I said. "Go home. Your parents are waiting." "I will," she said.

• • •

What I didn't know was that Rick watched us from inside. The fight had just happened. He skulked about inside, pacing, waiting for her to drive him off, waiting for her to come to her senses.

He saw me kiss her cheek.

It was as innocent as a snail sliding through grass.

When I was confronted by the board, I was shocked. I

had no idea a witness saw that simple, friendly gesture. We are friends. This is what friends *do*.

I had such a clean conscience that I hadn't a clue as to what the board meant.

"You have been charged with indecency," Glen Handard told me.

"According to the Code, this necessitates immediate dismissal. We are sorry and we thank you for your services."

"Apparent improper relations," Sylvia Gold added. Even Sylvia!

I watched the wind twist through the grass. I watched the grass shift in the wind. I watched the smallest dead parts of the grass slough off into the wind, carried off in it.

* * *

I'll spare you the angst.

I have found the city is a good place for me. It took me some time to figure this out.

I don't need to be perfect here. I have two rooms and they are clean enough for me. I vacuum once a week, watching the patterns in the rug appear and disappear as I run the vacuum.

My wife is happier, also. She feels less confined amongst the presence of others. She has friends and activities. Our relationship is better, seemingly.

I thank the board for the improvements. My life has been a matter of small adjustments, only some of which I control. Others are controlled for me, one way or another.

Janitorial work is not a bad way for me to go. The hospital pays me well and I am essentially my own boss. I steer clear of the pediatric ward altogether. Aaron, the new guy, takes care of that. I am eternally grateful.

I often think of Abigail and wonder what has become of

her. On several instances I began drafting a letter to her, my wife asleep in the other room. But I stopped myself, suspecting that it would not find a receptive audience. I crumbled those attempts and buried them at the bottom of the kitchen trash. Instead, I sat in the near-darkness and thought of her and attempted to make this thought visible to her in whatever way I could. I thought of the pool and the lake behind and the gentle breezes and Abigail sitting on the edge of the pool, her feet dangling in the perfect water. Me watching.

I'm Not Finished Yet

Dirk was playing in the baby pool behind us. He yelped—pretending he was a seal clapping for halibut entrails. I tried to tell him seals don't yelp, but I didn't want to explain too much regarding the intricacies of clapping or tail slapping (lest he start in on that, also). Dirk was five at the time. This was way back when.

I reclined there in that clunky piece of shit chaise lounge, our patchy lawn surrounding us. The weeds tickled my ankles. My X reclined next to me—a little circular plastic table in the middle holding my iced-tea, her vodka tonic. It was suffocating, swampy-like. I felt as if I was drowning in the air. My X was humming that insipid Marshall Tucker Band song I didn't even like when it came out. There was no sense to any of this.

We drank too much in those days.

I kneaded my sweaty brow and closed my eyes. I imagined I was on the Alaskan tundra, alone. I've always enjoyed solitude. But when I squinted my left eye open, I was still in Virginia in July. Dirk's squeals were transmuting into screeches.

• • •

I can only blame myself—my nether regions, to be more precise. In retrospect, I fell more in lust with X. It wasn't love, I know that now. She was the filthiest woman I'd ever met and this was exciting to me—more than it should've been. She wore flimsy lingerie; she got off on dirty talk; she was in theory at least, open to threesome possibilities.

Growing up in a conservative church-going household, X was like crack to my dowdy sense of ethics.

I met X at a local restaurant—more a café than an actual dress-up-and -sit-down joint. She was in charge of managing the floor—even though you picked up your orders at the counter (I could never reconcile this contradiction). It seemed a job without real purpose. X had a world class smile, a helmet of platinum blonde hair right out of the Marilyn Monroe handbook. Her lips were full and red and she knew how to move. I couldn't help myself.

I wasn't used to doing anything on impulse—I was a very calculated kid. My X brought out something in me I wasn't even aware of.

By the third of fourth date we were sweaty with sexual intoxication, lunging at each other on the floor like marmosets in heat. Three of four months later we were shacking up. My X was a rich girl (all that heiress bullshit), but I didn't know that yet. She had a sizable trust fund, but it was cloaked behind her intent to live like a "normal person." She was embarrassed by all of it.

I still remember going curtain shopping with X at Kmart, looking at stacks of hideous, cheap curtains—X went right along with the charade.

"Why don't we get these?" X said, pointing to some blue muslin ones. I shrugged. It was fine with me really—what did I know?

"They're as pretty as any of the others."

I didn't know she was playing house. Who does that?

• • •

Living together so early on was a mistake. I know that for certain now. At the time, however, it made my imagination race. I never thought of myself as the kind of guy who would have a smoking hot live-in girlfriend. We could have sex at a whim—there was nothing to it. I was, in my own way, playing house.

Our apartment was a simple one bed-room in a small garden complex. I was in awe of my freedom—a balcony overlooking a man-made lake seemed luxurious. We listened to the faint sounds of water lapping. As we were drinking or fucking we would often hear ducks or geese flapping around. There was this sense that we were living on the edge of some watery world.

• • •

I realized after a month or so with X, however, that dirty talk might be the only kind of talk we engaged in. At meals we were mum, scraping our food around our plates, looking off in the near-distance.

"Sorry, I'm being so quiet," she'd say. "Just tired." This was a regular statement, a factual dictum.

"It's okay," I'd say. "Me too."

We took to watching television as we ate—old episodes of *The Jeffersons* or *Taxi*—something to lighten the sense of dread on the margins of our existence. Something to drown out the silence.

It felt as if we were constantly in a waiting room together. We'd make small talk, but the conversation would never go beneath the exterior. Until later on I didn't know if she was a Republican or Democrat.

I always looked forward to sleep. The one true escape.

• • •

The problem with watching television as we ate was that

our conversations began to revolve around the lives of fictional characters (since our own lives were so dull). At least we agreed on some things, however—no courtroom dramas; *M.A.S.H.* was the best show running. Programs about couples squabbling were difficult to pull off—but then again, what else could be so privately exposed?

Our relationship became painfully normal. She'd work at the café. I was employed as assistant manager of a pet store (I usually came home reeking of gerbil pellets, for some reason). She'd cook some overly processed food—Kraft Mac and Cheese or Rice-a-Roni—and we'd eat it with a glass of cheap wine or a Budweiser. Then we'd drink more after that.

After a year, however, we discovered vitamins. A friend of X gave her a tip on supplements and she became fixated. She'd come home from the health food store with a box of clattering pill jars—fish oil and folic acid and glucosamine. I didn't know what any of that stuff was and still don't.

"If we take all these," she said, "We won't even need food that much. There's a ton of good stuff in these things."

"That doesn't sound healthy at all," I said.

She squirreled her mouth. "Well, what is food really? It's just vitamins and minerals. Why not just cut to the source?"

"Are these vitamins or minerals?"

"Not sure exactly."

"Well, if you're not sure, what's with the grand proclamations," I said.

"Give me a chance to look into all of it, will you? I'm not finished yet."

It's no wonder Dirk turned out like he did.

• • •

Fourteen months after X discovered pills, she gave birth

to our new son. It was oddly exhilarating to me at first—I was impressed by X's fecundity, for starters—and yet I felt absolutely zero connection to Dirk. He was just this product—something emitted from her body, like menses or urine. Only he was a living, breathing, crying, shitting tiny person for which we were suddenly responsible. He was just there causing turmoil.

X and I had a shared interest. We had something to *talk* about. Dirk—he was a question mark.

Except we did little talking—neutrally that is. When we talked we argued. She wanted everything for our son; my position was on the basis of pet store and café—we could only afford so much. This is when I found out about X's financial standing. Or lack thereof.

"Why did you keep this from me for so long?"

She didn't want to talk about it. She said not every aspect of everything has to be verbalized. What's the mystery then?

"I don't want mystery, really," I said. "I want clarity."

"I don't want to hash everything out. You see what happens when we do."

• • •

I don't know to what degree guilt motivated X, but soon after our lengthy financial row X decided that she'd use her "hidden pouch" to settle us in a three bedroom colonial on the leafy side of town. We traded our watery patio for a backyard of pine bowers and an expansive green.

I didn't complain—on one level I was grateful. But at the time—and even more in retrospect—it was emasculating. My wife *owed* me; as a traditionalist, I was unmoored.

If I was a drunkard, this would've been my opportunity to fall off the wagon. At odds with fatherhood, at odds with my exceedingly dull (but pretty) wife, I had little at home to look forward to. Other than the house—which was lovely. The windows were new. The wall-to-wall carpeting gave a hush to every moment. The airy house seemed constantly bathed in light. A gentle breeze seemed to constantly blow.

And yet I was despondent.

At the time, I told myself my misery was only temporary— that soon enough X, Dirk and I would be a real family, rather than a coalition of separate dinky islands. It didn't happen. What *did* happen was that X grew more and more inward, metamorphosing into a shell of her former self. We began eating separately—her and Dirk when they felt the urge. I'd fix myself something quick when I returned from home or scrounge for leftovers.

I maintained an optimistic front. I would spout uplifting clichés. In counterpoint to X's interior withdraw, I became a Pollyanna.

● ● ●

Reclining on the crappy chaise lounge in the middle of the lawn that sweltering day, I knew it was time to make a change. The problem: I was (and still am) adverse to change. I watched the air ripple with heat.

"I don't like plants," X said. She sipped her vodka, keeping her eyes closed. "That's why."

I wasn't sure at first what this statement was in response to exactly. Then I realized—about twenty minutes prior I made a point that we should do something about the lawn's dire state. For our own aesthetics, if nothing else. This was her way, I guessed, of saying "no."

"How can anyone not like plants?"

I sat up. It just seemed inconceivable to me. It was

tantamount to saying, "I don't like life."

"It's pretty easy, really," she said. She threw her arm over her head. "Too much work."

I didn't know what to say. But I knew what to do.

"I'm going to get a drink of water," I said. "Want something?"

She—almost imperceptibly—shook her head. Her hair slashed across her face.

As I walked into the house through the sodden air, I could feel the vile sweat glisten all over my body. Once I set foot in the cool kitchen I poured myself a glass of tap water, drinking it as I walked upstairs.

I pulled a new t-shirt on, slipped into my shoes and grabbed my wallet and keys. I opened the front door and breathed again.

• • •

This wasn't just change. I dropped an atomic bomb on my life. I'm now living in the nuclear fallout.

Deep-sixing one existence, however, does open up the possibility for another one. I not only left my wife and son, but also my job, my house (if I can use that possessive), and all of my things. Sometimes one has to go against one's very nature to find a better way.

I'm back to square one. Thirty-three years old, I'm living in an efficiency above an office supply store. I work at a garden center—answering questions mostly. I've met a younger woman—Kimberly—a barista at a local coffee shop. She can tell me the difference between Sumatran and Peruvian roasts.

I see Dirk once a month and that's plenty for me. I haven't seen X since the day I walked inside for a drink of water.

Kimberly is fascinated by my former life, almost as if she

doesn't quite believe it existed. At night, when she rests in the crook of my arm, I'll tell her stories about X (minus the sexual details). Kimberly is curious. She finds the window into my previous life fascinating. She's also plain, and a bit on the chubby side, but it is okay. Sex—that is something we're easing into. I'm not sure how many more chances I'll allow myself to have.

I don't tell Kimberly about the vitamins. I now have my own, different vitamins. Maybe someday I'll slip into my own skin.

Concrete Slab

It's a humid night and they're drinking warm water on Ed's patio. He wanted a screened-in porch, but his wife never went for it. She's dead now but he's stuck with the patio. Concrete block. Rust spots from something or other. A can of bug spray sits in the middle of the picnic table. They are surrounded by four citronella candles in tiki spears.

"I don't know," Ed says. "It seems too convenient to me. A big honking excuse."

"One man's convenient is another man's—"

"Or woman's," Jillian says.

"Or woman's so and so."

"Honking?" Kyle says. He asks if Ed has ice. Kyle is two years younger than Ed. They're brothers. Corea is Ed's adopted daughter. From Korea. Jillian is her longtime lover. The air is heavy and unsettled.

"I'm not judging," Kyle says, standing up. "It takes a lot to maintain a relationship. With anybody. Period."

Kyle goes inside to get ice. Ed hurt his knee years ago and has to resort to a cane on bad days.

"How 'bout something other than water?" Jillian says.

"Like what? Chocolate milk?"

"Smart tags."

"Like what then?"

"Surprise me."

Corea slaps at a mosquito. Her legs are dotted with bites. She's a dutiful daughter. Her face is flushed—too much time out at the lake? To Ed it looks slightly puffy, fuller than usual.

"This one man I know," Corea says. "I won't say how I know him. I just do. He's maybe fifty-six or fifty-seven. He has three children. He's not what I would call typically handsome. He has a belly. His face is kind of scaly. Maybe pitted—I don't know. He seduces all his daughters' friends. They come over and he hits on them and one thing leads to another."

"Right there? Right then?" Her father says.

"No, later. He works them over big time. He builds them up. He can be very charismatic."

"He must be like Julius-Caesar-charismatic."

Corea would use a different word for "seduces," ordinarily. She doesn't like to curse in front of her father. He doesn't always reciprocate.

"What kind of model is he? You know, for his children and everything?" Jillian has her index finger in a puddle of water condensation.

"I don't know. It can't be good though," Corea says.

Kyle steps back out onto the patio with a slight duck. He has a bowl of ice and a spoon in one hand. A beer in the other. He hands the beer to Jillian. It's already dripping with condensation. It's so humid the ice barely feels cold. Kyle is taller than his brother and always embarrassed of the fact.

"What did I miss?"

"Corea is talking about a pervey pop," Jillian says. "Wait, Corea—you weren't one of the friends, were you?"

"Hahahahahahahaha. Very funny. No. I knew even then that I was more interested in his daughter. I thought he was shiny."

"Nobody *drinks* anymore," Jillian says. "This would definitely be more entertaining with gin."

Ed Glowers. Kyle's on the program; Jillian knows. Ed hates how she just tends to get wrapped-up in her attempts to sound witty.

"So are you saying fathers can't be trusted with other people's kids?" Ed is perplexed. This is coming from his daughter.

"It's just a story I'm telling," she says.

"So there's only one father here, and that's Ed. That's a fact."

Kyle leans forward into the shadows.

"Here's the thing," Kyle continues. "We all had fathers. We know it's a mixed lot. Just like anything else. Our father, for instance. Our father would proclaim he was a "family man." He'd pronounce that shit all the time. But he was getting home from work at 8:30 most nights. The mysterious phone calls. Then that one time—you remember, Ed—that woman showed up. She wanted to 'talk.' Outside in the bed of tulips they're talking. Hashing out some sordid end-of-times. Our mother just ignored all of it."

"At least as far as we could tell. She was a saint."

"Yeah, I'm sure they had it out at other times."

Corea pulls her hair back. She likes the feeling of her hair taut against her skull. Jillian eyes her.

"But what does all this have to do with fatherhood?" Jillian says. "You can diddle all day long and still be a good father."

"Can you?" Corea asks.

Kyle shrugs.

"No," Ed says. "Not really. Let me explain something to you."

He plops two dripping ice cubes into his glass.

"Fatherhood is simple really. It's caring for somebody. Happens to be someone younger than you. Helpless at first, then not as helpless. But basically it's providing for this small person. Offering guidance. ll the other things—the distractions, the affair, the overworking, flaws—all of that; it doesn't even matter."

"So this guy—""It doesn't matter. That's what I think." They sit and listen to the traffic on the highway. They drink their water. Corea slaps at mosquitoes.

Kyle suggests maybe they should go inside.

"It's buggy," he says. "I'm getting chewed up."

Ed shrugs. His face is flushed. Corea looks at him. She wonders. Her mother would know, but she never thought to ask such questions.

They go inside.

Ed runs a load of dishes. He stands over the counter, shifting his weight to his good leg. He doesn't run the air conditioning. Corea knows he won't.

Everyone sweats.

They sit in the living room and Ed bring out two oscillating fans. Corea presses her glass of water to her forehead. Ed sits next to her on the loveseat. Kyle and Jillian are on the larger couch. Jillian sits legs crossed. She's thinking of her father, who she considers a saint. Throughout college she boasted that not once did he ever even spank me. Not even a little smack on the face. Kyle is yearning for a whiskey sour.

"So what did you do then?" Kyle says. He's looking at his brother. Had to be something, otherwise you wouldn't have said anything. Or at least not in that way.

"What is this, a confessional?"

"No, but you said a father's other baggage doesn't matter."

Kyle leans forward, narrows his eyes.

"That might seem true to the father," Kyle continues. "But

what about to the children?"

Ed looks at Corea. He expects a sympathetic shrug, a smile, something. She picks at a dry place on her knee.

"I'm talking in the abstract here. This isn't about me."

"Oh, really, Ed?"

Ed runs his fingers over his teeth, paranoid now. He can't believe his brother is sticking him on the grill. For what? Because Jillian's drinking a beer and he's too much of a fucking something or other? What?

"Do you have something to say?"

"I'm not putting words in your mouth. You're the father."

The fans are dusty. Jillian notices they blow dusty hot air. She can feel sweat balls dribble down her back. Ed stands up.

"I'll be right back."

Ed limps into the kitchen. He limps back with a bottle and a glass. He opens the vodka and slumps into the couch. He pours the vodka into the glass. He hands the glass to Corea.

"We need more of this," Ed says.

Corea looks at it as if it were a shrunken head. She has never in her life had straight vodka. She doesn't want to be rude to her father though. She can see he's suffering. She brings the glass to her lips. She doesn't swallow.

Ed glowers at his brother. Kyle watches the dusty air. He knows what's coming.

"We could never, you know…. As you know. I mean, Corea wouldn't be in our lives if we could. So it's a blessing."

Nobody says anything for a long while. They listen to the oscillating fans do their thing. A moth pings at the overhead light, even though the bulb is not on. Amazing, Corea thinks. What an instinct.

"Fucking A," Kyle says.

"Yeah, fucking A," Corea says.

They clink glasses and drink.

Sleep is still a long way off. There is plenty of time to kill.

New Slots

It wasn't, I admit, the most auspicious start to adulthood. A year into my marriage with Kat, I realized I had a problem. It wasn't as if I was drinking a bottle of Jack every night, but I could barely stomach the thought of dinner without a few beers, a few glasses of wine. Had to drink something before sex, after sex, after a long day, before a long day. Not just had to. Wanted to. I owe it to Kat: she brought the problem to the forefront—it wasn't as if I had a sudden bolt of realization. It wasn't as if I *knew* anything.

"You have to make a choice," she said. "It's me or all the booze you're drinking."

"That's ridiculous," I said. I thought much worse.

We were at the dining room table—flowers, candles, Jim Hall on the speakers. I had made paella and salad with goat cheese and $16-a-pound olives. I did the cooking. She had the high powered/demanding job. I freelanced, owed a laundromat. She was the breadwinner. I fulfilled shopping lists. Whatever.

I wasn't angry at her, just perplexed. She drank also. Albeit, not as much. Albeit, not right after work. Or before work. Or during work.

"I have too much time on my hands," I said. "That's all. Too many bottles just lying around."

I chose her—it was the obvious choice. We were young and college wasn't that far behind us. We were just starting off. At the time the health experts were constantly saying that a glass or two or three or four of wine was *good* for you. Good for your heart. Good for the circulatory system. I was indoctrinated into the fad of booze-as-health-food, perhaps.

So out went the booze. I gave all the beer and hard stuff to Jim and Sally who lived on Covington Court and all the wine to Geoff and Jillian who lived catty-cornered to us. I explained, directly, that we're giving up booze. We may as well have admitted that we had syphilis.

"Oh, I'm…sorry to hear that. Everything okay?"

"Yeah," I said. "Just taking a break."

"Sure," they said. "No problem." But they didn't mean that, I could tell.

So in all of the little beer bottle slots in the fridge—which previously, always but always, held cold craft beer at the ready—I kept yogurt. Cherry. Peach. Banana and strawberry. Plain, low fat. Something new for the old slots.

I started attending A.A. Those people knew what they were doing and were there to help me the first month or two. I found a sponsor—or a sponsor found me. But I just didn't want to talk about it anymore. I didn't want to listen to boozing stories. It was all well-intentioned and helpful and not in the least culty or overly religious or weird—as I imagined it might be. I just couldn't do it.

Kat didn't like this. She wanted me to be systematic and thorough, but as a fly-by-night guy I wanted to go my own route. So for months we had a silent standoff. I know how she felt and she knew I wanted to try my way. In the meantime I wasn't drinking. I wasn't. But the beer commercials on TV every five minutes. Mila Kunis pounding the whiskey barrels. Tequila ads dripping all over Kat's magazines. That guy from *The Sopranos* slamming them back in his shiny suit.

I was trying to be appreciative of her and grateful and take to heart the old "there but the grace of God go I" dictum. But when I cooked, I wasn't 100%. Not even close. I made us pasta one night and my sauce was nothing. Or so I felt. Some pinto beans and onions, maybe an old shriveled bell pepper. I shoved a bowl of it at her when I returned home. I wanted to retreat to the bedroom, complain of a headache.

"Eat up," I said. I watched the football game on my gadget.

She looked at the bowl.

"I'm sorry," she said. "I can't."

"What's the matter? Stomach upset?"

Her face was corkscrewed with inner pain. I wanted a drink.

"No, this wasn't cooked with *love*," she said. "I'm sorry, no offense."

She walked out of the room, her hand covering her eyes.

I thought of all the times I sent her off to work with a butter sandwich and a mealy apple or a crusty bagel and sandwich bag of unpeeled carrots. I could have done better, much.

• • •

We separated shortly thereafter. I stayed in the townhouse and Kat moved across town, closer to her job. A tidy efficiency.

We talked on the phone every other day. She said she still "thought about me all the time." She was in self-protection mode. She checked in on me but said she couldn't live in the blast zone. I couldn't blame her one bit, really. She deserved better and I told her so.

I tried to focus on work, but my freelancing was slow, covering a few zoning meetings here and there, sometimes a soccer game. Mostly I checked in on the coin-operated laundromat I owned (I inherited it), made sure everything was functioning.

The townhouse was nearly empty of furniture but I had bags of coins everywhere. I needed to roll them and take them to the bank, but that took effort.

I remember looking through an old cookbook. I had always loved cooking as a kind of therapy, as a creative outlet, and I realized while looking through this old cookbook that I rarely baked for my wife. Hardly ever. I began reading the recipes: orange peel bread, pecan muffins, popovers, chocolate rolls, parker brownies, coconut squares, linzer schnitten, banbury tarts, and all manner of cookies.

My imagination exploded and I simply had to make some of these things. So I went to the store and bought several hundred dollars' worth of baking goods: eggs and sugar and raisins and lemons, nuts and flour and salt and milk and tons of butter and oranges and baking powder and chocolate.

I went on a baking frenzy. Everything else ground to a halt.

And when I had enough to make worth my while, I put a sign outside my door and a note on our community Facebook page and started selling baked goods right from my front door. The neighbors came—slow at first, then in droves.

I was late on my articles. I had to check in on the laundromat less frequently. For two weeks it was all baking all the time. I wanted a drink.

The entire house smelled of sugar and chocolate, oranges and butter. There could be worse things in life.

• • •

Toward the end of my frenzy a woman appeared, bought three popovers and returned the next two days for twice as many.

Her name was Luisa.

By this point I had figured out that I'd sell more baked

goods and waste less if I set up a little plastic bench outside right under the maple tree. Customers could sit there in the shade and eat a little pastry and watch the dog walkers and old couples walk by.

I was in clean-up mode the second time she came by and she took advantage of the empty plastic bench. She dribbled honey over the popovers.

I swept the crumbs and detritus from the front stoop.

"Do you want some cold water or something? It's hot."

I was trying quite hard not to stare, not to creep her out.

"Oh, no thank you. I have the honey."

I started laughing. It just struck me as funny, as if honey could quench her thirst.

"It is moist though," she said. "It's *like* a liquid, right?"

Her beauty intimidated me. I had to summon the strength to ask her if I could sit down with her. She told me she worked for the state, but she hesitated and looked away, as if embarrassed.

"What's up?"

"I work construction," she said.

I had no right to judge.

She told me she just started the job ten months ago and that it's road construction. Small roads two and four lanes. She holds the slow/stop sign, rotating it with a turn of her wrists.

The image and reality—there was a disconnect.

She talked about managing the heat—hydrating and also just trying to find a way to not let the humidity sap her mentally. I wanted a drink.

"It's not the most exciting job. We have assholes on our crew. Ex-cons. And not the nice rehabilitated kind. But I was laid off a year and a half ago from a nice job—IT—and it's been touch-and-go since."

Her face was mesmerizing. She had a rather prominent nose, something from a Roman statue perhaps, almost mannish. Sturdy. But her skin was burnished and olive and gorgeous, which gave her an Italian look. Later she told me she was Irish on her father's side. She had these startling bluish green eyes which seemed almost alien, too bright and distinct for a human face. But the most compelling aspect of Luisa's face (I've always been drawn to faces, most of all), was that she never seemed to duplicate a facial expression. At times she had this fanciful, knowing smile. At others, she looked innocent and direct. At others she seemed almost maternal and protective. I have never seen such a pliant face—one which revealed so many personality strains within a span of two minutes. But soon enough I ran out of energy to pursue the baking much longer and Luisa only dropped by two more times for pastries. One time she was in her orange construction getup (she tipped her cap and said little—this was early in the morning).

• • •

She lived in a small apartment—on the second floor of an angular building tucked back behind a larger office building with a donut shop on the ground floor.

I had her phone number, several pictures—what I could find online—and her name and e-mail. I had her license plate number and street address.

Basic Internet searches are helpful. What I lacked was the wherewithal to knock on her door, to use her phone number or e-mail. They just helped me feel *comfortable*.

But I printed off the pictures I could find and taped them to my office wall. I drove over to her apartment building and parked at an angle so I could look up into her room. I sat there for a long time over many nights. If someone walked by I'd pretend to be on the cell phone and turn my eyes down into the darkness.

It wasn't as if I could just call her and explain I found her number on some sketchy virus-ridden Internet white pages. Perhaps I could "accidentally" bump into her on the sidewalk or in the donut shop but that would be just as difficult to explain, potentially. I wanted a drink. So I kept quiet and hunkered, knowing that as long as I did that, the more I might recede from her memory (if I was even in there).

I wanted a drink.

• • •

What happened is this—I found the gumption, walked up to her door and knocked on it. I thought she would be surprised or offended or taken aback, but she opened the door and waved me in. I still stammered.

"I saw you out there. It's not a big thing to me—I always *knew*."

I couldn't tell if she was being sarcastic or not. It's very possible she was.

She made tea and we both drank it slowly. It was a scene from the 19th century, I thought.

"I have this thing," she said. "I'm indebted to someone."

And of course I probed to the best of my ability, without probing too much. But she wouldn't go beyond the coy and mysterious. I couldn't tell if it was a relationship, a family thing, something religious. She wouldn't say.

"It's a kind of debt that I can't explain. Maybe someday. I'll have to leave it that for now."

Beauty is an odd concept, a kind of artificial construct, temporary and fleeting. As she was talking and as I was sipping my tea, I attempted to avoid complete and utter staring. She wasn't absolutely beautiful in a standard way, but her *uniqueness* was so striking and pure that it was all I could process.

When I was a child my mother would take me to the city museum downtown. It wasn't the largest museum in the country but it had a decent collection of European and American art. I was paralyzed. I would stand in front of an Edward Hopper or Tintoretto or small Picasso and just stare, unmoving.

In school when I found a girl who I thought was pretty, all I could do is stare. I was a big starer. I froze up, immobilized by beauty.

With Luisa, the same.

• • •

Luisa was generous enough to let me take her on several dates—once to the state fair, a second time to a film and coffee, a third time to lunch and we became physical at my place— which was an odd sensation. I kept thinking of Kat, despite myself. But as I was kissing Luisa, I mostly thought she is too beautiful to sully with my touch; she is too beautiful for sex.

Her arms were strong and her hands rough.

She agreed to meet me at the Windsor Hotel downtown the next weekend. It would—we implied—act as the consumption for our budding relationship. It was implied, not stated.

I arrived early and quickly became sleepy. This was almost inexplicable since I was revved on lust and expectation. But I must have exhausted myself in my overexcitement. I couldn't sleep. Instead, I just lay there under the covers, as if waiting for something to happen. I stared up at the sprinkler system jutting out of the ceiling. I stared at the open wardrobe hangers affixed to the wooden pole. Something cold and antiseptic about these two details—the hangers pre-fabricated and identical in every room of the hotel—cookie cutter.

Luisa showed and all but glided in, green and orange and black floral print.

But I stayed in bed, trying to beckon her into it with my passivity. She stood rod-straight, bemused. I wanted a drink.

"What's wrong? Are you feeling ill?"

I responded by pulling the comforter up to my chin.

"C'mon, let's go to dinner," she said.

This was my moment. I had to break through my wall of paralysis and dread, but I couldn't bring myself to say a thing.

Instead, I lifted myself from the bed and followed her out of the hotel room door.

We walked down the street a few blocks and ate dinner at the restaurant. We talked about furniture and antiques. After paying for the meal, I excused myself. I walked down the corridor towards the bathroom and past it and out the back door into the cool night air. There were six cases of beer stacked in the corridor. I walked past and away from it all.

A Straight Arrow

Kevin is the only one who doesn't sit. The others are pleated, tan and olive-drab and gray, sitting in armchairs, discussing the latest film version of *Wuthering Heights*.

His shoulders slump forward, not out of any lack of confidence, mind you. His body is hunched on the edge of the hearth, gargoyle-like. He is wearing a Bill Belichick-style ripped sweatshirt (Kevin's features ARMY in block letters) and his jeans are spotted with oil/grease blotches. He wears his VT baseball cap backwards. I wonder if college sports fans would find his dual-allegiances disturbingly contradictory—I'm in the dark on such matters.

I'm standing in the doorway at the edge of enlightened conversation. Kevin glances my way and offers me a snappy one-fingered salute—back to his temple and then forward. As usual, he's listening. A good listener. I watch his eyes dart back and forth from speaker to speaker. He doesn't look bored at all, even when the conversation turns to which actor made a better Heathcliff, and so forth.

My sister, who sits next to him in a wingback, pats his knee in sympathy. To me this gesture communicates something essential about their relationship. She understands his outsider stance. He never ushers a complaint or seeks to change subjects to something more closely akin to one of his interests.

Kevin nods and briefly tips the side edge of his maroon Tech cap upwards.

"Out of all the literary characters, which one do you find

the most compelling?'

The lists—Kevin loves rankings, pecking orders. Grand statements.

"Well, Hamlet of course. Lear and Othello," my father says. "Most of the Shakespearean tragedies and histories feature extremely compelling heroes."

"Bloom and Daedalus," my mother chimes in. She sips gently from her slender champagne flute. "Mrs. Dalloway. Emma."

"Jason from *The Sound and the Fury*," my sister says. The fire crackles and hisses behind Kevin.

He half-turns his head. He nods, takes it all in.

"Nothing surprising here," I say.

"I don't know, we could blabber on and on," my mother says. "What do you think?"

"Daffy Duck. Followed by Elmer Fudd," Kevin says, flashing a sly smile.

"Can never be serious, even in answering his own question."

• • •

Kevin officially entered into the family proper, of course, the day he wed my sister some years back. However, his *unofficial* entrance into our circle occurred several years before, during the stage in Cara's relationship which was, at one time, called courtship.

Kevin comes from a rougher family (to use my mother's terminology). His father owns a cinder block business and Kevin grew up believing in the potential of the cinder block. He ate cinder block food, slept under cinder block walls—not literally, of course, but this is the general idea. One balmy night (moths pinging against the exterior sunroom lighting)

Kevin confided in me that when he grew up he knew he would eventually fill his father's footsteps, even if he didn't want to. He did not utter the word "trapped," and perhaps I am reading too much into it. On the other hand…

Kevin's mindset strikes me as simultaneously medieval and fatalistic, but also refreshingly devoid of pretense and East Coast intellectual striving (what is left of it). As a counterpoint, I told Kevin that I grew up not knowing if I would be a doctor or a lawyer or an investment banker or an academic of some stripe (one must have a contingency). That I chose the latter path was perhaps as much a matter of slapdash luck as anything. Fate for Kevin; luck for me.

However, Kevin attended college anyway. When I asked him for what purpose (and implicitly if he felt predetermined to take over the cinder block business) he admitted he didn't really know: that's just what people did after high school.

"I didn't make it. Three semesters in and I found myself *distracted* for lack of a better word. I partied too hard—that's a definite."

Unlike many other people I know, Kevin thinks about what he says before he says it. He's rarely knee-jerk.

In college he played rugby (he went on scholarship). In high school he played football, but competition being what it was he found an entry point into rugby much easier (and profitable).

Kevin looks like a rugby player. He's six feet four and two-forty-three; muscles upon muscles; head like a bull. But his eyes are alert and penetrating and his face sharp and defined by a rather muted intelligence: I don't mean to sound patronizing, but Kevin is a lot smarter than he seems upon first glance.

Initially I thought he would find himself overwhelmed

intellectually by "the family." In a sense, maybe he's sidelined by overly bookish topics, but then when the topic shifts closer to Kevin's comfort point, he's as insightful as anyone else in the room. I am aware that I sound like a condescending prick.

• • •

All of this is to say that initially we thought Cara and Kevin's union was a mismatch, at least socially.

I'd see Kevin surrounded by our modern and Asian art, seated at our antique Arts and Crafts table—our house is very Lloyd Wright, late period—and I'd think "fish out of water."

But he never embarrassed himself early on.

Then about three months into his relationship with Cara he arrived at dinner with a nicely bound edition of Edmund Wilson. We were all ve-ry impressed—believing he couldn't *possibly* know who Edmund Wilson was (college drop-out and all). But he did. He gave the book to my parents as a gesture of my gratitude, he said.

"Be still my beating heart," my mother said.

"Sting? Really, mother?"

"No, he got that from Shakespeare," I said. "I mean…"

My father nodded.

"A very nice touch, Kevin," my father said. Kevin doffed an invisible cap, a sign of humor and humility.

This was a turning point for me.

Then we ate. I'm sure it was an oyster stew, plus chicken fricassee, and three grain bread.

I can't, at this remove, recall the topic of mealtime conversation exactly, but I do remember that after dinner, father drank his Martell and Kevin asked about the art.

"I never really took an art history class in school," he said.

"It's okay," Cara said—my mother was in the kitchen

arranging the mouse and preparing espresso. She pointed around the room with a pleased sashay.

"That is a Picasso print. That's a late Matisse rip-off. But that little one over there that's an original Modigliani. It's no big deal though: who *doesn't* own a Modigliani?"

Kevin formed a querying facial expression. He didn't say anything.

I felt for him; at this moment we became brothers.

• • •

Kevin's ability to rise above the fray of pithy conversation and superficial witticisms made him, in fact, superbly suited to our family. He became a kind of voyeur to our pseudo-intellectual blather. If Kevin was not able to either (a) participate or (b) ignore, his entire union with Cara would collapse. In fact, though my family remains dear to me, Kevin was the one who first opened my eyes to the rather artificial nature of our traditions. It's just stuff you like to do, he implied.

All of this is to say that Kevin and I began spending time together apart from family gatherings. Kevin's idea initially, but one which I quickly embraced.

Though I was indoctrinated into the belief that sports were the bastion of the ignorant—Kevin asked if I wouldn't just like to go "shoot some hoops."

"Sure," I said. I had played basketball a total of maybe six or seven times in my life, but I did always find it enjoyable. Diversions—and sports are, if nothing else a kind of mindless diversion—are part of human nature, also. Why not experience this? Why not live?

So I sat in Kevin's dusty Jeep and we proceeded to a park with two courts side-by-side and Kevin pulled out two tall water bottles and the basketball. The courts—from what

I knew at the time—were rough: weeds sticking out from cracks; the nets were down. As an uncoordinated, not-particularly-competitive guy I didn't really know what to do out there. I couldn't dribble the ball consistently. I could barely shoot. I ran lethargically and stumbled or tripped half the time (Kevin graciously blamed my shoddy footwear, not the feet in them). Despite his girth, Kevin moved beautifully. He would jump up and shoot the ball in one single, smooth motion, the ball rising and falling and sinking right through the unadorned rim.

I have never had so much fun in my life.

Our sweaty clothes heavy on our backs, we sat on the hot asphalt and talked.

"There's no reason to judge you," I said.

"Glad you're in the family. Gives me some hope."

"What do you mean?"

"You're different than Cara and especially my parents. But it's working anyway."

"Is it? I'm not sure. I mean your folks are good people. It's just not knowing where I stand sometimes. No big deal. Thoughts and feelings can't hurt me."

"They are subtle, you know."

"That's a good word for it," he said. "Do me a favor, tell me if I'm ever headed on the wrong track, would you? I don't want to do that."

"You got it," I said.

We drank water and dripped with sweat. The clouds scudded by and the wind picked up, but I didn't want to lift myself from the concrete.

• • •

I would have days like this with Kevin frequently. But when he and Cara had children, I saw him less and then more later on when he needed a few hours to unwind.

Inevitably he'd destroy me at basketball (or some such) and then we'd talk. Sometimes if it was too cold or too hot or rainy—we'd go shoot pool instead (he always won at that, also).

"The children," he said once. "They're changing everything. I mean…."

"In a positive manner, I hope, correct?"

"Well…you know how it goes."

"No, not at all," I said. And I didn't. A lifelong bachelor, I had no idea how it goes.

"I mean sex," he said. "It's not…"

"Different than before?"

"You could say that."

"Sorry."

"This isn't something you want to discuss, I'm sure."

"No, but…"

"There are other things as well. Your sister—well, you know her better than me."

"Not anymore," I said.

He said the children made him feel like an orphan somehow. He was secondary, all of a sudden, to his own progeny. Kevin's crisis was that he felt forced to compete for time and space. Often he felt shut out, at a loss. His feelings, he said, were taking over his own best instincts. I'm paraphrasing.

"Then again, it's just me," he said. I wasn't sure what he meant by that.

Often I'd change the subject. In those days Kevin particularly enjoyed discussing speculative historical theories (if he *had* completed college, I wonder if these wouldn't have withered). I patiently listened to his latest explanation for the emergence of the Easter Island statues, the Sphinx and so forth. He believed Neanderthals walked the Earth in the late 1600's. At the end of his conjectures, he'd admit: "These are just theories though."

· · ·

At family gatherings Kevin loved to ask sweeping questions, point blank. He was especially fond of rankings.

--Who do you think is the best musician of all time?

--What is the best movie ever made?

--Who was the greatest football player ever to play the game?

--What is the most delicious type of cheese?

--What is the tastiest beer you've ever had?

Part of me thinks his questions were designed not to promote discussion so much as to *provoke* it. Or—put another way—Kevin excelled at steering the conversation into his comfort zone with these simple queries. To me they were indicative of some key aspect of Kevin. He's a straight arrow. He wanted all cards laid on the table. I hemmed and hawed and I was *trying* to appease him. My father often demurred and my mother shrugged. "It's not a contest, is it?"

· · ·

Five years and change after the birth of their second child, my mother called me to relay the news: Cara was leaving Kevin. She presumed it was her decision, and that such a decision was based on her desire for a more "like-minded" match. It had to do with compatibility, she related; this was not an issue of high drama.

My mother was and is, I'm sure, torn. On the one hand she detested the idea of divorce and believed that couples who entered that level of commitment should not break it. On the other hand, my parents looked down upon Kevin, despite his attempts otherwise.

"This is a man who traffics in cinder blocks," she said. "That's who he is."

"*Traffics*—you make them sound like narcotics."

"He's not exactly an intellect, as you well know."

"I know nothing of the sort. I could feel my grip on the telephone tightening. He's a smart guy. He's just not in your mold, that's all. He's not a doctor or a lawyer."

"I'm not arguing with you, Daniel," she said. "Don't shoot the messenger."

"Sorry, isn't there some quote from Shakespeare you can pull out of your hat to illustrate *that* particular point?"

• • •

I still meet up with Kevin maybe once a month or so for basketball. Perhaps it's his best means of communicating with Cara. He has visiting rights with their children twice a month, which he explains as a strange circumstance.

Cara has—in my view—turned into a different kind of person. I love my sister, of course, but the divorce has diluted her. She has an *edge* now—and a wicked cackle she never displayed prior. She has a new husband—a pediatrician ("only a pediatrician," my mother says —not a surgeon), who is okay though I find him overly distant and of course tainted by the adulterous courtship. I play nice.

I've told Kevin, however, that he is still a brother to me and that if he ever needs anything I'm at his everlasting disposal. He must have, in his sincere way, taken me at my word.

"I need a place to stay," he admitted.

He's sleeping in my guest room indefinitely. My honored

guest.

Often I will lurk outside the room after I'm certain he has fallen asleep. If I listen closely, I can hear the soft whistle of air through his nostrils. It calms me somehow. We all endure in ways strange and unusual.

A Compelling Interest

Carol doesn't know what to do about Larry anymore. She's good at doing. She manages the two pizzerias they own, and manages the eight unit apartment complex, and takes care of the chores around the house and the errands, and gets Jonas ready for school and picks him up at 3:30 to shuttle him to soccer practice until 5:30. Carol knows that if she were a different brand of person, she could easily become addicted to speed or some rough equivalent. She needs to drink four or five cups of coffee a day as is, just to make it through. Just to keep her energy level up.

Larry rarely leaves the living room sofa. Carol would have more compassion if Larry had a compelling interest—some hobby or compulsion (something even quasi-productive). Instead, Larry sits on the sofa and watches television and eats cheese sandwiches and Doritos, drinking two percent milk. Carol wonders if Larry minds the cheese and cheese flavored redundancy. Obviously not. He loves to just sit there.

When Carol returns home from her storm of activities she knows exactly where to find Larry. She even knows what channel he'll be watching—CBS. Larry doesn't channel surf. He only watches whatever is on CBS: news, soap operas, golf—whatever it is. He's committed. He doesn't move.

Her mother has advised her to leave Larry. Even though Carol was brought up not to "believe in" divorce, her mother has told her that divorce might, in this case, be an act of mercy. Her mother characterizes Larry as "a good person gone awry," a "shackle around your ankle," or when she's tired or in a less generous mood, "deadweight."

"Something is off, I mean deep inside him," her mother said once.

"We know this. This is not news."

"Nevertheless."

Her mother ground pepper into eggs, stirring with a fork. Carol watched her: in the way her mother stirred the eggs she could feel the disapproval.

"Patience—you've established this. There's a time to draw a border. He needs a push in the right direction."

Carol helped her mother cook breakfast on Sunday mornings. This was also the time to talk, and often conversations took the form of unsolicited advice. She loved her mother anyway. Without her guidance…who knows? Her mother has always been *involved*. At times Carol has wished she lived in another state; mostly she's grateful. Still, Carol wonders how healthy it is.

Larry sits in front of the television. Carol sits next to him, clutches his sleeve. The nubby orange blanket rests on his legs.

"Are you cold?"

Larry shrugs.

CBS is showing *Amazing Race* reruns. To Carol it seems odd that reality television should have reruns. Isn't the point of reality partially that it is of the moment? Real reality doesn't have reruns.

"How was your day?"

Larry looks pensive. "Okay," Larry finally says.

It's difficult to get more out of him than this.

"Are you hungry?"

Larry shrugs, eyes on the screen.

Carol sits next to him, leans into his body, pressing her thigh against his. She thinks back. Carol believes they had sex the week before last, though perhaps it was the week before that. It blurs together. She doesn't need an active sex life to make her happy though—she knows this. Sex is just something on the fringes of her life and that's okay with her.

"I mean, I can eat," Larry says. Of course he can—he always can *eat*, Carol thinks. He's the one, who at family gatherings, gorges himself and then falls asleep on the couch. Last year at Thanksgiving the kids took turns taking pictures of him and laughing up a storm. They called him Rip Van Uncle. She laughed along, though the stripe of shame inside her is long. Sometimes the stripe widens, engulfing her entirely. At other times the stripe recedes and she can see her husband through it.

"I'll put something together," Carol says. "You just relax."

• • •

Larry knows there's not much left. He knows he's emptied-out, running on fumes. Yet he can't help it. He has nothing left to offer.

There are patterns. Larry can sense these patterns on some elemental level. The patterns of the universe, of which he never speaks. He doesn't admit that his focus is cosmic, not worldly—at least not exclusively worldly. The universe is exploding and nobody notices or cares! Neutrinos are vibrating! We live in a reality which will soon be radically altered and yet he's supposed to care about getting a job. Carol knows better than to press him. Nineteen years is a long time to go without employment. Even if he did return, he's not sure where he'd start. What would he even stick on his resume? Nothing is *easy*. Everything is a trial.

The fire consumed everything. They didn't have a problem putting it out. He watched them from across the street. However, by then it was too late. He sat on the curb across the street and watched the hose burn. In the days before cell phones, he had to walk to the pay phone outside the A&P to call his parents on vacation in Florida. At 17 they thought he was old enough—Larry knew they trusted him. The distractions were too much. If only he had ordered out instead of attempting to cook, his life would've been completely different. He was trying to save money so that he could use the money for beer.

He watched a cardinal flit in the poplar out the back door. He was transfixed by the flutter of red when the smoke pillowed out to the deck. He couldn't make it back in time. He could only step back off the deck, into the back yard. He could only watch the black clouds rise and run to a neighbor's house to make the call. If only it wasn't so late—11:45—perhaps it would've been different.

The smoke billowed high into the darkness even after the fire proper was out. He watched it for hours.

• • •

Carol heats up leftovers and they eat. As she's heating up the leftovers Carol thinks back to the days when she used to prepare complex "gourmet" meals for Larry and the kids. She'd hunt down exotic ingredients and spend hours carefully preparing the meal. She was partial to stews, slow cooking. She found a website specializing in healthy but complex meals that were tasty and would last for days. Carol would make them early in the morning and by the evening they would be done.

Why did she scale back? Partially, now that the kids are grown, she just doesn't have as many mouths to feed. Perhaps she burned herself out expending the energy all those years in creation. Carol needs a rest, also. But mostly, if Carol was honest with herself, she'd admit that Larry simply doesn't care if he's eating Kraft Mac and Cheese or paella. His level of enjoyment seems about the same.

"What would you like to do this evening?"

Larry is chewing the warmed-over grilled potatoes from two nights ago.

"I don't know," he says. She can see bits of half-masticated potato skins between his teeth. His mouth smacks. Parsley gums to his left incisor. She dabs her hand with a napkin. They haven't slept together in months.

"Okay," she says. This is one of those moments their therapist told her about. He said that, in moments of frustration, she should count to ten and focus on her breathing. She should resist the urge to "mother" Larry. She counts to ten. She breathes and is aware of her breath. She snaps a raw green pepper between her teeth.

Carol has to fight the urge to shake him by the shoulders and say: "Wake up, Larry. You are not the man I fell in love with. Get a grip on yourself, your memories, whatever it is that leaves you constantly somnambulant. Come back to me." But Carol knows this would only result in Larry retreating into his shell, pushing her even further away. No, she's better off just taking it, letting the frustration simmer if it will.

"Sounds good," she says, somehow without even a hint of sarcasm.

"What's for dessert?"

"I think we still have some cookies and cream, don't we?"

"I think so," Larry says, leaning back and rubbing his expansive belly. "I'll take some when you have a moment."

Carol remembers the beach house. For years they would go there—the kids loved it. The water seemed bluer then, more pure. She remembers the laughter, the walks along the beach. She knows her memories are maudlin, but she can't help it. What else is nostalgia but a gauzy refrain? Yet something that has been lost, somehow. They were happy for years. She can't forget that.

• • •

After dinner Larry decides to return to the stash. Forty-five shoeboxes of Polaroids from over the years. He still owns the old Polaroid, which hangs from his neck. On holidays he likes to plant himself in the corner with his camera snapping pictures. His socialization usually consisted of holding pictures against the backdrop of his chest to those he captured moments before.

Few Polaroids in the box feature him. Fine with Larry.

He sits cross-legged in front of his closet, pulling at shoebox after shoebox, flipping through the contents. He wishes he had the motivation to organize and label, to place the Polaroids in albums or even date the photos. Instead, he just enjoys casually flipping through them—all those smiling faces: cousins, uncles, parents, siblings. The shoeboxes are, for him, more than anything—a record of themselves.

Carol has seen the boxes, on occasion. But she always seemed befuddled by the disorganization, the casual clutter. Larry prefers it if she doesn't look.

The photos make him feel lethargic. Larry wants to sleep for fourteen hours. Dazed, he rubs his eyes and shuffles to bed. He surrounds his body with pillows and heaps blankets upon himself. This way he feels protected, surrounded by fabric. This way he can sleep.

Larry has had heart issues before. For the past three years he has suffered from hypertension. High blood pressure. She was there when the doctor told him he was in "high jeopardy." He didn't have to spell it out to her. Larry must embrace a more active life-style, cut drinking from his diet entirely. Exercise. Larry hasn't so much as lifted a leg since, except to use the bathroom.

Carol knows nobody will be surprised by this. Her mother assumed it was an anxiety issue all along. The Lozol and Midamar weren't particularly expensive two years ago, but that was when Carol was still unsure about whether she could go through with it or not. The side-effects have not been kind. The doctor said that nausea might be an issue, and it has been. That and the constant need to pee.

• • •

Carol wishes she had a better outlet of any kind. Kim has encouraged her to take up crocheting. Kim says it relaxes her; "It's a kind of puzzle, mom. You have to think, but it's light thinking. Which is good. Plus, your hands are moving. It keeps everything occupied." Kim gave her a crocheting set for Christmas one year and Carol tried—she did try. Carol just has trouble sitting still. There is so much to do and so little time. A hobby seems like frittering time away.

• • •

Because she still loves Larry, she has to. Loading the syringe with the liquid takes time. Carol isn't confident in her abilities—she's not used to this. But she manages to fill the syringe somehow; she uses her deep reserves.

Peeling back the layers of blankets takes time, also. They

are heavy and she doesn't want to wake him. She unpeels the blankets deliberately. In a few minutes, he's exposed. She finds a vein in the back of his thigh, a place she read nobody will look. She watches his sleeping form under the covers. This man she has mothered for decades. This poor man.

She inserts the needle, watches the liquid descend in the dropper. Then Carol withdraws the needle and pulls the covers back onto him. Larry rolls over, sighing slightly. She read that it will take fifteen minutes. She read that the effects are akin to a heavy sleep, just slipping under. Carol takes the syringe to the bathroom, flushing it down the toilet. She puts the seat down and sits on it. She sits there on the cold porcelain, arms crossed at her stomach. She sits there, unmoving. She can feel the cold porcelain against her legs. She crosses her arms at the stomach, tries to focus on her breathing—she is so numb she wonders if perhaps she accidently inserted some into herself. In and out, Carol tells herself—just breathe. It's all she has. Maybe all she's ever had.

Cucumber Sandwiches

For fifteen minutes Ethan watched the single pine needle swirl in the water near the ladder in the lap lane. It was stuck in the whirlpool that began with the circulator, but the air vent underneath played counterpoint. For the first five minutes Ethan thought the pine needle was actually two conjoined needles, but then he realized that this illusion was the effect of refraction and his scratched sunglasses and the distance from which he watched the needle swirl around and around and around and around. His lifeguard chair was at least twelve feet from the pine needle, at least six in height, and another six across.

It was another steamy day and the mugginess sapped Ethan's energy enough that his book of Chekhov short stories sat in the strange holster to his right, uncracked for over an hour. Even in the shade Ethan could feel the heat rise from the concrete.

At 2:30 on the nose, Butch wheeled Mrs. White down the AstroTurf path behind the azaleas—Ethan could just see over the crest, a head and a torso—and he took a hard right to the shaded umbrellas near the shallow end. Butch wore a sleeveless black shirt, which exhibited several serpentine tattoos and another featuring some dramatic Japanese or Chinese lettering. A demonic tattoo sprouted from underneath Butch's shirt and the head jutted out onto Butch's neck—all pointy teeth and bulbous eyes and fiery breath. He tucked an orange kicker under one arm.

"There you go, Mrs. W," he said. "Easy does it." Butch held her arms and led her to the steps that angled down into the pool itself. One step at a time, slowly, Butch helped Mrs. White descend into the water, as if she were entering a baptismal.

"Ooh, not too cold." Mrs. White said, laughing.

She was almost always amused at something, usually herself. Ethan noticed this. He had little excuse not to—she was one of the only residents to use the pool.

Once Mrs. White was up to her shoulders in water, Butch slid the floaty board under her arms and she beamed.

"I can take it from here," she said, suffused with kindness.

"You got it, Mrs. W. I'll be here if you need me."

"Don't pee in the pool now, hear?"

Slowly, Ethan watched Mrs. White frog-kick her way across the pool, directly toward him, or perhaps this was just wishful thinking.

He zoned-out, watching the sun glint in the dirty water. Waves of heat rippled through the air and Ethan took a long pull on what was left of his lemonade (more diluted lemon water at this point).

"Ike, have you listened to the Satie?" No "hello," just slipping directly into what they ended with the day before.

She called Ethan "Ike." He never corrected her, feeling as though, if he did, she'd stick by her guns.

"I did," Ethan lied. "It is very soothing, calming. You are absolutely right."

"Good. And you listened to Gnossienne?"

"I forget, they all kinda blended into each other. I think so, yes. Moody."

"Listen to it again. And did you sleep better?"

"Oh, that's right," Ethan said. In a moment of weakness he admitted to Mrs. White that he too hadn't been sleeping well. Yesterday Ethan fell asleep when she paddled up to him, her little head bobbing above the rim of orange plastic.

Mrs. White was of indeterminate age—Ethan asked Butch once and even he wasn't quite sure. By virtue of her hunched back and gait, Ethan would guess at least eighty-five, but he was petrified to ask. He felt pity for her and feared his big mouth might disrupt what could be the remaining days of her life. The Tea Garden Retirement Home was, as far as he was concerned, a dumping ground. Ethan wasn't sure if Mrs. White was lacking relatives, but she was in the unfortunate position of having to depend on Tea Garden itself—which was an unenviable situation. If it was him, he'd rather up and croak. Frankly.

It wasn't as if The Tea Garden Retirement Home itself was in dire disrepair, but it was certainly run-down. The rooms, when he walked by them to purchase a candy bar from the vending machine, seemed serviceable enough. But the building itself displayed ancient windows, peeling paint, surrounded by a fringe of cracked sidewalks. Little to no grounds maintenance. Butch and others told him they were perennially short staffed, and on the one occasion Ethan nearly decided to eat in the cafeteria, the grub was nearly inedible—it made homeless soup kitchens seem gourmet.

"How is Mrs. Lily treating you?" Mrs. White floated in front of him. He wanted to doze.

"I don't know a Mrs. Lily, I'm sorry," Ethan said. He felt formal, but ineffectually so.

"You know, that sweet thing."

"I told you, I don't have a girlfriend, not now at least." They had been through this particular conversation a thousand times, but it didn't stick. It never did.

Mrs. White smiled at him—her teeth somehow clenched—and stared. She bobbed in the water like that for a long time. Ethan remembered the staring contests he had with his younger brother. What were they, nine or ten?

"Would you like to be my girlfriend, Mrs. White?"

"Now you know—I'm taken already," she said. "Ike, I have a beau!"

Butch paddled over behind her.

"Let's get you in the lap lane before it gets too late," he said.

"Oh you hush," Mrs. White said, splashing him lightly.

Butch reached back behind Mrs. White's head and did a triple fist-pump.

Exactly, Ethan thought.

• • •

For the past three summers, Ethan served as a lifeguard at Tea Garden, mostly because the duties were light and he could sleep or read or just siesta and still make enough to cover his bills. Often not a single resident was in or around the pool area, and those were days when Ethan did sleep, if he could. Perhaps he could download some Satie to help, Ethan thought. It was an easy, brainless job.

Ethan was $120,000 in debt. This was a problem. His parents covered the first two years of undergrad, but after that they agreed that Ethan would be on his own. He tried to work and attend school at the same time, but it was akin to pissing into a volcano. By the time he graduated, whatever he earned at the restaurant plus adjuncting and at the lifeguard gig went toward bills and debt. Even with a decent full-time position he couldn't envision paying off his student debt for several decades. He had to also *live*.

Ethan was twenty-seven years old and lost, or that's the word that came to him often. "Lost." "Floundering." He thought of himself as "in transition," yet he was only a year out of graduate school. Initially the two classes a semester he taught at his alma mater were a heady thrill—there he was back where he started, teaching the young and starry-eyed. But when they slumped down into their chairs and began texting under the desk as he lectured or led a discussion, his heart drooped. He couldn't bring himself to play the role of hard-nosed disciplinarian. The reason he finished his graduate work in the first place was to avoid the high school mentality and its idiotic trappings. At the Black Stump, a mediocre grill downtown that specialized in stuffed baked potatoes, potato skins and thick slabs of fatty meat advertised as "lean and mean," Ethan felt that he gained five pounds a week snacking on French fries behind the register.

In the meantime, Ethan lived in the Harrison's basement. He had a bedroom with a pocket door, a tiny bathroom, a linoleum kitchen and access to the shared washer and drier at the foot of the stairs.

His apartment smelled of mildew and Ethan frequently woke up coughing. He bought fans and anti-mildew spray, which he utilized frequently, though not once did he complain to the Harrisons. His hobby was smashing spiders and roly-polies with an old pair of tennis shoes (he couldn't bring himself to look at the soles—and he felt bad for those he smashed). He contemplated getting a cat, but Ethan couldn't afford to feed an animal and he wasn't sure if cats cared about spiders anyway—and he'd have to deal with the yowling and the guilt of being negligent.

Ethan parted ways with his longtime girlfriend when she landed a position teaching in Santa Barbara. There was nothing for Ethan, and he didn't see how he could afford to live in California anyway. In addition, even though he wasn't exactly surrounded by friends and family, they were a two-hour drive north. It was more comfortable to stay put.

Also, Ethan wasn't sure he could survive in a relationship when his partner was more successful than he was. Bad dynamic.

"Let's touch base in, you know, a year and circle back."

"We're tabling this, is that it?"

Ethan avoided her eyes.

Her work was strong, Ethan knew that. The one story she wrote about the marathon runner with the prosthetic leg—Professor Lind loved that story and cited it as an example of "kick-ass workshop fiction" ("kick-ass" was one of his go-to expressions). Lind usually dressed in Hawaiian shirts and corduroys with a belt seemingly made of woven hemp, chest hair sprouting from the neck of his shirt like heather on the moors.

But she struggled in her assistantship and Ethan had to often help her keep up with the grading.

"I have to warm-up to my work," she often admitted. She would hide away in the study for hours, the door closed. Silence.

Later, Ethan would ask if she had a productive writing session.

"No," she would say. "I just thought about my characters. I meditated on them. I'll write soon, I know it."

That entire year she only produced four stories—the four required for the two workshops. Ethan must've written a hundred, exhausting himself. But since graduate school, Ethan hasn't written a paragraph.

Something is missing, he knew. The mix was off.

• • •

Ethan heard the voice: "Hey, buddy. How are you doing?"

Ethan jumped in his seat.

He had been asleep.

It was four o'clock in the afternoon, the sun angling down the sky, making it difficult to see.

Harvey had a brown paper bag in his hand. Ethan was just relieved it wasn't Bill Walker, his Tea Garden supervisor (who rarely swung by—too busy day trading tech stocks in the dingy Tea Garden office).

"Oh, it's you."

"I come bearing chicken," Harvey said, handing the bag to Ethan. "I took the day off today and cooked up a bunch. Thought I'd drop over and see what's doing."

"Not much, as you can see," Ethan said.

"Least you don't have to stress out."

"If I'm not here, I'm there, or the other there. Always at work these days."

Ethan realized Mrs. White hadn't gone for her daily mid-afternoon dip today (unless she did so when he was unconscious). He took out his cell phone to text Butch.

"Hold on," Ethan said.

"Doesn't feel well," Butch responded. "Do me a favor. Humor her."

"Don't I always?

Emoticon, smiley face.

Butch never graduated high school and yet he had a better job than Ethan. Maybe Ethan's parents *were* right. Maybe he should've gone into law, like everyone else.

Harvey squatted in the umbrella shade and they talked writing. Harvey graduated the same year and had similar results so far. He was a substitute teacher and found little time to write. He was working on a kind of roman a clef, but "it's formless and lacks pull," he admitted. Two years ago Ethan bar-hopped with Harvey, but now they had to wake up early the next morning. They either stayed in and drank alone or just went to bed early.

"My brain is slowly turning into a wet noodle," Harvey said.

"Mine is a fat blob of jelly," Ethan admitted.

"That sounds better than wet noodle."

"At least a noodle provides sustenance. Jelly is nothing. It's sugar and fruit diarrhea."

"So any hot chicks at this pool?"

It was empty, the pool water littered with mosquitoes, desiccated cricket legs, moths, pine needles. The other (one) lifeguard, Sally, couldn't make it the day before and they had to shutter the pool for the day entirely. Ethan knows he should've cleaned the pool when he first arrived, but who was watching?

They reminisced about Professor Blighton's "workshop" where he ordered students *not* to write. They spent all semester studying the meaning of "it." Lyotard, Habermas, Wittengenstein. They were both lost and paying a bunch of money *not* to write. They still were. What was it all for?

"My students hate me," Ethan said. "I make them work and they want me to write their shit for them."

"My students hate me more," Harvey said. "Because I actually teach them shit. They just want to watch a movie. Sub! Movie time!"

The pool water smelled clammy and medicinal

simultaneously. It lapped gently against the crumbling concrete.

• • •

"Have you ever had a cucumber sandwich, Ike?"

Mrs. White was dangling her feet in the water, sitting in the blazing sun below him. Her stomach was too upset for her to swim, Butch explained. Butch sat in the shade, head down into his smart phone.

"Can't say I have, Mrs. White. Doesn't sound that exciting really."

"Oh, but it is. You have to understand the subtle art that is a cucumber sandwich. You have the Melba toast and then the soft stuff. The cucumbers and butter and herbs and things."

"That does sound good, Mrs. White."

"It is a summer delight, quite refreshing on a hot day like today."

The humidity made breathing difficult for Ethan. He was thankful he wasn't responsible for children.

The pool was more crowded than usual. Mr. Stiles was doing the side-stroke in the lap lane. Mr. Ronald Currant and Mrs. Sturgeon held hands in the shallow end, the water at waist level. Mrs. Gillette and Mrs. Parlet sat at a table in the shade playing cards. The activities roster must've been thin as a Kleenex inside, Ethan thought.

Ethan took it all in.

"Ike, would you be so kind as to let me make you a cucumber sandwich? It would be my pleasure."

Ethan shrugged. "I don't see why not. Do you have a kitchen available?"

She waved off that question as an insignificance.

"I'll call on you one day. The pool can go on standby for a few minutes."

"That's for sure," Ethan said.

Ethan wasn't sure if it was his imagination but it seemed as if she kicked her feet slightly. Girlish almost, gleeful.

"Humor her," Butch said.

After a while Butch walked over and helped Mrs. White to her feet. He had her cane in his left hand and he transferred it slowly into her right. There was a simple grace in the way Butch cared for her, Ethan thought. It was almost shocking in a way.

• • •

"I'll need your help with the refrigerator," Mrs. White said.

They were in her constricted little room, maybe twelve by twelve—all of her possessions crammed into one space, the kitchen a single burner and a mini-fridge.

"And you have all the stuff to make it?"

"I eat cucumber sandwiches just about every day. I'm dainty, remember!"

She rattled off the list of ingredients to pull from the mini-fridge: butter, cream cheese, mayo, and the package of herbs—tarragon, watercress, and cilantro. The salt and pepper are on the counter, she mentioned, along with the other ingredients. The counter sat low, beneath the stove. Ethan handed her the knife and cutting board, as instructed, and she did the rest.

Ethan watched her hands. He thought they would be jittery and frail, but as she peeled the cucumbers and sliced them into thin, almost translucent discs, he was surprised by their agility and strength.

He watched her wrists as she stirred the cream cheese, mayo, and Worcestershire sauce, onion salt and lemon pepper.

"I know, I'm used to doing this," she said, as if she could tell what he was thinking. She slapped the cucumbers on each slice of Melba toast as if she were dealing cards at a Blackjack table in Atlantic City. Then soon enough, she was finished completely. She slid four sandwiches onto a paper plate, handed them to Ethan, topped each one with a little watercress at the last minute, and directed him to her little table.

The cucumber sandwiches were delicious and Ethan savored them, chewing much slower than normal and making sure to taste the herbs, to taste Mrs. White's intent.

"So now you know something new," she said.

"That's true," he said.

And when he was finished eating he decided to tell her. He watched her hands. He couldn't look at her eyes—he wouldn't be able to.

"My real name is Ethan, Mrs. White."

"Ethan! Oh, and all this time I have been calling you something wrong. I'm mortified."

He didn't want to crush or disorient her, but she was doing so well—he figured she could take it.

"Ike is my nickname," he lied. "Unofficial, of course."

She shrugged. "Oh well, live and learn. You are young still."

Ethan wanted to tell her so many things. His sense of disappointment and boredom. His aspirations. The gaping hole yawning inside of him. It wouldn't help anything. He dug a nail into his palm to force himself not to delve deep.

"May I have another?"

She pointed behind her and nodded.

"You know where they are."

He stood up to take one or two, but when he saw them, he knew he'd bring all of them back to the table with him; he did. They sat there and ate them in silence.

Five Visitations

I sleep and I wake; I wake and I sleep. I am not sure entirely which is which. When I sleep I remember so much. Images rush into the forefront of my mind. And yet I do not know if they are *my* images or not. They could be.

There is a pink robe swirling. She speaks my language and feeds me. Sometimes hand to mouth. Sometimes I suck on metal.

"It is spring," I am told. "Would you like some fresh air?"

I get some fresh air. I smell the most delicious floral smells—a warm wash of petals and I don't even know what they are called. It is a cloud. The petals form around it.

I stare into the whiteness. There are flecks of paint and it so reminds me of something. Is this déjà vu? The whiteness has a purpose, but I just can't recall it.

I have a sudden urge for apples, for playing cards and listening.

The pink robe swirls. The room is empty. I listen to my breathing. I am good at breathing. I excel at respiring. These things mean something. I'm not sure what.

• • •

Who is this individual crying in front of me? He has a bowl of—what *are* those? Colorful "orbs"—is that the right word? Yellow and green and orange things. What do I want with these? I'm no spring chicken here. I'm a good egg though. People always said I was one. I come from a legacy of good eggs.

"I just, I just don't know," he's saying. "It's tough."

"You should stop with the blubbering. Be prideful," I say.

He can't look at me. This is the sign of weakness. And I can tell by the way in which he holds himself, he's short and insecure. He lets life drag him around rather than the other way.

The lady in pink comes. She has one arm draped over the short man and she's speaking softly to them.

It's not polite to whisper.

"Turn on the television," I say. "It's very cold in here." The short man leaves the bowl of color on the tray next to the other things. The lady in pink reaches over to the black thingy with buttons and presses it and the television comes on like a miracle from heaven. Finally, some peace around here. What does a woman need to do?

"I'm so sorry, Mrs. Blackburn," the lady in pink says.

"It's okay. I'm just...emotional."

"Oh. No."

The short man stammers out and I hope he stammers for good. I cannot abide such weakness.

The walls are all a dull white—don't they have *any* sense of aesthetics here? It's white outside from that stuff falling and it's white inside. Overkill if you ask me.

• • •

The red maple leaves distract me. They blaze in the sunshine outside the window of this place. At some points the window almost seems to be on fire. At times the effect is almost threatening. At other times the fire tells me what I need to know: it is happening.

He sits in front of me. He is such a kind son and I tell him so. He holds my hand for a moment, which is nice. I know he brings what's-her-name sometimes, but not this time. I for-get—he told me there was a reason why she couldn't visit. He holds out some fruit and I take it and thank him.

"These things look delicious," I say. "You know I love the green ones."

"Yes. Yes. You're welcome, mother." His eyes seem vaguely misty. "You've always loved apples."

"And what are these yellow things?"

"Bananas, mother."

"Funny word. 'Banana.' Isn't it? Ba-na-na."

"Yes, it is."

He tells me about losing his store. He says it's going under and there's not much he can do about it.

"Nobody buys books."

"Used? What kind of store is it exactly?"

"A bookstore. A used bookstore." He tells me that he had to carry board games and stuffed animals and even video games recently and that these items now account for more than half his revenue.

"Are the animals really *stuffed?*"

"They aren't real animals, mother."

"Oh, they aren't?"

"No. Can we change the subject, please?"

He cuts an apple up for me and I eat it. He starts to inquire about my stool, but he knows I don't want to think about what's coming out one end while I'm tending to the other. It's not supper talk.

I watch the fire in the tree.

We sit for a while and take it all in. He holds my hand again.

The nurse lets him out soon enough. Her pink robe—what

is it called?—really stands out around here.

• • •

The air vibrates. I can see it vibrate. The vibrations ripple through the heavy green leaves and the air is pregnant with things to come. Is that thunder?

Joel is late, which is unusual. This concerns me because usually if Joel is late this means it will be a bad day for him, an "off day." Joel loathes lateness, in himself most of all.

I fall asleep waiting. A hand presses my shoulder—Angela, the nurse. Her uniform is a bright reminder of where I am: a cotton carnation.

Joel sits next to me. I can see pity in his eyes—which I don't like. Someone else used to express this. Names slip most easily. Dr. Oswald says the slipping will only increase. The white pills help prop me up. For now they do.

"I'm thinking maybe fruit will help you," Joel says.

"Help me with what?"

"What we spoke about—you know, your bowels and all."

A side effect of the white pills. One of many. Laxatives help, but not enough.

"That would be wonderful," I say.

His fist clenches and I know why.

"I don't want to hear it," I say.

The last time Angela had to call security. Joel is a good son, but his temper still gets the best of him. Just like...it all seems so long ago now. The lake, the pungent aroma of skunk cabbage, the apple trees by the bank.

"Where did we live? I mean, all those years..."

"Oh, God," Joel says.

"Was it by a lake? I'm thinking it was by a lake, or maybe it was a pond."

Joel says he showed me the photo album before, that he tried to jog my memory that way. He says he's working hard.

"It worked, too. You did remember."

The fan oscillates nicely and I'm sleepy. When I'm drowsy my conversations with Joel seem dreamlike. When I drift off again it's as if he was a spirit visitor, an apparition from some long forgotten era.

• • •

What kind of tree *is* this?

Angela stands at the doorway, cross-armed and smiling. A contradiction. She says she's from Trinidad: I wonder if this is a common mannerism there.

"I believe it is a maple tree, Miss. See those red blossoms?"

I do. The tree is stick and branch and little red buds. The thin sunshine leaks through it into the room where I sit on my bed. I read and sleep. I don't like television except to block out the noise. Only then does it relax me.

"Your son is coming today, Miss. You have a visitor."

"My very *first* visitor!"

I eat lunch—vegetable soup and something hard and crispy. Not a cracker. Bigger than a cracker. What is the word? I wash my face and hands.

Joel arrives with flowers—a cluster of carnations. I kiss his cheek. He is a sweet son. I have so many rich memories, a lifetime's worth.

"This is a nice setup," he says. He crosses his hands on his lap. Edward would sit in this exact position. We would rock on the porch swing and watch the dragonflies zip over the lily pads and upward to God-knows-where and then zip down to the water again. We called it Joel's Pond. I'm not sure why now. Why 'Joel's'? Edward was a watchful man and had a great birding eye. He'd point out the Junco. He'd point out the Grackle. He almost always saw them first, and I loved him for this.

"Yes, it is," I say.

"You'll be fine here. They'll take good care of you."

"Yes, I think that, also."

We play cards. Gin Rummy—my favorite game. All those years we played at the house. All those blissful years.

"You look content, mother," Joel says.

"I was just remembering," I say. "Forgive me, I was lost in thought."

"That's great, mom. That's a wonderful sign."

We look at photos from the old house. I wonder what ever happened to it. I should know this, should remember. This is one of those missing bits. One of those holes…

The photos are delightful and he laughs and smiles so much. Joel points to a photograph of a young child, but it is not Joel; I can see that.

"Who *is* that man?"

Joel shakes his head.

"Never mind, mother. It's okay."

But I remove the photo from the album and flip it over. On the back: Jacob one year and seven months. All these lost moments….

I have so many questions, most of which I don't ask. I'm afraid of what I might remember. I'm afraid of what I might blur.

"I need to rest now."

Joel kisses my forehead and I lie down. The sheets are white and I'm surrounded by white walls. I slip easily into sleep. In my dreams my memories—everything—are right there. Sleep is good. It is a place I want to be. But then I must wake up again and forget.

Glory Be to Those Who Choose the Light

When Mildred Fennester Smith passed we knew rested on uncertain ground. Ms. Mildred had been our sign lady for as long as anybody could remember, and our memory trickled back to the edge of time. Ms. Mildred was ninety-three, at least (some say she was older and that even she couldn't herself pin it exactly)—she wrote a sign the week she passed. As the parish assistant, I was slated to handle the manual manipulation of the sign proper, but that was the easy part. The Reverend called me God's own assistant, but the sign was my pleasure—it was just maneuvering letters around is all. Ms. Mildred heard the spirit and provided the transcription.

Thankfully Ms. Mildred passed in her sleep. They say that's the best way to go, and if anyone deserves a best way, it was Ms. Mildred. What with her handmade potholders (mine in the shape and resemblance of an acorn squash), her visits to sickly children and benevolence to the poor in our parish. She truly was a blessing upon us.

• • •

"The Clothes on your Back are More than You Need"
We carried forth much discussion in the parish at large and amongst the Reverend and volunteers who assisted him in some capacity: who would replace the utterly irreplaceable? Who could inscribe an inspired sign? Who had the *ear*? We

pondered possibilities for weeks, while the Reverend recycled Ms. Mildred's recent chestnuts to fill the void: Jesus is our lifeboat! The cross is not mere wall decoration! God's house is *never* for sale!

The parish did not mind a reprise, but after several weeks of mourning they were hungry for the new and unseen breath from above. They wanted inspiration. The sign had become a community guiding light and many among the parish considered themselves followers of the sign, and as such it bore almost as much meaning to them as the weekly sermon. Some felt it was the *beacon*.

Jim Nettles was thought by some among the parish to be a natural replacement for Ms. Mildred, but he was acrimonious in personality and political and some thought he would abuse his given powers. Mary Rison was also considered, but some among the parish fretted over her steadfastness or lack thereof (and Ms. Mary had health problems herself). Finally it was decided to hold a contest: the best sign would result in the position. We decided to leave it open to pure inspiration and go from there.

Over one hundred and seven entries were received (from our blessed town of nine hundred and eighty-seven). The judges consisted of the Reverend, Bill Bullis, Pam Voller, Lisa Seethan, and Michael Balken. I assisted. I have been around a long time and didn't have much else to focus upon since my husband passed several years ago.

After eliminating the nonsensical and prosaic, we decided on the author of "The Clothes on Your Back…" This struck the judges as witty, poignant, relatable and mysterious (but not too mysterious) enough for the layperson.

The author, shockingly, was Nettie Heslin.

· · ·

"I am Lost, Forgotten, and Without the Wings of Youth."

"Nettie Heslin," Ms. Voller said. "That old oddity. She cannot by any means or ways be our sign lady. She's *nuts*. She talks to the clouds and eats beetles for breakfast."

"Fair is fair, is it not?" The Reverend said. "We cannot go back on our word, not this church."

"She may be a *pagan* even," Ms. Voller continued.

The Reverend shrugged his shoulders stoically. "God speaks through her pen, clearly. Perhaps he ignores the vessel. That is enough for us."

And so it began.

· · ·

"You are only Voiceless if You Fail to Listen."

Our town of Midgeville is a pleasant enough place, but nobody ever ever leaves—which gave us, for many years, a rather parochial reputation. Most likely we were deserving of such standing. The residents of Midgeville were often born, bred and died within the confines of the town without scarcely seeing so much as the state capitol. Some residents are afraid to cross the town line and rarely, if ever, do so. I have visited Lincoln County (twice and Wilson County (three times). I am, as a result, considered worldly.

Nettie Heslin was one such homebody, though. However, she took it to a rare extreme which made others in the parish queasy. Only five or six (little Timmy Croslin is questionable) members of the parish had even *seen* Ms. Nettie in the flesh, since she doesn't leave her property. Nettie had a young lady— one Jillian Wilton, who did her weekly shopping. Sadly, Nettie had no family to speak of. She only saw the light of day in the backyard and cultivated a weakness for gardening, by legend. However, she kept her hedges high and somewhat unruly—that was known.

I was instructed to make her acquaintance, as I would be the go-between. The parish was only asking for one single sentence from her a week; yet the prestige of the position warranted at least a courtesy face-to-face.

• • •

"Imagine a Field of Poppies. With Fangs."

I knocked on the door expecting strange shuffling behavior and avoidance, but instead it snapped open. Before me stood Ms. Nettie in a brilliant blue robe adorned with orange birds (was it silk?). Her hair snaked around her neck in an odd pattern, covering the entirety of her neck and coalescing in front of her in a wide horse brush array. It looked quite uncomfortable. She gesticulated wildly as she spoke, guiding me to the divan, then she clicked a heavily lidded lamp, blowing dust from the bulb self-consciously.

"I don't often receive visitors, as you may observe." Her hands continued their desolate movements. I thought she may have been simultaneously translating into sign language for an invisible audience of her own making—her fingers were that vigorous.

"I have heard this," I said. "I just came to discover the source of your beautiful words."

She pointed upwards with both index fingers.

"I am just a mere go-between. I listen and let my pen capture what the Lord distributes."

She talked non-stop about her routines, her gardening, the books she was perusing, the villanelles she composed in her mind, the photography she takes with only the assistance of her eyelids. I expected to find a grouch and hermit, instead I found a woman with immense and seemingly boundless creative energy. Then she showed me her paintings—wild effervescent, swirling patterns of orange and blue and black and purple, like airplane contrails though a morning sunrise.

"Sometimes he speaks to me with words," she said. "Sometimes he speaks to me in images. I have to be ready."

• • •

"The Spirit Within is the Spirit Without Within."

The parishioners were, at first, entranced. "When she says 'without' she means Jesus before Gethsemane—that is clear," Mr. Robert said.

"I think it refers to Job," Ms. Rebecca said.

"I think it is *all* of us—the common sinner," Ms. Voller said.

"What about 'you are only voiceless'," Mr. Robert asked.

"Who is voiceless and who should they listen to?" Ms. Voller asked.

"God himself, who else?" Ms. Rebecca replied.

"It's a riddle," Ms. Voller said. "A twisted little nugget." We couldn't tell if this was a compliment or not. The way her voice hung on "little" made it sound demonic somehow, or perhaps this was my false and contorted impression.

They found her signs enigmatic. But perhaps a shade *too* much so. Perhaps too odd, not what they expected. They wanted the sign to offer them something from which they could learn. Some grumbled, complaining that Ms. Mildred's signs were for everyone. Ms. Nettie's signs seemed for the close reader—obtuse and far afield.

• • •

"The Cancer that Lies Dormant in your Heart can be Deferred."

"By what? By whom? Help us out," the Reverend said. "Main Street Baptist gained twenty last Sunday. We lost a few."

Main Street Baptist was the interloper—having started just twenty years ago and stolen countless budding parishioners with their fire and brimstone. We suspected a corporation behind their signs—Holy Land, Inc. It was no accident: they ran and operated the vast majority of churches in our state, including Main Street Baptist (though they kept the author of their signage in the dark). It was direct and plain, a counterpoint to Ms. Nettie's vagaries.

The Reverend enjoyed the artistry of Ms. Nettie's messages, but he simply hoped the cryptic messages would not drive more parishioners into the arms of our bitter rival.

"Give us something we can *use*," he said.

"I have enough on my plate at this juncture."

"Sustenance is the world's temptation."

I mentioned this to Ms. Nettie but her eyes stared holes through me.

"I can't steer these messages," she said. "They steer *me*."

I liked her. My mother was lost to me at a young age and I had a weakness for the wisdom of older ladies. Plus, Ms. Nettie was authentic—odd, but true.

I respected the Reverend, also, but his motivation was often directed outward toward strategy and the best interests of the community.

I also suspected he had eyes to move on—I witnessed him several times glancing through the classified section with interest.

"Sustenance is the world's temptation." I watched the reverend read it, ticking each word one by one, savoring the resonance. He stared at the sign, at the gladiolas in front of it. He shook his head with a tinge of defeat.

"I should go and make the acquaintance of this woman."

• • •

"The Path to Righteousness is Littered with Broken Hearted Sinners."

I took him there. Ms. Nettie was in especially rare form— arms and hands flailing and whipping about as she spoke. She served iced tea and orange wedges and little oatmeal cookies. The Reverend averted his eyes from her paintings.

"Can you do me a personal favor?" The Reverend kept his hands clasped down on his lap as if he were containing wild rodents. Every hair on his head was perfectly arranged, a wax statue of himself.

"I can certainly try."

"Can you just include the words 'Jesus' or 'Heaven' in your phrasings more often? It does not have to be all the time—just on occasion. We need efficiency and we need to make sure we bring it all back home, if you catch my drift."

Ms. Nettie sunk into her flailing explanation about being the translator of God's statements, offering that the words come directly from Him untranslated. After ten minutes of this, sensing an opportunity, I stated: "Perhaps we could just add that in an afterwards. It's implicit anyway."

"What does 'implicit' mean?" the Reverend asked. "What do you mean 'afterwards'? This isn't that difficult."

"It's already in there."

"What is? We just tack God onto the message board? It's *about* him."

"It's *from* him," Ms. Nettie said. "This comes direct."

I nodded and Ms. Nettie did a kind of half-gesticulation, half shrug and looked off into the wall. That was good enough for the Reverend, perhaps.

"The spirit within Jesus is the sprit without within," he said, as we were walking back to the car. "What does that mean? I'm not sure, but it sounds better with Jesus in it."

He shook his head twice. I knew what that meant.

• • •

"Heaven is a Place on Earth."

I couldn't bear to tell Ms. Nettie that she had been replaced. She still sent her messages from God, but we didn't post them. We had a computer for that. Attendance was still down and "trending down" the Reverend said. "We need holy behinds in the pews."

The ones who hadn't died or moved on.

I missed Henry so. We lived a good, simple life and he would have had the right advice for the situation. I had to return to our photographs for consolation.

Ms. Nettie's surreal compositions with Jesus tacked on (the ones we didn't run) seemed even stranger than her original compositions. "We of the people, are within the people and the spirit sings. And Jesus." "It is a lonely man who dances with others. Says God." "The highway of thieves and gamblers glistens with the spirit underneath and because of the corruption. Says God."

I continued to drive over every Monday morning to pick up her latest lines (as she refrained from using the phone or a computer). We chatted and I went on my way. I was forced to tell her that we weren't using them.

"I was swimming in the corn on Friday and it was as if he

was inside the stalks. It is difficult to describe. He was sprinkled everywhere, speaking to me."

How was I supposed to just walk away?

For a year and two months I visited her every Monday. She rarely asked about the Reverend, the parish, or anything else. She just handed me one or two sentences.

"I usually fall asleep in church," she told me once.

But I moved. I decided that in the time I had left I needed a larger scope.

I heard from Ms. Crystal that Ms. Nettie passed in the cornfield about nine months later. Stroke or brain hemorrhage, she suspected, not sure which.

According to Ms. Crystal, Ms. Nettie became lost in the stalks and began grasping them for a way out. Yet the field was large and, as a result of her struggles, Ms. Nettie lost her way and stumbled. She had a smile on her face, one brimming with inspiration I had no doubt.

The Reverend bought an updated computer program to automatically churn out randomized weekly sayings as needed. He kept the computer in the basement, by the secondary freezer and beverage fridge. The fridge was always stoked with Pepsi, Sprite and Coke. All ice cold.

Good Filth

The Professor's VCR began beeping incessantly. This was a time before widespread technological competence. Rather than simply unplugging the VCR from the wall, the esteemed went ballistic, lost his shit. He began banging on the television, as if it was the television's fault. He shouted, "My life is a fucking farce." Our jaws dropped, unsure what to say or do. Eventually the professor figured he could unplug the VCR, but he didn't stop there. He unplugged the VCR from the television and walked over to the window and chucked the whole beeping mess four flights down to the quad where we could hear the VCR smash against the sidewalk below. Then silence. It worked.

I think of this little anecdote frequently. Though Dr. K was normally even-handed (if intense), something clicked in his head that day and he simply couldn't reign it in. He had to throw the VCR out of the window, had to hear it smash on the sidewalk (we wanted to cheer, but didn't). *My* life is a fucking farce five times a day. Though I haven't thrown any electronic equipment out of the window, I'm not above it one bit.

My life is farcical for different (non-academic reasons).

• • •

Have a daughter who lives in perpetual crises mode and is seemingly always a day from dying (or believing this to be the case).

My wife threatens divorce at least twice a week.

We have ants in the house. Lots of ants.

We have or had mice—unclear which. Most likely the former.

Birds constantly smack into our new windows. When we spent the twenty-five grand on windows, nobody mentioned the bird-slaying possibilities.

I'm a writer who never writes.

I'm likewise a writer who never publishes.

An overly solicitous politician, Phil, comes by the house every other day to check in our welfare and discuss the latest local issue. This despite our clearly marked "No Soliciting" sign.

We have a handyman doing some odd jobs for us who is not only incompetent but doesn't have a car or any tools whatsoever.

I'm a house daddy.

• • •

So here's how it plays out: I'm sitting at the blank screen typing. But I'm not writing. I'm taking notes. I am a kick-ass note-taker. I can research a novel concept all the live-long day. I'll detail a slew of interesting characters. I plot. I plan. I have a particular historical period in mind and I am well-informed about its various mechanisms. I have a good sense for how the people in this particular time and place (1836 Oklahoma Territory, say) speak and act. I take reams of notes for weeks and months. But when I arrive at the point where most writers would actually write the novel, I balk. I lose gumption. I lose interest in the project. I go back to social networking or Words with Friends or check out old famous clips on YouTube or dangle my cat upside down like a bat. Anything but the writing. I'm not experiencing writer's block exactly—I just lose the desire, for whatever reason.

I have extensive notes and ideas accumulated for a total of forty-five different—possibly exhilarating—novels. I haven't written one of them.

It's an exhausting cycle.

I have actually pondered the possibility of placing an ad in *Poets and Writers* in search of a writer who needs copious notes to begin his/her novel in exchange for an acknowledgement and a few hundred clams. It's probably worth a shot. Someone could use all of this preparatory work.

As I'm immersed in this utterly fruitless project, if one can call it a project, my four year- old daughter comes up to me and says: "My brain is bleeding." Ranks up there with the worst possible sentences a parent can hear. She leans her head toward me, already anticipating my inspector eye. And there it is—a thin trail of blood trickling from her head, down to her face.

"John F. Kennedy," I say. "What happened?"

"I don't know. It's just coming out of my head."

So I have to press the pause button on the note-taking for a book I will never write (and if it *is* published by someone else—I'll never read). And I'm annoyed. I was producing some excellent research on various plains rattlesnake dishes.

We rush to the E.R., wait nine hours and upon being finally seen by some kind of exhausted nurse practitioner, we discover that Dina accidently spilled some Halloween blood and forgot to tell me.

"Whoops, sorry Daddy. I forgot." She thought it was real. She convinced herself it was.

"That's okay," I say. "These things happen." My favorite appeasing cliché because it covers virtually every known problem or situation.

It seems I have a dumbass attention-whore for a daughter.

So I call my wife at work. I can hear her typing the entire time we're talking. Hate that. I relay the basics of the story—including my fury at our daughter's early onset dementia.

"She's *four* years old," my wife says. "Cut her some slack."

"You have no idea," I say.

"What does that mean?"

"It means I'm bending over backwards to raise this kid and she pulls a day-sucking stunt like this?"

"I'm going to speak to Marty about, you know," she says. "This is getting out of hand."

Kate drops the D bomb as if she's speaking about stopping the newspaper delivery—casual and non-stop.

"We'll talk about it when you get home," I say.

As if there's any doubt about where Dina gets her sense of melodrama.

Dina's dancing around the dining room. Our dining room is in name only—it's devoid of furniture, as we ran out of money years ago.

"What are you doing, Din?"

"And there are bugs," she says. She does this—begins her sentences as if we were already in the middle of a conversation. She's slapping at her knees and pounding her feet. Her dance could very-well be the next hot maneuver at the clubs downtown. Very self-flagellating.

I saunter over thinking it's yet another Dina fixation. But this time it's not. Five lines of ants crisscross the room and rise up the walls and to the ceilings—large, bulbous black ants. They look peeved.

There's a moment when, insect annihilation spray can in

120

hand, I experience a moment of clarity. I realize I should absolutely not spray exterior insect spray in the dining room with a young child prancing about.

But then I think, Fuck these ants, I'm doing it anyway. I just go bonkers—firing away at the ants indiscriminately. Watching them flail and they fall from the dining room walls to the gray carpet below.

Then: "Daddy, I have blood coming from my eyes." And she does. And this time it's not Halloween blood.

I'm a shitty father.

• • •

"How can you even think of such a thing?"

We're at the breakfast bar—the designated contrition spot in our household.

"I know. I just didn't think it through."

"Thank God she's okay. The two of you could've been killed."

"I know. My mental capacity is very limited these days. It's all that pot I smoked when I was sixteen."

She doesn't even have to utter the D-word. She shakes her head in a divorcee manner. Or maybe it's her purposefully unflattering do. She knows I don't like all that Jennifer Aniston-y layering and frippery.

"Also, we have mice," she says. "Don't spray bomb the house with poison, okay? Let's just call someone."

"How do you know we have mice?"

"There's mice turds all in the utensil drawer."

I look. It could be flattened peppercorns or wild rice. I don't know, maybe barley husks? I make the argument.

"I also *saw* at least three. I didn't tell you until now."

So now there's another thing. Maybe when Dina feels

better she can try to whack them with a shovel. It might stop her face from bleeding for two seconds.

When Kate takes off for her book group at the hip bar slash coffeehouse, I e-mail a few exterminators. First I do a cursory research job on Angie's list. Then I type up a brief form letter. Finally, I send it off. I figure they're all basically the same.

I tuck Dina into bed. She blows me a kiss and I do the same.

We're good.

• • •

In the morning I get a response from Taylor's XXX and I ask the guy (Taylor?) if he can make it over today and he says yes so I give him directions.

After she eats her Coco Puffs (I keep them in my den— her mother is against them), I hand Dina a shovel, tell her to whack any fuzzy smelling brown things she sees running on the floor. Dina squats two inches from the floor, shovel in hand, ready to pounce.

Taylor's XXX truck pulls up and a thick black guy with no neck and a gangly white dude with tattoos up and down his face trudge up our walk. They look like ex-cons and probably are, but what the hey.

As they're spraying and setting traps and whatnot I ask no-neck what's the deal with the name.

"My name?" His eyes widen, sensing a judgment

"Nonono, Taylor's XXX? Sounds kinda risqué, don't you think?"

"The X stands for death," he says. "As in poison."

Doesn't anybody have a sense of irony anymore?

"No, I get that," I say. "I think it's just the triple x." No neck shrugs. Tattoo face stares at me, unblinking.

As the mice killers are leaving, two birds thwack into our addition windows. Two sparrows.

This has been happening on and off all year—ever since we upgraded our windows.

We find robins and blue jays and grackles and wrens and cardinals, necks broken, wings flapping limp in the wind.

I'd like to bury each one individually.

Instead, we have a makeshift mass grave. It's a hole behind the pine tree in back next to the shed. We cover the hole with cinder blocks so the scavengers can't get to the birds. But there's nothing to feel good about here. Dina cries every time. We go back there with a newly deceased bird. I do the cross on my chest and say a few trite words of uplift about the lives of sparrows. Dina looks away.

"Do you think they were in love?"

"Like a husband and wife?"

"Yeah."

If I say yes it makes their demise potentially all that much more grueling for Dina to deal with. Not that I'm into protection. Just the opposite. But why roil relatively calm waters for no apparent reason? If I say no then we get into a further call and response regarding the nature of sparrows, how sparrows relate to one another, and the innate random cruelty of the universe.

"I'm not sure, Dina."

"Yeah."

"It looks as though they knew each other. They were probably friends, I guess?"

"Yeah."

"So that way at least they have someone next to them in

the ground."

"You mean in heaven, right?"

"They don't?"

"I think they probably just decompose into the ground."

"What's 'decompose'?"

"You know, when the beetles and worms have to eat them. Their bodies rot and slowly they turn into dirt. More dirt, I guess."

She shrugs—the same exact shrug no neck offered earlier.

She doesn't say much after this. We go inside for apple juice and some crackers.

• • •

That evening is peaceful. I have a couple hours of interrupted me time. Dina is taking a nap (perhaps having nightmares about bird-eating worms) and Kate is off at work plus whatever she does after work—pre-divorce support group? This gives me time to not-write. It's what I'm best at—procrastinating my novel writing, while vaguely pondering it. Every year I win the NaNoWriMo contest for laziest fuck who doesn't write shit.

But I *do* write this time—it's just not novel writing. Instead, I recline on the couch, sip a Yuengling, and write a piece about how I can't bring myself to write. It's an essay/memoir/blog entry/glorified Facebook status update/Tweet/whatever.

I know I'll do absolutely nothing with it. And yet, just the process of putting my phlegmatic words on the page helps immensely. It could lead to "real" writing. Which could lead to growing a pair so that I might someday submit my drivel for publication. That would be nice.

Then Kate comes back from work/post-work, tipsy from several glasses of wine (white, I'm sure). She wants to have sex.

So we do. This is about the only scenario whereby this happens. Alcohol is our friend.

And yet, alcohol is not our friend for waking up and being responsible adults.

I hear a knocking at the door. Kate is still out cold next to me. The clock says 10:32.

I'm in my boxers and my wife beater. But I don't really care—it's only Phil the Politician.

"Greetings, resident," he says. "This is me." Phil hands me his card.

This is his usual boilerplate intro despite the fact that he's dropped by the house at least twenty times.

"Phil, I have about fifteen of your cards. We've talked a thousand times before."

"It's just my way of—"

"I know, I know. What's up?"

"Well, funny you should ask. Do you know that…."

And Phil the Politician launches into some spiel about the school board's attempt to control blah, blah, blah. Here comes the monologue Phil the Politician assumes (wrongly in my case) that all suburban parents give a rat's ass about the school board. The school's safe. The teachers are good. What's the problem?

We have a No Soliciting sign clearly posted on the door. Phil the Politician pays it zero attention.

"Can we change the subject?"

I'm brash with Phil because I have to be to avoid getting sucked into the vortex of his verbal diarrhea.

He's a good guy and I'm sure he'll make a great whatever-he's-running for. Politics just don't do anything for me. Change I cannot possibly believe in.

So then—to attempt to answer my request to change the subject—he rotates through a series of possibilities, like some kind of topical jukebox gone haywire: the environment, crime, identity theft, speed bumps, rats in the neighborhood, unemployment, suburban drug abuse.

"Phil," I say. "I like you. I do." I hand him a twenty. "My donation for this week."

"Oh, thank you, thank you."

I close the door with a satisfying snap.

As if he didn't see it coming.

He'll be back for more in a day or two. He's like a well-dressed panhandler. Except most panhandlers are smarter and more interesting.

• • •

We find twitching, dying mice all over the house. Dozens of them. Dina smashes them with her shovel, as I instructed.

"You don't have to smash all of them, honey. Not now. It's overkill. Literally overkill."

The carpets are pocked with blood stains.

"How will we know if they are alive or not then?"

"Forget it," I say. "Carry on."

• • •

My wife wakes up, goes to work (thankfully).

Dina is going over to one of her little friend's. Nina and Dina. It's vomit-inducingly sweet.

So again. Me time. But I decide to take a different tact. Rather than frustrate myself with the whole writing/not-writing dichotomy, I decide to do something nice for Katie. A cynic would say this is in response to sexual pleasure the night prior, but the cynic would be wrong because I didn't receive much pleasure and I'm also acting sheerly out of fear. I. Don't. Want. To. Be. Alone.

I call a handyman who comes highly recommended—at least from Jake, a father of another one of Dina's little friends (Winnie).

Kate wants a new shed. She's wanted a new shed for years, though I've poo-pooed the idea. It's a *shed*, I've argued. It's supposed to look crappy. But, as Kate has indicated, looking crappy and moldering are two different things. The shed door swings off its hinges. The walls are collapsing and/or rotting. About the only component of the shed which *is* actually functional is the roof.

So Jack Shore tells me he can rebuild our shed for under $500. Which—aside from being a good deal of money—is music to my ears.

"The only thing is, I don't have a car."

No problem, I say. And pick him up from the local bus station. We shake hands.

Jack is a giant of a man—at least 6'8 in my estimation and probably three hundred pounds. I want to ask him about football or basketball, but figure he's heard these questions before. And I don't want to aggravate a 6'8 plus giant.

There is one small problem though. Jack doesn't have any tools. Not only that, he doesn't even have a tool belt or box or bag or anything.

"Wait, aren't you missing something? I'm lacking equipment."

"That's one way to put it."

"Sorry, buddy." Is it just me or does the term "buddy" mean exactly the opposite of "buddy" in most contexts?

"So what do we do?"

"Do you have any, you know, tools?"

"The basics. A few hammers, a wrench, a couple screwdrivers."

"You have a level and a saw?"

"No."

So we go get a level and a saw. We get plywood. We get cinder blocks. Other things to do the job. This is the hidden cost of a $500 job, I think.

I contemplate buying Jack a tool belt. But I don't. I just can't bring myself to do it.

Jack is slow, molasses slow. Chinese water torture slow. On the phone he estimated a one-day job, but five days later he's still out back hammering. I bring him water, check on him. He usually smiles and says it's going well.

"It's going to be a really nice shed," he says.

Dina prances outside and watches him in full wonder.

When Jack is there, we're all transfixed.

Then he's done. It's a gleaming, perfect red mini-barn shed. It's a shed from the shed-lover's Annual. It's a masterpiece of sheddography. I'm in love with that shed.

"Before it gets all mucky," I tell Kate. "Let's, you know, *christen* it."

And when Dina is asleep, we do. At least until I get skeeved out by the crickets which have already made their way into the inner recesses of our brand new masterpiece. But it doesn't matter. At least for a few hours, it doesn't.

Something will go wrong tomorrow morning. I know it. Kate knows it. But standing half naked in the shed, we couldn't care less.

"Did you come?"

"My brain did," I said. "It's good. It's fine. It will all be okay."

She taps my hand with her hand in concordance. A little love tap.

A Little Blood Company

What they dreaded was mud. T&T could handle the heat and the cold, but when it rained Taylor She's white dress spotted up and smeared no matter how delicately she walked. Taylor He wore boots and a pull-over, but the mud found its way through regardless, like some ruthless omen.

The fall was the dry season, Taylor He reminded her.

"Don't fret. We're in an excellent position here."

They walked.

To find the obscure households through the valley they had to hoof it—the car was never enough. They had to leave that forlorn spot, parked on the non-existent shoulder of Rural Road 187. They had to lumber up the scarp.

As a result, Taylor He bore the burden of the backpack clinking with "The Product," as they referred to it. Taylor He worried, despite himself, that a bottle or two might crack during the journey, but it never did.

They could see the house up on the ridge and a thin grey plume of smoke snaked upward through the branches. Taylor She could smell the burning cherry—she thought it was cherry. Somewhere in this fine country boys are throwing around pigskin, she thought. It's that brand of weather. Light air and the sun some distant anecdote.

"I was thinking about what you said last night," Taylor He said.

"Yeah. Ain't that something?"

"I don't feel the burning. That's the thing. You said it must be something smoldering inside you—not knowing what. Me? I'm trying to get a few sparks from the flint. Get my meaning?"

"I do. Felt that way when I had pneumonia once," Taylor She said.

Taylor He light a cigarette, saying they still had time. It was still early. Best not to knock on any superfluous doors during breakfast, he thought. Not a winning stratagem.

"Not talking about an illness," He said. "Mean to tell you, there's nothing left propelling me. Not like you."

Taylor She knew that was, in part, because she was nubile and still fervent. At 18 who doesn't have a burning? If they didn't they might actually no longer be of the corporeal. She knew that He had been twice betrothed, even though she was afraid to inquire about the finer points. No use asking about defeat—there is something mean spirited about even probing there. She just knew it cannot be a *contented* feeling for He. Those dashed lives.

Thankfully the slope was pebble and rubble, not dirt. If it was dirt, it would be mud.

"But you're good at *this*," She said.

He tipped his cap with an overture of sarcasm.

"Why thank you, cousin," He said and winked.

"You're welcome, cousin," She said.

He picked a stone up and pitched it down the hill, hearing it click against the others and roll in the leaves and then stop.

"It's a citadel here. They don't make it easy," He said.

"I'll be on the lookout," She said.

"Tact A, alright? If we hit a hitch we go to F, not B."

She nodded nippy and turned.

• • •

"We don't usually cotton to passersby, especially

door-to-door types." The lady of the house was wearing a red and white striped dress, which tattered in places and thin in others. She looked young to Taylor He, but he wasn't the best arbiter always. He had learned this the hard way, in the villages. There was a reason he clung to Taylor She. She wasn't *just* a piece. He trained her, but she trained him, also—though he'd never admit as much. Her forehead seemed a whit too wide. Her front teeth revealed a gap.

"Are you, by any chance, newlyweds?"

"Yes, sir. How did you know?" The lady's posture loosened and she let her neck muscles slacken and she pulled at her hair and she smiled broadly. This was good.

"Just a lucky stab in the dark. That first year of marriage is a delight and you seem to bear the stamp."

"It sure is," she said. "We've only been here nine months now. And it *is* a delight, you are correct."

"Well, that's what we're here to speak with you about," Taylor She said. She wanted to cut to it, do what they needed to and skedaddle before somebody hounded them or worse. She felt like an intruder, a fraud, even if *they* didn't exhibit this suspicion. Some unseen tautness rippled the air.

"This here is my cousin," Taylor She said. "We're in this together—a shared family interest. Our little blood company."

"Oh, I thought you two were a couple—you had me going there."

Taylor He and She exchanged slight cringes. Taylor He knew they had her then. They practiced this expression many-a-time in his cracked shaving mirror.

"What we have to share with you is a way to make your marriage even sweeter, even *more* delightful, if that's possible. And it *is* possible. Quite. There are always unseen possibilities."

Taylor He reached back into his pack and withdrew a bottle of The Product.

The substance was orangish yellow and from inside the glass it almost glowed in the autumn light.

Taylor He cracked the seal and asked the lady of the house if she had a small glass he could borrow for the purpose of offering her a sample of The Product.

He poured a small line of The Product into the glass and handed it to the young bride.

"Now, before you drink this, let us kindly tell you something about it," Taylor She said.

"The all-natural ingredients within this concoction contain absolutely no chemicals or additives," He continued, "and this concoction will stay safe to drink for up to a month, if kept cold. You have an icebox, so that is helpful."

"But, if I may ask, what does it *do*?" the housewife asked, tugging on her hair again. "What is the purpose?"

"Ah, but it has been proven that this elixir will add two *entire years* to your life," He continued. "If you drink one bottle a month for a year, you will absolutely gain two years. Just like that. This is a scientific *fact*, not an exaggeration or something I like to spout because I am selling this fine elixir. It is a scientific *fact* proven by accredited factual sources and most impressive statistics."

"No, I believe you. You seem certain."

He mentioned the literature was utterly convincing—a tad technical, a tad complex, but utterly true—and Taylor She slid a packet of it across the kitchen table to the housewife.

She glanced at the study and nodded along.

"Well, it does look very scientific. As long as the two years are good years and not spent in misery, this truly could be a real bargain. Something extra and unexpected."

She downed the sample, gritting her teeth.

"Won't taste great. We apologize for that. But…two entire extra years. Just imagine!"

The housewife shook her head in disgust.

"It tastes a little funny, like spoiled vinegar or something."

"That's the taste of medicine working. It wouldn't be medicine if it tasted like maple syrup."

She nodded along.

"How many bottles would you like?"

She bought a year's supply, saying that she'll surprise her husband when he returns from hunting grouse.

"Your husband hunts?"

"Well, not all the time—but often. Too much really. I do miss him often when he is out and about and simply hope he will be back before he said he would."

"That is so sweet," Taylor She said. "What young love birds." She didn't mean to echo the prey. She regretted this.

Taylor He whooped and hollered in celebration.

Taylor She wanted to run to the next house before hubby returned and demanded their money back. Taylor He wasn't overly concerned. The woman of the house—Mrs. Bauten, she said her name was—mentioned two more households on the ridge, both worth a roll of the bones. Not too many out here, she proclaimed. The next house over, she said, was an old man who lived there with his nephew who took care of him—Mr. Closter was his name, she said. And then there were the two ladies on Poplar Ridge. This is why leads didn't usually matter. Word of mouth was worth its weight in gold, Taylor He thought. He said this often enough to bore She to tears.

Mrs. Bauten was the perfect buyer, Taylor He said—young,

dumb and in love with life. Free spender wanting to improve what they had and prosper into eternity. It wasn't a fountain of youth exactly, but it was a bottle of extension and sometimes that's all it takes.

His usual plan B was to launch into "Can you imagine what you could do with an entire year of life…" Which often worked if the sheer factual basis did not.

Around the corner, Taylor She yanked Taylor He to the tree.

"I need a break," she said. She pressed his hand to her dress and up into it, his knuckles scouring her inner thighs. "All this selling."

"I think she could tell," Taylor He said, tonguing her. "I don't think she bought the cousins line at all, not deep down. Who knows though? Perhaps it offered her something else to think about, perhaps distracted her."

"It doesn't matter," She said. "Maybe we're just *special* cousins. They have those."

Taylor She thought back to their wedding night, to the way his eyes glowed cat-like in the shadows of the hotel room, the way the ocean wind whistled through the slats of the blinds, the way the candle popped and hissed in the humid air.

"Maybe we are, in fact. Distant ones. You never know."

"That's disgusting," She said, gently tamping down the edge of her drawers, careful not to rip it. "Is this going to be bad luck?"

"Next time we tell them we're cousins who also happen to do other things. Might get us somewhere in these forsaken parts."

She pressed into Taylor He.

"You'd do anything for a sale," she said.

136

"That, young lady, is the absolute…." He said, pausing in pleasure. "Verity. That's the word I was searching for."

• • •

"Mr. Nelson doesn't receive visitations," the young man said. His teeth reminded Taylor She of ancient lichen-covered boulders and his eyes bore a droopy negligence. Taylor She was hoping Taylor He would just let it go. Sometimes his unwillingness to move on simply wasted time they could fill more productively elsewhere. "You know this," she told him once. "It's a weakness."

"I'm subject to my own competitive drive, I'll admit it."

The young man had the door propped half-way closed, his foot wedged in the opening. Taylor She shot Taylor He an evil glance, but he avoided it.

"We would like to take the opportunity to share with you our product which, at bare minimum, can add several years to your life. Interested in hearing more?"

The young man shuffled and looked behind him into the darkness.

"I'll be right there," he said, back into it.

"It won't matter in his case," the young man said.

Taylor She saw an opening.

"What about you? You still have a long way to go. Couldn't you use two extra years *on top* of the years that God grants you? This is a beautiful world chock-filled with wonder."

They could hear woodpeckers thock behind them at dead branches.

The young man turned the nob to make sure he didn't lock himself out of the house. He closed the door behind him, gingerly, lifting his finger to his mouth.

"It's not a good circumstance I have here. Can you take

me with you? Get me out of here."

He bent forward and his left hand trembled. He didn't look up to them.

"I am in need."

Taylor and Taylor looked at each other and found themselves lacking words in the company of the troubled soul before them.

The woodpeckers continued ominously in the deep woods.

"We cannot, I'm sorry," Taylor He said. "We have our own obligations and a constricted schedule we must stick to. Our company employs us individually. The best I could do would be to pass along information as to prospective employment and a word to someone who might be able to help, once we get back to civilization."

The young man threw his head back in frustration, pulling at the skin on his arm.

"This old man is going to drive me mad. What's worse, there's all this excess medication at arm's reach. I don't want two more years. I want a bullet in the head. *That* would be a grace."

There was no plan F or anything else after this. Taylor He tightened the straps on his sack and offered the young man their best. They turned and headed back into the thumping echoes of woodpeckers and the dead wood around them.

• • •

The third and last house on the ridge was lower down on the Eastern side and Taylor and Taylor had a substantially longer hike to get there. The pine trees reached higher into the gray sky and the path itself was less traversed, as evidenced by the briers and moss underfoot. It was a dark and mangy patch of woods.

In a meadow on the left Taylor She spotted a sign and the cemetery behind it. Six or Seven headstones tucked in the high grasses, though it was difficult to approximate an exact count.

Taylor She couldn't help but think.

And what exactly have they achieved so far? How would she be judged?

The woodpeckers sounded off far in the distance.

They trudged on, past fern and crow's feet and skunk cabbage. The woods reeked of unseen and moldering vegetation. These were the days of their youth, Taylor She thought. And yet, look at how they conducted themselves.

"Who is it?" The voice reverberated from within. The house was a split log cabin. The porch was mossed and half rotten, though the two rocking chairs upon it looked freshly painted.

"We have a health product that will make a vast difference in the quality of your lived days," Taylor He said. He had a fine voice that would have suited him to radio.

"I have a shot gun," the voice replied. She was a woman. The voice was graveled with age and one too many packs of cigarettes, one too many bottles of brandy. "You git."

She clanked the barrel of the rifle against the inside of the door to punctuate.

"There's no danger here," Taylor He said. "Just me and my cousin came to show you a health product."

They heard her speak to someone else inside—a murmuring.

The chain loosened but stayed in place. A crack in the door revealed long gray hair and an almond head. A few strands of hair stuck in the woman's mouth.

Taylor He and the woman eyeballed each other. Taylor

She lurked behind him. The woman behind the door sighed profoundly.

"We're outliers," the woman said, after some consternation. "We're trying to live the life up close here. I'm sorry, we haven't had a guest up here for some time. It's not personal."

"How long has it been?" Taylor He asked. "We come as friends."

"At least six months, maybe more."

"We only have a product that can add years to your life if properly consumed. It is an all-natural concoction and one which you can purchase a great quantity of from me today if you'd like. The risk is miniscule and the reward is huge. Do you want us to tell you about what we have? Do you want us to come in?"

The woman lifted the barrel of the shotgun to the door so Taylor He could see it.

"You stay right there is what I want."

Taylor He sensed that she was interested, despite the dispiriting tone so he went ahead with the pitch, detailing the usual high points, interesting tidbits and footnotes worth keeping in mind. If he kept talking they would be fine, he told himself. Keep talking. Keep talking.

"You and whomever else might reside on your esteemed property are guaranteed a two year boost to your life expectancy, just from consuming the product on a regular basis for a year."

Taylor He heard more mumbling and he turned around to Taylor She and shook his head.

"I don't have a good feeling here," She whispered.

But the woman asked if she could see a bottle of the product, to sample and further investigate.

"Absolutely you can," Taylor He proclaimed, handing it through the crack in the door.

Taylor and Taylor waited, trying to listen through the crack they were provided.

After some time the bottle landed on the porch, nearly missing his shin.

"Get the hell out of here," the woman said. "That's nothing but corn starch, vinegar, some bitter herbs and a little seasoning of this and that. You think I was born last week?"

"Let me explain the contents," Taylor He started, but the door slammed in his face. "It's not what you think."

"Take one more step, I'll shoot your legs off," the voice bellowed.

Taylor She picked up the bottle and they high-tailed down the path, out of range, in an outright hustle.

• • •

"Well, at least we had the first one," Taylor She said, trying to derail the suddenly dour mood. "It wasn't a complete loss."

Taylor He passed no objection. He simply wanted the haven of car and road and something cold to drink away the pain in his legs. He didn't like to find himself exposed out here in the sticks where he lacked backup, where he was separated from any mode of quicker transport.

The woodpeckers pocked closer and louder and the sun was a distant memory, cloaked behind the tree boughs. The day dimmed speedily.

Taylor She saw him first and froze and the blast came seconds after. She ducked into the leaves. When she looked over at Taylor He, his head was missing its left half, as if suddenly sawed in two from some unseen celestial saw. His mouth smirked as if he knew this would happen, as if he appreciated the irony of it all. Then He was down.

Taylor She ran. It was pure instinct, she knew. She had no other option. She ran. She ran as the blasts continued, one exploding the bark of a tree next to her, another disappearing into the briers.

"And you'll give us our damn money back, you frauds! Cousins, my ass!" It was a deep bellow, as if emanating from within the earth itself.

The hunter.

She tumbled down the ridge, hitting rocks and logs and tearing her white dress to shreds. She rolled and ran some more and heard only her breath and her feet through the leaves and debris. The explosions ceased. She couldn't hear woodpeckers. She couldn't hear anything. And as she ran she realized everything they had was on his back—the car keys, the Product, everything.

She told him not to push it, didn't she?

He always had to push it. The air damp on her cheeks and hot on her neck. Her feet through the leaves. They sounded like the cold wind of another season.

July in the Sticks

Bill never imagined much would happen to him after he retired. It's not as if he had the world's most exciting life, after all—high school then forty-five years working for the state—accounting. Marriage, two lovely daughters. Bill's life was tragedy-free, but dull.

When Bill and Janet moved downstate to officially let go of their previous life (the "damn rat race," Janet called it), Bill hoped for another ten or fifteen years before disease and death took root.

For years everything worked out as planned. He played golf twice a week, went fishing three days a week and puttered about the house and garden. An exciting day was when one of his daughters sent them an e-mail. Once a year, however, the daughters—Kim and Liz—would pay them a visit. Kim was unmarried and owned a small vintage clothing store in Philly— "she turned Yankee on us," Janet complained. Liz was married and had a son, Phillip, and a daughter, Crystal. Phillip was older now and had his various sports and clubs and friends—he was too busy to worry about his grandparents. Crystal, however, just turned five and loved seeing Ma-Ma and Pee-Paw. Bill fell head over heels in love with the girl and he wasn't afraid to admit it. He thought she was even sweeter than his own daughters when they were young. Well-behaved, too. Crystal hardly ever said a negative word. No whining. No complaints.

After golf one day, Bill returned home to an e-mail from

Liz reminding them that Crystal was taking the train down this year and that she would be arriving at 4:30 on Sunday, accompanied on the train by her au pair from Holland (Isa?) who would see her to the station and then continue on to Florida. "Please be prompt, as Crystal will be alone at the station." She probably talked it all over with Janet already—all the finer points. Bill showered and drank a glass of iced tea, eyeballing the sports page. The thin paper was little more than AP reports and box scores anymore, but Bill scoured it anyway, just like the old days, as if well-written columns and feature pieces may have blossomed on the page in the hours since his departure. Janet cleared her throat and asked if he wanted some Swiss cheese and crackers. Bill fluttered his hand. She said she'd save them for later. Why she couldn't eat them on her own was beyond him.

"Odd that she's coming on the train this time," Bill said. "All the way out here." He liked being able to say that. The sticks—he loved the solitude and space out there.

"Not really though. It'll be easier this way. Definitely easier for poor Liz. She's so overworked and probably wants to get stuff done with the kids off from school. Remember those days?"

"I'm just concerned. 'Worried,' really. Better word."

"It will be fine. I just hope we don't bore her to death like last time. Remember?"

Bill wished that Janet wouldn't cast a bad omen, jinx it. He didn't remember boredom. He remembered bliss and bonding and laughing on the rug like a child, his legs rolled under him.

Janet was right though; no reason for his daughter to take two trips—gas prices through the roof.

Janet ate a pickle. She would eat pickles standing over the sink.

"We'll give her a whirl," Janet said.

"You know it."

• • •

When Sunday came, Janet and Bill drove five minutes to the Amtrak station.

Bill wanted to stay in the car so Bill left her there to "keep the seat warm." It was a weekend in early August and it hadn't rained in forever. Bill could see the dryness in the grass out in front of the train station, in the browning boxwoods pressed against the façade. He took his time walking to the platform. No real hurry—he was still early.

Yet when Bill stepped into the train station, Crystal was already there swinging her feet on the bench next to the little wishing well. It was a lighted pool to collect good luck pennies, and it sent her reflection shimmering onto the ceiling. Bill picked up the pace.

"Hey there, youngster," Bill said, kneeling down in front of her. It was probably a bit much. He liked to talk to her eyeball to eyeball. She was probably too old now for the crazy faces, but probably not too old to appreciate the attempt and laugh at it anyway.

"Whew," Crystal said. "You're here."

"Did your train arrive early?"

"I don't know," Crystal said, still swinging her feet.

She wore red sneakers with pink laces.

"You must've been a patient little grand-daughter."

This was what Bill feared. Five is too young for this kind of trip, Dutch au pair or no Dutch au pair.

"Yeah."

Bill sat next to her, gave her a quick hug. She had grown three or four inches since he saw her last—when was that, Easter? Her hair was longer, and Crystal's face revealed an intensity and awareness she didn't have before. Her hair was also much lighter—all that poolside sun, most likely. Crystal liked to purse out her lips in a kind of simian mimicry which got Bill every time. He called her a "monkey" frequently, which would send Crystal into squalls of simian noises and arm waving. She half-pursed her lips right there on the bench, though Bill saved the reference for later, sometime after dessert.

He couldn't possibly be happier. Bill felt lighter. Breath of fresh air.

"Are you hungry? C'mon, let's go get some pizza. Still your favorite?"

"*With* pepperoni."

"With pepperoni."

"Yeah, it's still my favorite. But sometimes I like macaroni better."

Bill carried her backpack and handbag. Crystal took one finger and leaned against him.

• • •

Bill knew the challenge ahead would be as much entertaining Janet as Crystal. Janet quickly became bored of "kid's stuff," and found playing dolly with Crystal akin to Chinese water torture.

"I'm just not built that way," Janet admitted. "At least not any longer."

Bill remembered Janet used to exhibit quite a bit of patience as a young mother, but perhaps she was cowed then or intimidated by her own children, or simply caught up in the moment. Different when the child is not your own. Perhaps she simply blanched at the prospect of disappointing them. If Bill was honest with himself, he'd have to admit that Janet wasn't the best grandmother in the world. She half said so much herself when they moved downstate: "I don't want to be so caught-up in family." "That's why we move far enough away, so that it's not an option."

She did her time; Janet was an excellent though purposeful mother.

Janet was a different kind of grandmother.

Last time Crystal visited, Janet shut her in the guest room for half a day instructing Crystal to "mellow-out." This was when Bill was playing a round of golf—he only found out about the showdown from Crystal (Janet admitted the truth to it days later). This time, no golf. He'd bend over backwards for his granddaughter if he had to.

When they returned home, Bill ordered pizza from Vito's and while they waited he played hide and go seek with Crystal (Crystal wanted *him* to hide—she liked being surprised).

"You're going to get her all riled up," Janet complained. She leaned back in the armchair, stretching her shoulder. Her neck and upper back were often knotted in pain. She was watching the news again—some political talk show on Fox. All that rage and froth. They're eroding my wife's brain cells, he thought. Fox News morons.

"And we're getting Cokes, too," Bills said. "Aren't we, Crystal?"

"Root beer!"

"Sorry, root beers."

"Christ on a cracker," Janet mumbled.

• • •

The next day Bill took Crystal hiking into the state park.

Janet opted for seclusion.

"She's going to get tired," Janet said. "She's only five and barely five at that."

"Well, we'll just have some fun, see what we can do."

"She seems tired from the train."

"She'll be okay," Bill said.

Janet didn't unglue her eyes from the computer screen.

Some help would be nice, Bill thought. Was that passive aggressive?

When they walked through meadows Crystal asked about the name of each flower. When they walked through the forest she asked about the ferns and mosses. When she heard birds chirping in the underbrush she asked what kind they were. To Bill she wasn't annoying in the least; he enjoyed these kinds of questions. He wished he had better answers. He knew some of the names and admitted when he didn't. He also made up ridiculous names, which Crystal could tell were fake: "That fern is called the Ozzy and Harriet Head." It was sticky and hotter than it usually got up in the hills. But it was late July, so perhaps there wasn't much they could do.

"Noooooooooooo!"

They ate lunch by the thin little trickle of creek on an incline in the shade. Few hikers passed by.

"This would usually be a waterfall," Bill said, pointing to the creek. "Or at least a rapids."

"What's a rapids?"

"A small waterfall—fast!"

Bill told Crystal about the drought and how when it doesn't ran the river becomes shallow and slower. Creeks, also. Bill ate a cheese and tomato sandwich. Crystal ate a butter sandwich. Then they both ate apple slices and chewy granola bars embedded with chocolate chips.

"Are you tired?"

"Nah," Crystal said. "I want to see more. Animals and things like that."

"Maybe. Animals are hard to see. We'll have to stay quiet. Our voices will scare them if we don't."

"Okay," Crystal said.

So they walked in silence, Crystal covering her mouth with both hands. This is good, Bill thought. Otherwise, I might laugh at her facial expressions.

When Crystal heard a squirrel skitter through the brush she stopped and pointed.

"It's a Southern rhinoceros," Bill said.

"Nooooooo!"

"Shhhh, you'll scare the Dixie elephants."

• • •

When they returned from the hike Janet wasn't home. Instead, a sticky note on the door: *"at store."*

Crystal took a nap in front of a DVD. Bill read the newspaper in the armchair and watched her.

If only her name wasn't Crystal, he thought—stupid redneck name.

When Janet came home, everything changed.

"Have a nice walk?" A notch too loud.

"Good hike. I think I tuckered her out."

Janet didn't lower her voice. Bill pointed at the sleeping lump.

Janet shrugged. "Can you help me with the groceries? I did a full trip and my shoulders are hurting me."

Bill nodded and helped her carry the bags in.

"I got some nice steaks," Janet said, a bit too firmly for

Bill's tastes.

"That's great—can you keep your voice down just a bit? She's sleeping."

"This is my house," Janet said. "Is it still my house?"

Bill stepped back, as if struck.

He didn't expect that one, and worst of all he didn't feel as if he could argue with her while Crystal slept in the living room. Instead, he bit his lip and helped her unpack silently.

"What's wrong?" Janet asked.

Bill shook it off.

"Little melodramatic, don't you think?"

"I'm just saying that I live here, also. I just spent an hour shopping for us. I can speak."

"Who said otherwise?"

"Kids," Janet said. "Everybody loves kids. We have a whole culture which coddles these children. What about the *rest* of us?"

Janet pivoted and marched deeper into the house. Bill wasn't sure what her little sermon meant, but he knew it wasn't helpful. He only saw his granddaughter a few times a year, if that. He wanted to savor his time with her. Now he had to apparently also think about some nebulous spousal infraction and the pent-up wrath that could last weeks. He wasn't going to bear it any mind with Crystal present.

● ● ●

If there is one aspect of his life Bill loathed analyzing it was his marriage. Bill was no fool. He wasn't in denial. Bill knew Janet can be prickly and selfish and aggravatingly political. Their lives together was never cloud nine. Her interest in politics was all-consuming in its scope and to Bill disconcerting at best. Ten or fifteen years ago she wasn't much of a political person. Twenty years ago she had no interest whatsoever. However, like many, Janet found herself swept up in the talk radio tide and propelled forth into a world where suddenly everything was an overheated debate, everything skewed and presented, every point questioned.

What happened to simplicity?

Bill often felt nostalgic for the Janet he married—the woman who was content to read a good book and go for a walk around the neighborhood. That rendition of Janet took pleasure in the small things. Then she didn't feel the need to "be involved." She didn't check Facebook and Twitter fifteen times an hour to read the latest counterpoint regarding some obscure discussion about a solar company or tax credits or where the President was born or the latest possible vote on some congressional whatever. How do these things add to your life? Bill wanted to ask her.

But he couldn't. Janet became her own person, in a sense. Her retirement "hobby" was the welfare of the entire world—most of which, in her view, depended upon the revocation of liberal "ideology" (one of Bill's least favorite words). They used to play cards and sit in front of the fire and listen to the wood crack and hiss. Now others have intruded. TV people, the computerized political world where every single utterance must be discussed, hashed-out, picked apart. He didn't understand it.

• • •

When Crystal woke up from her nap Bill already had dinner prepared. Janet had locked herself in her office.

"Did you have a nice rest?"

Crystal nodded and buried her head beneath the afghan.

"You're alive!" Bill shouted and went in to tickle her.

Crystal shrieked with joy.

"I have all of your favorite foods. Pizza from yesterday. Hot dogs. Mac and cheese. Ice cream.

"All together?"

"In a big stew."

They ate. Crystal smiled and Bill felt worthy again.

From the kitchen he couldn't hear Janet at all.

• • •

On Crystal's last day with Bill and Janet, Bill proposed fishing. He knew this was a risk, but he also knew it could be different and relaxing to Crystal. Also, though Janet didn't fish, she would probably come along and maybe it would put them on the right footing again.

"Okay," Crystal said. "But I don't know how."

"I'll show you," Bill said.

"Oh, good."

Bill took Crystal into the back yard and showed her how to cast and then they went hunting for worms. They had scanty luck in the back yard (the recent drought didn't help), so Bill drove them to the convenience store and they bought some worms there. He opened the top of the Styrofoam container and Crystal watched them squirm. Some things don't change, or only imperceptibly so.

"Do you want to touch them?"

Crystal shook her head in quick little motions.

After lunch he strapped boots onto Crystal's feet and put his own on. Janet agreed to come along; she carried the chairs and water. They drove down to the river and unloaded the car and set up a spot in the shallows. They sat there in the sun while Janet sat in the shade behind them and read. Janet wore her dark blue American flag and shirt. She looked as though she were waiting for some unseen fireworks display to unfold on the horizon in full patriotic pomp and bluster.

They cast their rods with bobbers and worms as bait and Bill whispered to Crystal that if they were very quiet and didn't move an inch, they might snag a trout.

"Have you eaten pan-fried trout?

Crystal shook her head, her hair bobbing.

"It is mighty tasty."

"Let's get one."

"Or two. One for me. One for you."

"What about grandma?"

"Let's not worry about her. She doesn't like trout much anyway. Let her eat hot dogs."

But it was a hot day and Bill knew they picked the wrong hour for it. The fish wouldn't bite—not even a nibble. The only prospect was a snagged stick, and this came at the end of their time in the river. Two hours in and Crystal's face rested in her hands and she dipped her boots in and out of the water. Bill watched the birds fly over and the breeze tickle the leaves. He was bored, also.

"Would you like to go home? We could watch a movie and cool off. Get some ice cream."

Crystal nodded and Janet took her rod. Without a word Janet and Bill packed up the car and called it a day.

"Sometimes this is the way it goes with fishing. Don't always catch something," Janet said from the back seat. Bill appreciated this. "There are worse things, aren't there?"

"Yeah," Crystal.

Back at home Janet brought Crystal a small bowl of ice cream and asked Bill if he wanted one, also (he didn't). Bill could tell Janet had relaxed her previous stance, and that was a positive. If he wanted to be caustic Bill could suspect that Janet felt guilty (and she probably did) but that wouldn't get anybody anywhere. She knew who she was and what she was doing. He had to give her that.

"We will miss you tons, Crystal."

She clinked her spoon in her ice cream bowl.

"Mummy will be happy to see me," Crystal said.

"Yes, she will," Bill said. Janet stood behind him, then moved next to him. They looked at the girl together.

Bill already imagined waving goodbye to her on the platform. He'd have his side of the house, Janet would have hers. They wouldn't talk about things that mattered. They would occasionally meet in the middle.

A Fresh Launch

Lance was on vacation when he saw the ad pinned to the white picket fence running along Route 236. "Miniature horse farm for sale—includes seven minis!"

"Would you look at that," Lance said. "Tiny horses." Kaitlin's eyes widened. His daughter was an animal fiend, in the best way.

"I didn't know there *were* little horses."

"Something new every day. It's certainly not something you see very often, is it?"

Lance slowed the car down and pulled off onto the shoulder. From where they sat idling, he couldn't see any horses though. He wanted to see the tiny horses. Something calming about them. There was a barn pressed against the spruce and maple and some kind of smaller auxiliary shed next to that. On the other side, the grass ran along the road for acres; hilly, but not steep, the land set up higher than the rest. He bet it had a nice view of the other farms below on the Western flank, lower down.

With a grubby magic marker he wrote the phone number down on his hand. What the heck—you never know, right?

The next morning Lance drove them back to the city. Their little weekend getaway was over and Kaitlin was glad to be back. She missed her friends, and even missed school. Kaitlin was a good girl; she tried hard. Lance was decidedly *not* glad to be back. He was sick of the congestion, the rudeness, the brisk competitiveness of everything and anyone. People behave as if their little lives are so utterly important, Lance thought. It's absurd. They're all just pencil pushers—most of them, anyway.

Lance ran his own marital counseling practice, amassing numerous clients over the years. His track record was solid and it was easy to stay busy. For the most part, he was able to bring couples together, or closer together than they were before. He felt as if he was doing some good. Not always, of course. Some couples simply didn't belong together any longer and as he told them, "this is not the end of the world. It's a human relationship and human relationships ebb and flow. They are in flux." Mostly the job was rewarding, though not always—and when it wasn't, it was incredibly stressful. Mr. and Mrs Lux, Tom and Diana, gave him nightmares (that image of Tom shaking a knife at Diana in the kitchen until she curled up into a little ball on the kitchen floor).

However, Lance knew that the years of involving himself in the problems of others lead him to be cynical about human nature, or at least *skeptical*. He knew that people could stoop to immorality. He knew that people could be vain and disconnected and selfish and easily waylaid. Sometimes it was difficult for Lance to develop his own relationships; he knew too much about what *could* go wrong. His own marriage with Patty fell apart for different reasons—she was aloof and painfully shy and Lance was a people person who loved (despite its sometimes exhausting qualities) to immerse himself in humanity. She never, ever wanted to socialize. He usually did. An introvert and an extrovert—it was a difficult dynamic that lead ultimately to a severing of the relationship, a mercy killing, perhaps.

Still, Lance felt tired, worn down. He had started his practice in the early 90's and now, over twenty years later, he was still churning out advice and providing a listening ear. What about himself? What about *his* needs?

• • •

The phone number had already bled off his hand the next morning. He was kicking himself for not at least putting it on a piece of paper, clicking it into his smart phone, something. He remembered the name of the little corner grocery store though a few miles from the farm and he called there.

2.

I live down the road a piece, so I don't know everything. That much is certain. But I got eyes and ears just like anyone else. I've been called street smart, to paraphrase.

Benny's wife died suddenly is what happened. That's how all of this got started. She was suffering for some years. Lupus is what got her. She had it for a long time, it seems, and then it burst forth dramatically. She was always tired, but it was against her. Ultimately, it was too much fighting, too much battle. Benny came over one day and we were shooting the shit and having a laugh. We had a six pack and the radio and that was plenty. Listening to golden oldies. We shot some pool downstairs and I can tell then and there something's not right. He just couldn't concentrate is all—missing easy shots.

We're sitting on the benches next to the wood stove when he tells me Jenny's not going to make it much longer.

"We're making our plans," is all he says. He's trying not to get emotional, so he's looking off into the knotty pine. Some of them knots look like owl eyes.

"It's tough," I say. I didn't know what else *to* say. "This is very hard."

He looks away. "I'll be selling the farm," he says. Then his eyes grow fierce. "It's not going to be a good place for me to be after."

"Yeah," I say.

Things happened quick after she went. Funeral, then the signs were up a week or two later. A week or two after that and the farm was gone. I didn't know the buyer and neither did Benny. Said he was from the city coming out, trying to make a go of it in the country.

"Nice guy at heart," is what Benny had to say. "Honest. But he has no idea."

See, I haven't mentioned the minis. Benny wasn't just selling some cabbage patch, he was selling a miniature horse farm. "Mini Neigh," he liked to call it. I'm not up on horses, but Benny sure was. He had seven of them. I can't remember all of their names, but the most important ones were Shadow and Peaches. Peaches was a mini-Appaloosa mare, who gave birth to two of the others—so she was the matriarch of the farm, really. Shadow was the father, and the largest mini. Almost show pony-sized stallion. So the minis were his family of minis not just some discombobulated assortment.

He put a lot of work into those horses. Not only did he breed and train them and provide food and loving care for them, he was also always with them. He'd bring them into the house, walk around with them. He'd talk to them, play with them. They were a hobby of sorts, his collection. But they were also more than that. Jenny could never have kids of her own.

I was pretty shocked he'd sell so quickly—just like that.

I imagine his thinking went like this: too many memories in that house. Refresh, wipe the slate clean. Move somewhere else and you get a fresh launch. Shame he had to sell the minis, also. He loved them so much. They were part of the memories. So was I. I haven't seen or heard from Benny in years.

● ● ●

Few days after Lance moved in, I went over to make friendly neighborly introductions. Welcome him to Lansburgh. We say Lansburgh, but the town itself is three miles down on 236 and it's only two shops and a gas station. I knocked on the door three times, real polite and restrained. Didn't want to be pushy or force him into a corner from the outset.

But it was a big eyed girl who answered the door, flat iron face, with arms just a tick too short for her body, seemed to me. Nice enough.

She goes, "May I help you?"

"Hello young lady. I'm looking for a Lance. I'm sorry, I don't know his last name."

"That's my father," she said. She's about to make a move to fetch him when I realized here's an opportunity for a bit of insider knowledge. Dr. Lovett was always telling me to take advantage of my opportunities (he's my guide to this day). My wife can't stand him.

"Wait, wait," I said. "How're you getting along here?"

"It's okay. I don't know anybody though. So it's pretty quiet. Sometimes at least."

I nod in recognition. She has a halting, pondering way about her. And even if you do know somebody, I think.

"I'll go get him for you."

Then I'm standing there in the foyer I stood in so many times with Benny. But now the walls are empty of Benny's

159

horse photos and Western motif drawings. It was no longer the same place.

"Hey, I'm Lance," he says, hand outstretched.

"Ned. I live down the road."

"Neighbor Ned. Good to meetcha, Lance." Felt he was trying too hard, to put it simply.

He was friendlier than what I thought he might be. Imagined some big-money guy in pin stripes. Stood tall with wide shoulders and his posture was rod straight. His face bore signs of sorrow though, and it was pocked by little marks or zits or something. He looked far off, eyes on the horizon line.

He invited me into the living room, which seemed smaller somehow without Benny in it. Plus boxes were still stacked in the corner.

"Excuse the mess. Still getting settled."

We make small talk, which leads to me asking him how he's managing with the minis.

He snorts and kneads his fist into his palm.

"Big learning curve," he said. "Huge. I'm gaining traction though, I think."

"Yeah," I went. "It's tough."

"You know anything about these horses? I'm at a loss really, if I can be frank."

I tell him about me and Benny and how far back we go, how I'd seen him through everything. I tell him what little I did know about their core—all that Benny put into them.

"But no, not really."

"I'm up all night doing research on the computer, trying to figure it out. One of them just wants to sleep all the time and I don't know if it's normal or not. Maybe I should take him to the vet."

He called all of the minis "him." He said he knew that Benny had names for them all, but he didn't write them down and now he's plain forgotten.

He leaned forward.

"I got it under control and everything," he said. "I'm just learning as I go, to be honest. Benny said it would be a challenge at first and he gave me some pointers, but for the most part I get the sense…."

"Yeah," I say, knowing what he was thinking. "It's true."

● ● ●

I checked back a week later to check in on Lance and his girl and his mood had changed, or so I thought. I knew I should've come by earlier. He was out there in the pasture with them. The minis were running here and there, and he seemed much more relaxed somehow. Being outside probably helped, also.

So I thought everything was going to be okay at that point.

I was standing next to Lance and his girl was running alongside Ginny, or so they called her (I think Benny called her Feathered). He figured out that some were not boys.

Things change quickly sometimes.

3.

When it came down to money, Lance was an unskilled operator. He just didn't have the wherewithal to always make the best financial decisions. For starters, taking on a second mortgage was a risky maneuver on his part. Though his practice had boomed over the past ten years—due in part perhaps to the increase in Internet-based infidelity (post-Ashley Madison revelations were a boon)—he hadn't socked away enough savings. The house which Lance and Patty had bought was larger

161

than they needed and they were stuck paying pre-recession rates. Now that Lance was the sole provider for Kaitlin (Patty got her on weekends), it was difficult to simply pay the mortgage. He thought about selling, which would get the monkey off his back, but he'd lose vast amounts of money he already sank into the house. Plus he wasn't sure he wanted to cut all ties. It was lose-lose.

Buying the horse farm on top of this was financial sabotage, and how he got the loan was beyond him (he went to his uncle's broker—the inside connection helped). Additionally, though Lance theorized that he could sustain both houses with the increased income from his practice, by moving so far away from his practice it was seemingly put to rest. A few clients said they would be content to continue sessions on the phone, but Lance lost seventy-five percent of his client base.

He didn't know what he was thinking.

I will just find new clients out there, Lance initially thought. However, Lance failed to take into account the vastly diminished population base and the lower economic status of his neighbors. Despite his intellectual acuity, he fell victim to cloudy thinking far too often—and he knew it.

Once they settled-in at the new farm Lance realized the extent of his removal. Three hours west didn't seem like much at the time of purchase, but the reality of three hours hit him hard: he couldn't meet with clients, no more Indian food, his friends said they would visit but would they drive the three hours? Not often. Same thing with his family. Three hours felt closer when he was in the car *already*.

Lance didn't think of himself as impulsive and he frequently counseled those who truly are—especially in the sexual realm—but perhaps, he realized, he was as well.

The mini-horses were a nightmare. On paper they sounded so easy. Benny wrote out instructions for each horse and offered pages of tips—everything from diet to health to the finer points of breeding. Right away Lance thought he'd ignore the breeding issue altogether and just focus on being a "recreational owner." He mentioned this to Benny at closing even.

"But just in case," Benny said. "You should be able to cope."

He bought the house in early November. By late December half of them were sick. He didn't know what was wrong exactly, just that one of the horses wouldn't move or eat and another was dry-heaving, like a cat with a constant hairball. Then the older one had a colt.

The veterinary bills cost thousands.

They were adorable though and Kaitlin loved them. The minis followed her around and one even slept in her bed on occasion. Lance would wake up and drink his morning coffee as houses walked around on the hardwood. Little horses everywhere. My friends must think I'm nuts, Lance thought.

But the smell—to Lance they smelled musty and muddy, like glamorized pigs. He knew intellectually this was his city background speaking.

Nights, Lance would walk around the property flashlight in hand. It was the one truly calming aspect of the move. He would look up at the stars and see the eyes of deer in the brush and his feet through the reeds. Some nights he would walk for miles. Even though the property was not extensive, he would do a loop—all the way out, back to the house and back out. But only at night—he didn't want his neighbors to think he was nuts.

• • •

They started dying when the cold snap hit. First, one of the colts, then one of the yearlings, then Snoopy. Kaitlin went berserk—crying and yelling at Lance to stop it, to call someone. *What's wrong with them? They are just not moving.*

The minis would suddenly sit in the grass and refuse to budge out of sickness or weakness or both. And then a day or two later, the afflicted mini would be dead.

Eventually Lance did call the vet—he had to. Kaitlin said she would simply stop speaking to him if she didn't. *Forever.* She was utterly apoplectic. "These are my friends and they are dying and you don't care!" Personally, Lance could do without the minis altogether, they were expensive and you couldn't even ride them. They were just like mangy, smelly dogs to him—he only fed them at all to appease his daughter.

At night Lance would walk and the minis were sitting in front of the house like statues, sitting in the grass starting down into it. He walked faster, away from them. Spooked out.

4.

After a few died, the vet's van was parked at Lance's farm for several days. Triage. I drove by a few times thinking I'd see if everything was alright. All I could see was icy stillness. The shadows loomed.

When I finally got up the courage to pull in the driveway, the vet was nowhere to be scene. Lance opened the door, shaking his head.

"I guess there was nothing I could do," he said. "Bad luck."

Always a loser's mentality as far as I was concerned.

"Yeah," I said. "Bad luck."

I stepped around the issue of what got the minis, but as I stayed and consoled him, I got enough clues to piece it together.

Maybe it *was* bad luck. Maybe it was sheer ignorance. The more I heard, the angrier I got. If Benny was here those minis would still be alive. Why did Jenny have to die? Why was the world such a twisted knot of shit? I wanted to tell Lance to go back to the city where he belongs before he killed off the other four minis. Or sell them to someone who knew what they were doing. But I didn't say anything at all.

"It's tough," I said and stood there, my skin itching with perturbation. I knew I'd never set foot in Lance's house again. It was Benny's, always.

A month later the rest of the minis were in the ground, also. Potomac Horse Fever was the official diagnosis from the house doc. I know because I called pretending I was Lance's brother. But it could have been avoided, we all know that. The neglect, the poor diet—it all weakened them. Moron. If Benny was around it would've never happened. And I still suspect rat poison myself, and nobody can convince me that's not exactly what happened. My wife said perhaps the minis died of heartache— they missed Benny. But that's not what it was at all. Animals have feelings but I've never heard of an animal *dying* that way.

A month after that the sign appeared in front of Benny's farm. Except the owner, if you can call him an "owner," was nowhere to be seen. He had taken his short-armed girl and all his urban crap and moved back—or moved somewhere else at least.

He must've sensed that I was done with him because he never came by to provide the grand explanation. That or perhaps he was so ashamed he couldn't face me. He should be. If you're going to take somebody's palace from them, make sure you know how to lock the doors. That's for starters.

The Hill

"Why don't you work that hill?" Mrs. Whitten said. It wasn't a question.

She pointed up the slope past the woods towards the Millers' corn field hexagon. Her "estate", as she called it then, was just outside of town, but it felt like somewhere else.

I hurried to the barn and emerged with the trimmer, slipped my goggles over my glasses and started bushwhacking the hill. It was a sizable job. Mrs. Whitten said the kids liked the hill—"best hill in town." She had a generous spirit, I could tell. I'm a decent read of people. Kindly to her core.

I had a half gallon of water in a plastic milk jug sitting in the shade.

It was hot and humid and the gnats peppered me from the woods. Dust and grass thwacked my face.

Every molecule in my body told me to get out of there. But I had to think big picture. My daughter was about to turn four and she barely knew me, and the only way I could change that was to do whatever Mrs. Whitten needed me to do. Money. I felt on edge and for some reason my hands shook. She was the key. And the key to the key for that moment was that hot, dusty hill gnarled with thistle and ragweed. My whole life was there.

I completed the job as the sun slanted down the horizon. Everything looked silhouetted and beautiful as I walked back to the manor. Mrs. Whitten was sitting on the porch drinking tea, cold crescents of ice clinking in her glass.

"Did you finish up already?"

"I did at that," I said. "Yes, ma'am."

"Put everything back where you found it, and I'll see you tomorrow."

"Thank you," I said. I half bowed; I didn't want to say too much or ask too many stupid questions. She was already kind enough to bring me on board. I knew she didn't actually need me. I needed her far worse.

I put the goggles, gloves and trimmer back in the barn and stood there for a minute just feeling the heat radiate off me. I was dying for a drink of something cold and a bath. Both would have to wait.

Then I called Stevie and he came and got me. We didn't talk much on the ride back. I was glad my efficiency had a window unit is all. Small blessings.

• • •

I had been in the pen for eighteen months. There were things I would talk about and things I wouldn't talk about. Most people wouldn't even find out about the eighteen months, but if I knew you well enough, I might give it up.

Thing was, I didn't *have* any real friends—nobody who mattered enough. The friends I *did* have didn't want to talk to me any longer. They blamed me. I was banned from homes—talk about a shitty feeling. My family was a help, but even they held me at arm's length.

I found out about Mrs. Whitten through the moving company I worked for prior—two months of sweeps across the county. Hard labor, boy. I was forty-seven years old and I was having a hard time keeping up with guys half my age. I felt *weary* around them and then they found out—which made it harder. We mowed the yard of the Millers and Mr. Miller asked Chuck, our crew chief, if anybody needed some odd jobs. Chuck looked right at me. I was grateful. I'd take all the odd jobs I could get. Work kept me out of the shadows.

At first it was just weekends—on top of the moving company—but then she hired me to do work around the house "pretty much full-time," she said. Four times a week, minus Fridays when she had to be in the city. Handyman jobs, yard work, everything would be outside she said. No men inside.

"I'm just not able to do everything," she said. She explained that her husband died two years ago and she just didn't want to give everything up.

"I can do little jobs."

She knew nothing about me, as far as I knew. She wouldn't find out if I could help it.

• • •

The next day I was back on site at the normal time. I arrived on-site a bit early so I waited around until she came out onto the porch. That's the way she liked it.

"Can we take care of the windows today? Everything you need is out in the shed."

She called it the "shed." Perhaps this way she would make me feel less insufficient.

I found the ladder, Windex, rags and started in. It was a large undertaking, as the manor was an old Victorian with three stories, dormers and multiple windows. If I was smarter I would've been scared, but I didn't even think about it.

Instead, I watched Mrs. Whitten when I could see her. I hadn't, at that point, been invited inside the house itself, so this was the closest I had come. I memorized the interiors—what I could see.

At one point, when I was cleaning the sitting room windows, Mrs. Whitten walked into the room and sat in a winged back arm-chair. She was looking through a box of photographs, her eyes tight. When she looked up to catch my gaze, I glanced away.

I'm sure she had to wonder about me, even though she was a few decades older than I was. She reminded me of someone.

If she could've seen into my head, she would've known what I had been through. I learned things. I had the ability to take everything she had, like that. But I knew I had to restrain that impulse with every muscle I had.

• • •

My cousin Stevie understood me; he had gone through something similar a few years back. We weren't close, but I viewed him as a kind of model. His life was scoured clean and he patched it back together from the basement up. At that time he had a decent job at a hardware store, where he had worked for several years. Stevie had a kind of credibility that I was shooting for.

There was a day I showed up fifteen minutes late. Mrs. Whitten was on the porch waiting for me, running her palm along the painted white rail. She must've been beautiful in her own day; I could see that. She kept her hair done up in a bun and I was thinking it would look better down on her shoulders, flowing.

"Good morning, Ray," she said.

"Good morning, ma'am," I said.

"Are you planning on arriving late frequently? If so, I won't be needing your services, to be perfectly frank."

I explained what happened, or tried to, but she just raised her palm up, as if to say, "I don't need to hear any more." I stopped mid-sentence.

"I truly apologize," I said. "It won't happen again."

Mrs. Whitten squirreled up her right eye and swallowed. She told me I needed to help her repaint the shed. This was good news because if I was smart, I could work in the shade for most of the time, I realized. My skin felt leathery and baked-in already.

I could smell the lilacs around Mrs. Whitten's porch. For a moment I almost felt dizzy from the aroma.

• • •

It took me five days to prime and then fully re-paint the barn. I wasn't in a hurry and, in fact, I took my time—dragging out the process and taking long breaks.

I happened to finish on a Friday, which was the day when she was supposed to pay me for my week's work. She had paid the two previous weeks in cash. She did the same that day. Stevie was waiting for me. He didn't know.

I was standing on the porch steps watching her glass of white wine bead up and sweat. I watched the condensation drip onto the table, though the stem stayed dry. Something collapsed inside of me.

I walked up the stairs and the porch itself—it felt like forbidden territory. A knot in my gut. White paint and sunshine, standing on the manor house proper. I didn't think; I just walked straight into the house. I was sunbaked and needed a cool dark place. I was inside the foyer—rugs and little statues and paintings on the walls. I just stood there, leaning slightly against the wall.

When Mrs. Whitten turned the corner, cash in hand, she started. I watched her swallow.

"Now what are you doing?"

"I'm hot," I said. "Do you have something cold I could drink?"

But when she reached out to hand me the money I clutched her wrist instead. I don't know why I did it. Something about her earrings swaying. Something about a tickle in the back of my throat.

It *felt* like an accident.

I knew, of course, the mistake I was making. Unredeemable. But I was not myself. The sun had fried my good thinking. I was outside of myself—someone else was operating my body.

"And where is the rest of it now?" I yelled. My other hand rose upward. I could see the shadow of it before I let it fly. There was a moment when I knew I had to stop, that I could still keep this from being the worst thing, but I couldn't. My hand fell, and again.

• • •

She had barely anything, which made it even worse. And I knew I had to leave right away. I didn't tell Stevie about my misstep. Instead I asked to hear some blues on the radio. But he couldn't find any. The closest was some old Lynard Skynard with lots of ads about jewelry and expensive resorts. I had him drop me off at the bus station.

"I have to meet someone," I explained.

"You want me to wait? I can wait."

"No, go on. I'll get a lift."

I had enough for a ticket to the middle of the country. I had done plenty wrong in my life and it was time to pay. I bought a hamburger or two at the fast food stand inside the station and boarded the bus.

"No bags?" I shook my head.

Only invisible ones, I thought.

But two weeks later I was under wraps all over again. I laid low, grew a beard, slept out under the stars. I bought some cheap sunglasses and avoided public places. Snuck into town to buy food at the little, grubby market. It was no way to live.

I still don't know how they found me. Might've been my phone. Should've tossed that thing in the station garbage can. When I had the chance. Just that thin little filament is all they needed, I guess.

Too bad.

Part of me was almost thankful, though. I was down to my last couple of dollars and was getting the runs bad, drinking from the creek out back. Even though I knew where I was headed, I also knew they had to feed me and there was a sink. I could drink as much water as I liked, which is all I wanted.

Someday I'd count my blessings and be a good man, I thought. I was in the car and the blue and red were whirling. I don't know why—they already had me. It wasn't an emergency. I felt the cool air conditioning against my cheek and I had a pebble in my mouth to keep my saliva going until I could drink something again. They didn't take that from me.

I said nothing, turning my tongue over the stone over and over.

Cascade Falls

So you're on your honeymoon, is that it? Lovey-dovey? Oh, just a garden-variety vacation? What does that mean—"garden-variety"—anyway? Is there something wrong with gardens? If you look over there—just past that big rock, the boulder, no the other one….yes, there. Now that looks like a little garden, doesn't it? A little hamlet nook. Something out *of The Hobbit*. Little bunnies hopping around, little foxes eyeballing them from the ferns.

Vacations are good for all of us. Goodgoodgood. It's good to take a rest isn't it? I mean, I haven't really done that in a long time. Not a real one. Not a long one. No, I live over in Cambridge, two ridges over. This is a little day hike for me. A stone's throw. This is just a little jaunt. Is that the right word? "Jaunt"?

I'm intimate with these trails. We converse regularly. We hang out. We're friends—these trails and me. I mean, I see a little salamander or a skink or a black snake and I think, "Oh, good—here's a friend to talk to me." Hello, little amigo! Hello, muchacho! Did you ever do that—talk to animals? I do. We converse on a regular basis. We chat. It's difficult to always understand their little burblings and squeaks. But I do try. When we talk slowly we understand each other. We show mutual respect and admiration. But I'm sure I'm boring you. You know all about this.

It's fine and dandy. It's all good. I'm just joshing. Don't you hate that expression? Did you know "it's all good" consists of three absolute ambiguities (if that isn't an oxymoron)? It's. All. Good. What "is"? What is "all"? What does "good" mean?

Sorry—my sincere apologies. You did say you're on your vacation. I should leave you to your vacation mind-set, your well of peace and relaxation. I'm sure you have better things to do than listen to my disjointed ramblings. Well, I can stay here and you can walk ahead. I can proceed in silence like a grubby jerk-off. Then when you get to Cascade Falls I can take your picture and go on my merry way.

Okay, well then. No, I'm not attempting to be difficult or intrude on your prized little nature moments. During your little vacation. I'm sure, I'm sure. It's all anthropomorphized, isn't it?

Let me just say this: Cascade Falls is a bit of a redundancy, isn't it? I mean, isn't a waterfall a cascade? So the name is "waterfall waterfall"? Someone just was phoning it in on that one.

I don't mean to be rude, but I have to say you do look fetching in your little shorts and tank top thingie, if you don't mind me saying so. I mean, is that what you call it—a "tank top"? I mean, I'm sure you have a boyfriend or maybe many boyfriends. Maybe a whole town of boyfriends. Or maybe you are married (is it a husband)? I don't see rings on your fingers but maybe you're one of those couples who is all "modern" and doesn't "do" rings and the ring is a ring of stellar clouds around your heart, or maybe you just take your ring off when you're hiking. Rings are kinda superfluous, if you ask me. There's a whole history about rings you can read about, which doesn't make much sense. I mean, if you love someone you don't really need a ring, do you. Or maybe the ring is a way of reminding oneself that one *should* love that other person.

Maybe it's like a piece of yarn around the finger.

(Or maybe—well, you get the picture). But this doesn't really matter to me. Today, you have my attention. And I hope this goes the vice versa way, and so forth. Ditto, ditto, ditto. If you don't mind me being so bold as to speak directly.

Yeah, yeah sure—you just go ahead and walk up ahead to the little cascade….to the waterfall waterfall. I'll hang back here and let you have your moments of silent reckoning. And I'll watch you from behind and I'll catch up to you when you are near the edge of the waterfall and then we'll compare notes, so to speak.

I promise I won't push you! That would be a bad way to make the news, wouldn't it? I don't want to be that guy.

I can see your form through the trees up there. Man, oh man—I bet they don't have bird and larch where you're from. Snooty Brooklyn brats don't know ferns from falafel. That's one thing Dad taught me well. Identification. I may have had to teach myself in reaction to what he was doing. In utter rebellion to everything he brought to the table (or didn't bring to the table, respectively). He was all huff and bluff and bluster—you know anyone like that? He claims it was as a result of sleeping in the woodshed when he was a kid. My question is— why did you have to sleep in the woodshed? He implies that his father muscled him into the woodshed, that there was a kind of quid pro quo unleashed upon him as a result of vengeance of the sort fathers like to wreck upon their sons. I'm doubtful. Did you hear me up there? I'm doubtful!

I know you're not as far up the trail as you think you are because I can see your cute little Birkenstock footprints and I can tell it was just ninety seconds ago that your feet impressed their little toes upon the path here. Didn't anyone tell you that

Birkenstocks and hiking don't mesh? This isn't Disneyland. This is the wild and wooly. Look around you. It's trees and rocks and water and cliffs dropping down to God knows where. It's *elemental*. Hear me? And the elements don't care a whit for your pedicured little princess nails. This isn't the Hamptons. Okay, if you just respond I promise I'll stop being so forceful and loud...and abrasive. I apologize. I will. But only if you take me off the trail. Show me the meaning of life. Show me at least what it is to be young and flirtatious with some guy who just happens to be trudging his middle aged cloddy body up the same trail as your highness on the same day, same time. It's fate, isn't it? Or kismet? Or Karma? I don't know—it's something.

And by the way. Just because you aren't responding to me right now does not mean I'm not going to pick up the pace—with the talking *and* the walking. It doesn't mean I'm giving up. I don't give up. Ever.

Fine, I like silence, also.

Ask my son about the persistence. Gavin knows. Little shitheal fuck. Sure, run off to preppie camp with all the other spoiled little shitheal fucks in Richie Rich Hotha, center of the hippie-dippie crystal crowd. Sure, don't return your father's phone calls. Tell him "if you friend me on Facebook it would be better—that way we can stay in touch. That way you can see my pictures and read what my friends have to say."

Since when do I care about your friends?

Not yours. His. Shitheal Gavin.

Don't ask about the name. That was Katherine's idea of creativity. Trust me, names are one area where creativity is over-rated. My name, for instance, is Joe, in case you'd like to know. Doesn't get much plainer than "Joe," does it? And when you take me behind the larch trunk and my jeans are around my ankles I'm sure you'll tell me your name is Jessica or Julia or Jamie. I'm guessing J names here (if you missed that) because we're in synch and I can tell our in-synchness extends its beneficence to the contours of your name. I'm sure there are lots of contours.

Looklooklook. I know I run my mouth a lot and say some bizarre things. I know I seem like one of these guys—one of those creeper guys who won't shut up and doesn't respect you a whit and can't constrain himself. But I'm not. I'm actually quite a polite and gentle human. I could provide you with a series of. What? No. I could provide you with a series of references, if you'd like. I can put you on the phone right now with women, exes who could attest to my gentlemanly behavior. Because my behavior is something I take seriously.

You are not required to answer at all. I hope this helps.

Whoah, look at this. I've never seen a lizard with two heads before. Have you? This is not a ploy, not a game. Oh, wait. It's not two heads, it's two lizards. The one lizard is eating the head of the other lizard. Right here on the path, that's where. From the first angle it looks like two lizard heads sprouting forth from the same lizard neck. If you want to backtrack and come here I'll show you.

Nonono. I know that would be too much to ask since you East Coast types have to always hustle and bustle to the next thing—to the latest greatest. It's just a waterfall really. To be frank, that's all it is: waterfalling down from one plane of space to the next. You've seen it a thousand times before. In your life I'm sure you've stood overlooking fifty-eight waterfalls, if not more. This doesn't even count the number of images imbedded in your nubile little brain from photos, films, artwork.

Which painter was it that painted the fucking Niagara Falls thousands of times? Really original, guy! Nothing about Niagara Falls seems remotely—

Oh. I meant "young." Nubile just means young. I mean, no—I don't have a dictionary on hand. I don't usually hike with a spare copy of Webster's. You might. You're on a different intellectual plane than meager little me. You're different.

I don't mean anything "salacious" at all by the word. Nonono. I mean "young." Aren't you "young," technically speaking? I mean, you're younger than me, correct? From my perspective this makes you nubilesque at the bare minimum. Language is funny.

Sure, yes—I'd refer to lawn as nubile. Well, perhaps not in that context, but yes. The word would, in fact, apply.

I'm glad you were listening. Delightfully glad. Did you hear everything I said? Yes, my voice is fairly…whatever…. and gruff. I mean, look at me. Look at my body. Nothing about me is understated. No subtlety here.

Okay, so you want to enjoy yourself. Go ahead. What's stopping you? Enjoy. Go, go. Walk by yourself and listen to your own loneliness.

Enjoy.

Have a great time.

I can see that. I can see that now. Yes, I can see that. Your ordinariness. You seem unique and intriguing but you're actually quite ordinary to me.

So go ahead. I'll just sit right here and watch the lizard eat the other identical lizard. I would really like to see how this turns out. I am curious to see if he can swallow a mirror image of himself. That would be something, wouldn't it?

You don't need that really. I get the message. I can see

the seriousness in your visage. Okay, eyes. Eyes. Your…young eyes. I was going to say…the other one. But, you know.

Encontada. It means "nice meeting you." Go ahead. Walk on as I sit here on the trail. The jaws are unhinging. The head of the victim is sliding in slowly. I can't wait to see the arms and tail slide into this gaping mouth. It's amazing. It's as if he's ingesting himself.

Be careful on those mossy rocks. Those are the dangerous ones. They look safe and green and as if your footing would be more, you know, grippy. But they're not. It's deceptive. They lull you into complacency. Many things do.

Encontada. I'll be waiting here when you walk back down. Or had you forgotten about the return voyage? There's one way up, one way down. I'll be right here, waiting.

Scarfers

If food is the new sex, I wonder, what is the new food? I'm thinking this as I stand at the junction of two white lines—a parking spot catty-corner to the one in which my car sits. My car is equipped with a stack of pancakes on the hood, maple syrup dripping down onto the windows, down the doors. A cone of whipped cream adorns the pancakes, a cherry on top.

This is not a dream. My conscious mind processes the sensations.

I get in the car and drive away. As I take a left out of the parking lot I watch the pancakes slide off. For a moment they stick on the rear-windshield. When the pancakes fall, they leave a sticky mark. I think of slugs.

• • •

I'm heading to my tutorial. My tutorial is in the art of competitive food eating. I'm not speaking of enjoying the gustatory pleasures of food. I'm a wannabe pro food eater. I'm learning from Wayne Guthrie, one of the all-time greats. If there was a pro food eating wall of fame, he'd have a golden plaque in the "lobby of champions." He's won $1.25 million, lifetime. That's close to the record.

In past tutorials Wayne has taught me how to visualize a boa constrictor, how to maximize what he calls the "inner lining" of the stomach (the stomach's stomach), how to stretch properly for a competitive eating contest. He plays techno music to "get me pumped." He has me do pushups, run five miles, swim laps. "The more you exercise, the more your body will crave nutrients." His teachings are controversial.

IFOCE (the International Federation of Competitive Eating) discourages training per se, but everybody does it. Most at least "drink in." They drink as much water as possible in the weeks leading up to an event. This increases the stomach's elasticity. Nobody mentions Timothy Kerrigan, who drank so much water in preparation he completely depleted his electrolytes. He died at Mercy Hospital in Chicago.

Everyone in IFOCE, even in AICE (the Association of Independent Competitive Eaters) wants to win Nathan's Hot Dog Eating Contest, of course. They want to be featured on ESPN, win the prize money. It's human nature.

They're willing to drink two gallons of water a day, if it helps.

• • •

Today Wayne has me hang upside down. He has me do crunches, lots of core exercises. Then he makes me ride the stationary bike for ninety minutes. A "sweat down," he calls it. By the end of it I can barely walk. Then I drink a gallon of water.

Finally we watch *The Big Eat*, a film about professional scarfers. Wayne calls us "gurgitators," but this sounds like a disease. He makes me drink three glasses of water as we watch the film.

He fingers my calf. "I hear something else expands the stomach, also."

"Does it now?"

We've been down this road before though.

• • •

I knew Wayne put the pancakes on my car to egg me on. I can't prove it though. I don't like mystery. When I first started with Wayne, I thought he was lecherous. I still do; but he's also sweet. He roots for me. I only feel like a whore sometimes, and usually only at three in the morning when I wake to pee. It's like clockwork.

We now schedule the sex in along with everything else. Now I see why there aren't more female scarfers.

Wayne also has me do drills on occasion. Eat fifty hard boiled eggs in ten minutes. Down three pizzas. One hundred chicken wings. Three dozen donuts. Two jars of mayonnaise. It's good practice. Major league scarfing revolves around, mostly, junk food. So practicing high-cholesterol intake is what it's all about.

My husband doesn't approve. He shows me photos of small, malnourished Sudanese children with engorged stomachs, flies hovering around their sickly mouths. I tell him I get it.

"I'm not them," I say. "It's competition."

"It's a mystery to me people don't puke their guts out at these things," he says. If I make light of it I'm better off. Nobody asked him for this, I know.

Jeremy tends towards political gravitas. He's on all these lefty Facebook clusterfucks. Health care. Minimum wage. Environmental crap. Political. It's annoying. I wonder if my scarfing is a way to subvert in some way. I'm sure it is. There's nothing redeeming about cramming your face with peach pie crust. I like it anyway.

● ● ●

At the AICE tournament in Raleigh, they have us lined up on picnic benches. The wedding cakes sit four deep in front of each contestant, additional cakes underneath. The identical cakes are all three tiered, completed with edible bride and groom. White frosting, columns, the works. The cakes are so identical, in fact, it's as if they were baked in a mold. I wonder if that's possible.

We have half an hour.

The starter shouts "go," clicks the redundant stop-watch around her neck. Redundant because the digital scoreboard in front of us ticks. She's the only other woman on stage.

I begin cramming icing down my face. The icing, thankfully, isn't as sweet as most. The cake itself is on the dry side, however. We are not allotted water.

First tier.

Second tier.

Bottom tier.

The crowd cheers us on.

I eat the candy bride and groom last, breaking them in two, swallowing them whole.

I'm on my second cake. Don't look at the others, I tell myself. I don't. I do hear a guy gagging on icing a table down. I don't stop. I'm an eating machine. Eat the cake.

Half an hour up I've eaten six cakes.

Some guy three tables down has gulped seven and two thirds of a cake. I came in third. Not bad, but I could've done better.

I think I was slowed down by the dry cake. I collect my $150, head home. My mouth is gummy and heavy. I feel as if I've eaten ten pounds of wet sand.

• • •

My first (unofficial) food competition was at Denny's. Jeremy and I were there for dinner off Route 95 in Delaware.

We were headed to New Jersey to visit my sister. I was sitting there eating my hamburger and fries, side salad. Jeremy was eating his omelet. This guy across the aisle from us eyes me with the hamburger.

"I bet you can't eat ten of those," he says. He slaps a ten dollar bill down on his table. I eye it.

I've always had a high metabolism, so I tell him I could.

"I pay for them all if you do." So the waiter brings me five hamburgers, then five more. I down all of them in ten minutes. The last one was a mite tricky, I have to admit. And I need water to wash it down. But that was that. He handed the ten to me with both hands.

• • •

Wayne gives me a stomach massage to increase my stamina. I tread water for half an hour, then lift, then hit the stationary bike for an hour.

We are training for the big French Fry Festival.

We hold off on the extracurricular activities. After all, he's kind of a father figure to me.

It's that time of the month.

I wonder if menstruation helps or hinders my scarfing performance. I ask him about the pancakes. He says it wasn't him. I stare at him, but he doesn't flinch.

• • •

I've never liked French Fries. But liking or not liking is beside the point. Time slows down for me. I'm in some kind of French Fry trance, as if the fries are liquid and I can simply let them wash down my throat.

I win ten grand by just one basket.

Wayne lets me on top tonight. It doesn't get much sweeter

than this.

• • •

"You're not going to like this," I say. Wayne and I are sitting at an ordinary diner; I'm drinking a pitcher of water and eating cantaloupe and melon and French Toast.

"What?" He stirs his coffee.

"I'm out."

He lets his spoon clink on the side of the coffee cup.

Wayne's face compresses, tightens. I've only seen this twice before—once when he couldn't get it up; the second time when he thought he accidentally gave me sour milk (we were training).

His fingers interlock and he starts in on a speech designed to sway me in another direction. "Just because you won doesn't mean we can rest on our laurels. You should at least test yourself, shouldn't you?"

I tell him I'm emptied out. I have nothing left to test.

"I didn't feel anything in winning, Wayne."

I tell him I need a break, but he can't swallow that. Or at least that's what it appears.

Back at the hotel I'm packing up. He makes a grab for my wrist, but I elbow him in the groin.

"You stand over there," I say.

For some reason he listens to me.

I back out of the hotel room. Then I bolt.

• • •

In the very back of my mind I suppose I still consider reentering the food competition circuit. I know I can go a lot further than I already have. But recently I've been reflecting on the nature of competition itself—mostly negatively.

I don't like aspects of my own impulses. And yet—can I help them?

My husband and I eat light. I convinced him to go on a mostly fruit and vegetable diet—supplemented by a light smattering of the other food groups. Usually this means cottage cheese. I light candles every night and we eat in the flickering half-light. It's romantic. I haven't told him about Wayne. But that was the old me—the competitor.

If I feel competitive, now we play a video game.

I like thinking I'm retired now, in my food competition dotage. Mainly. My husband and I hold hands a lot. He doesn't know why I squeeze them particularly tight. But I do.

Queen Bee

737 Pounds

Kelly died of cardiac arrest after eating three steaks, a dozen hardboiled eggs, and a bag of sour cream potato chips—her favorite. She took a long drink of ice water, and it was as if she were suddenly struck in the chest by a hammer. She couldn't breathe. She clutched at her heart, deep within the fatty recesses of her chest. Her liver was also failing, as she knew. As her consciousness receded, she wished she could peel back the layers of fat, massage her heart, hold it gently until it calmed—a baby bird. She thought this.

Kelly could still taste the potato chip salt on her lips. She licked them one last time.

For a long while she knew it would happen in this way. Could not be avoided.

"Take your time," her father told her once. She eased into it. She accepted it. The ceiling peppered with black dots. The blackness ate the gaps of whiteness. She wished she was sitting, but she wasn't. She was on her back, too large to move. Kelly thought of a queen bee. That's what she was to herself. If only I could admire myself, she thought. If only I could. Except she lacked soldiers. Without drones she was a queen bee craning her neck, tongue lolling, heart screeching, stopping.

• • •

632 Pounds

"Hiya, Kel," her father said. She lay in a half-sleep. No energy to move. Her limbs felt weighed down by ten cinderblocks. She was glazed in sweat. She could smell her own fetid body odor, streaks of sweaty fecal matter underlying the flaps of fat she couldn't quite reach. The bedsores wouldn't kill her, she knew. If they became infected that would be a large problem. But to take a shower she'd have to find a way to lift her body. And she'd have to (somehow) fit in the shower stall—no easy task. Baths were even more difficult.

"Hey, dad," Kelly said. She could hear his keys jingle in his pocket, his feet on the stairs. Job two, she knew.

He popped his head in, around the corner. If he felt disgust he didn't say a thing. He would make a good poker player.

"Guess what."

"What?"

"They won't need me tonight. Schedule mix-up." Aardvark Security—his second job. Even though she didn't like the sins he committed, she admired the way he attempted to rectify. She knew he felt loads of guilt for his financial mishandlings. It wasn't wise.

But now he was manning-up.

Breathe, she told herself. Breathe deeply.

"I need a shower," Kelly said. "But I can't seem to…can't find a way to get up."

Her father held her arm and tugged with all his might, but this didn't help. Kelly didn't budge. It was difficult, physically. It was difficult psychologically. Tired, he eventually gave up. He fetched a tarp from the basement, and he unreeled the garden hose inside and up the stairs. Kelly was able to shift her body in such a way that her father could slide the tarp

192

under it. He put the setting on "mist." Kelly tried to position her arms in such a way that he couldn't see her intimates—a near impossible task. He averted his gaze. Kelly averted hers.

It doesn't matter, she knew. It felt good, and it was necessary—all that matters.

After the pork chops and mashed potatoes and gravy dinner she polished off a tray of chocolate cupcakes. She downed a liter of Dr. Pepper. He's a good doctor, she thought. Maybe the only doctor who can help me.

563 Pounds

Breathing for Kelly became a serious burden. She could barely lift herself from bed in the morning. She ignored the phone messages from C-mart. No way she could stand for eight hours anymore. She told them about her disability.

"Being a fat ass ain't a disability," Mr. Stokes said.

If she had the energy to hire a lawyer she would've. But she didn't. Or the money. So she stopped going to work.

She ate bag after bag of sour cream potato chips, then cookie dough ice cream, washed down with root beer.

She hoped her father wouldn't be too mad at her for the lost income. When she told him he said, "Well, okay. It's just temporary."

"Yeah, I hope," Kelly said. "Hope so."

"You wanna go for some of those popcorn shrimp tonight? Make you feel better."

He was singing her song. In heaven she wanted a Red Lobster, a booth always available.

498 Pounds

Kelly usually didn't smoke but Brandi was, and since they had nothing else better to do in the break room anyway, she figured why not?

"They're really bastards, aren't they?" Brandi said.

Kelly lifted the cigarette between her thumb and forefinger. Brandi laughed, said she was holding it like a blunt.

"Ladylike," Brandi said, showing her how to insert the filter between her middle and forefinger. "Like this."

Kelly chewed on a Snicker's bar.

"Yeah, I guess so. Nobody likes a chubby girl."

"I do," Brandi said.

"You think I'm fat?" Kelly said it serious, threatening.

"No. Well, you know…" Kelly laughed.

"I'm just playin' with ya. I know what I look like. But I ain't getting one of those stomach-staple jobs or lipo or some bullshit. It's wrong. Dangerous too." Brandi nodded, scuffed her shoes.

"So what are you going to do?"

Kelly flicked her fourth chin, rippling her face.

"I'm going to just do what I'm doing for now. Survive. Just like anybody else."

"Come in here, waste my life."

"Oh shut up."

"You shut up."

She popped the last nub of Snickers bar in her mouth and chewed. I think I would just about die without chocolate, Kelly thought. Half an hour later she ate another Snickers bar when nobody was looking. She stood at the cash register and chewed and chewed.

458 Pounds

Kelly's sense of dejection spidered in many directions. She felt dejected for living at home again after three plus years on her own, independent. She felt dejected because she was

194

smart enough to get accepted at the elite liberal arts college, but lazy/stupid enough to find herself withdrawing as a result of her own moronic fatness. She felt dejected that she couldn't exhibit more willpower, that she didn't have more fortitude. She felt dejected that a boy hadn't touched her in a long, long time—at least since she crested three-fifty. Her heart sagged.

Her belongings were in her Jeep—her step-mother drove that. She slumped in the back of her father's car. Kelly's step-mother hit the ignition and drove around the corner.

"It'll be okay, honey."

She picked at her fingernails. This was one of those times when she missed her mother something awful.

"Is there something you want to hear on the way back?" Her father pulled out onto the street.

"Something mellow, I guess," Kelly said.

Her father put in James Taylor's *Greatest Hits*—a CD they used to sing along to when Kelly was in elementary school.

Kelly watched the old brick buildings pass by. Then the pine trees. Then the wildflowers. It was October. The air was sweet and dry.

396 Pounds

"Look at me," Kelly said. "I'm *disgusting*. I look like a fat sow."

"No," Danielle said. "That's just what they want us to feel. We are the Other in the culture of thin. We're the new blacks. Skinny people are the racists."

"I hate when you talk like that," Kelly said.

"It's true. Fat power, motherfucker! What you need is a heavy dose of fat acceptance. Love yourself, will ya? Anybody who can't…."

"I know."

"Fuck 'em."

Danielle was her best friend in the newly minted fat studies program. Danielle, however, was much more brash and aggressive than Kelly could ever hope to be. She had eyebrow piercings, a tattoo on her shoulder. Danielle had done heroin a few times. She bragged about how she didn't get hooked. Not the addictive sort, she said.

"Easy for you to say. I got about two hundred pounds on you."

Danielle didn't have much to say to that. She opened the top drawer of her desk.

"I have friends who want to say hi to you."

She tossed a two pound bag of M&M's to Kelly. It felt like a bag of pebbles. This part of Danielle both frightened and exhilarated her.

She suddenly had the urge to kiss Danielle. The fat studies program taught them to indulge, to do what they desired. Let society judge them how it wishes. "Fat is beautiful"—and all that.

Kelly eyed the bag, with its personified, colorful smiling candies. She opened the bag and took a fistful, then another. Danielle did the same. They finished it in ten minutes.

315 Pounds

The summer before her sophomore year of college Kelly worked at her aunt's snowball stand. It was hot and sticky that summer and being obese didn't help. She felt constantly overheated, sweating. The shaved ice helped, but only a bit. Ice couldn't cool her down quickly enough.

Aunt Julia thought it would be a good place for Kelly to work—snow cones were not too caloric, and she'd get a chance to interact with people. "You could use a friend or two," Aunt

Julia said.

Kelly had heard it all before—she should diet; she should work out—go to the gym (even though she hated working out). She was tired of wearing homemade clothes because she couldn't find—or afford—plus sizes. She wished she had the metabolism of her cousin Amy, all one hundred and six pounds of her made her sick. But she didn't t tell any of this to Aunt Julia. Kelly let her aunt's comments roll over her.

That summer Kelly organized her childhood room. It was an experiment in self-loathing, regret and anger. She looked at her little fat girl pictures from elementary school and wished she could have it all back—that body, that innocence. Kelly hated even the memory of picture day with a passionate intensity.

One July afternoon Chad showed up at the snow cone stand. There's no way he tracked me down, Kelly thought. She spied him before he saw her, so she at least had time to mentally prepare herself. Unfortunately, she was the only one working the stand. Aunt Julia preferred them working in pairs, in case the line got out of hand, but Amy was on vacation in the Bahamas. Kelly was doing double-duty.

"Can I help you?" Kelly said flat, hoping maybe Chad wouldn't recognize her.

"Oh, my fucking God," Chad said. "It's fat ass Kelly. You're so fucking fat I didn't recognize you at first. Jesus, it's like you ate a replica of yourself. You're huuuuuuuuuge."

The woman standing behind Chad shushed him saying, "There are children in line." Chad ignored her.

"Fucking lard-ass Kelly. What're you doing' here? Have you drunk all the syrup?"

"What can I get you?"

Chad eviscerated her—another five minutes of insults intended to make her cry or jump off a bridge. She thought perhaps by virtue of graduating high school he had matured. Apparently Kelly was overly generous. When he ordered his chocolate raspberry he asked her if it reminded her of anything. He grinned.

When she returned home she opened the window and screen, tossed the family bathroom scale onto the lawn.

"I'm going on a diet," she told her father.

"Good for you, Kel. I'm proud of you."

She wished she could exercise. She wished she had the gumption for it, the innate desire. She just didn't like sweating. Sweating made her feel somehow fatter, even more miserable.

264 Pounds

Kelly wondered if she just set the record for the fattest eighteen-year-old. Her father told her she was gorgeous, but she could see the truth behind his eyes.

"Back in the 1700's larger women were more fashionable. Look at Rubens.

So she did. She went online, clicked on various Rubens paintings. They were prettified, she thought, glamorized. Yes, the women *were* large—they had bellies and fatty breasts. But she was fatter than they were by a wide margin, she thought. These women are just *hippy*, Kelly thought. I'm *huge*.

Her father and step-mother took Kelly out after graduation. She thought they would just take her to a Chinese restaurant or something subdued. Instead, they took Kelly to her favorite—La Casa Bella—an elegant Italian restaurant, with the works. That night she ordered gnocchi and eggplant parmesan and veal piccata. Nobody pointed out that she had three entrees. When they returned home there was cake and ice cream. Then the coup de grace—the Jeep (slightly used) parked around back to help Kelly get back and forth to and from Williamsburg.

"All that extra space for your stuff!"

It wasn't until a few days later that Kelly realized that her father must've known that she could barely fit into her Civic any longer. At the moment it didn't matter.

"I love you, Daddy," Kelly said.

"I love you more than anything in the world, Kell," he said, kissing her forehead.

198 Pounds

"Hey, Jabba the Hutt," Chad shouted from behind her. Kelly ignored him—it was the best option left really. What could anyone *do* now?

He threw something at her. It went whizzing into the forsythia. A pen? A pencil? A ruler?

"Why don't you talk to me anymore? Aren't we *friends*?"

Why was her father never there to protect her when she needed him? She would love to see Chad get his, but who would give it to him?

He was only a few steps behind her now. She felt nauseous. He'd catch her in a minute, and then what?

Kelly decided she needed an out—something other than ignoring him. Otherwise it could end up worse than before.

"I don't feel good," she said.

"Probably from the three fucking pizzas you ate at lunch, you lard-ass hog."

She bent over. Skunk defense-or something akin to this. She mustered up her loudest fart and then, still bent over, stuck her finger down her throat. The only tragedy, Kelly thought later, was that the vomit didn't land *on* Chad. Splattering from the sidewalk onto his leather boots was a decent second, however. And the smell—the stench of stomach acid.

"Disgusting," Chad said immediately. "You sow."

Kelly stayed bent over, watching Chad wipe his boots with leaves. He walked back where he came from.

164 Pounds

In eighth grade Melissa told Kelly that Chad was kinda cute.

"I think he likes you," Melissa said. This was in science lab, over a Bunsen burner.

Chad didn't call her names in eighth grade. He pinched her and snapped her bra. He grabbed at her pigtails. He whistled. He told her she had a "juicy butt." He told her he wanted to kiss girls just like her. Chad was short in eighth grade. Kelly leaned over him, and had breasts. This is what he meant, she speculated. Big ones.

One day Kelly found a note attached to her locker. It read, "Kelly" in all capital letters.   There were two stick figures. The male stick figure was on top of the female stick figure, his angry stick penis jutting forth—proportionally as long as his arm. The female stick figure had her arms thrown up helplessly. In the cartoon bubble the single word "No" leapt off the page, leaking from Kelly's mouth. The male stick figure was grinning. His teeth looked raggedy and sharp, fang-like.

133 Pounds

On the first day of her first year of middle school Kelly brought a bag of grapes and a butter sandwich. Her lunch was in a pink and purple lunch bag. Her mom packed it for her and enclosed a note on a heart-shaped piece of paper which read, "Love you, Kell!"

When Kelly returned from school she told her mom all about her first day—about the friends from the old elementary school she saw; about her teachers; about recess and the building and the positive feeling she had about her new classmates.

A small bag of Hershey's Kisses sat on the kitchen table.

"That's great, Kell," her mother said. "You're doing so well. I'm proud of you."

Kelly sat at the kitchen table and drew and her mother told her stories of growing up in Colorado. To Kelly Colorado seemed like a world away, and faintly exotic. The biggest mountain Kelly had ever seen was maybe three thousand feet max.

"Those would be considered hills out there," Kelly's mom said.

Kelly's mom talked a lot about how she missed Colorado, the open space. She said she never felt claustrophobic out there, like she did in the East sometimes.

As Kelly drew, she looked up. She watched her mom stare out the window. Her eyes looked off into the distance. Kelly watched her mom staring.

There was nothing she could do about it.

Kelly dropped her drawing pencil. She reached into the bag and unwrapped a Kiss. Then she ate another. Faster than she wanted to.

Shards

It's shards. We are a conglomeration of them—a mosaic. The shards aren't painful. It's the simple actuality—the structure of my existence. I'm describing what is there.

I lick his wounds. The trails slice him up, summers. Briers and thickets. He returns slashed and lined. He disrobes and I tongue his gashes. Five licks for a small one, ten for a larger one.

"Mama bear," he says.

Even his blood tastes sweaty.

• • •

When I was young I wanted an older man. It wasn't a father figure thing. I had a wonderful father. I just wanted an older man to take my life in his.

Now that I embody my own ambitions I want the product of it.

• • •

We're in the maternity ward.

I point to the mothers, the babies.

We don't speak.

He knows my thoughts on this. It would unite us. He won't allow it to happen on its own accord.

• • •

Once I tried the sexless route. We ceased the act—something I didn't need anyway. This provoked destruction.

"I don't feel for you," he said at our lowest.

We tried the sexed route—every option. There were obstacles.

. . .

"There was one," he said. "He had almost an adult face. It was something to see."

"I remember my father telling me the man I will marry will be the one who taps my maternal instinct. The one who makes me feel womanly."

"No, I get that."

"I want to come back to Earth."

"And this is the way to do it?"

. . .

I dream of a boy with a tree growing from his mouth. And on this tree a man lived, deep in the branches of the tree. This man wept every morning knowing his condition, a hermit living in a tree within a boy's mouth. He was burned by self-awareness.

. . .

"I'm not going to propose," I say. "It's not how it's done."

"Okay," he says. We are sitting in traffic, unmoving. Four lane highway. A dump truck sighs diesel exhaust upwards. We close the windows.

He snorts. "What do you really know about me? What does anyone know about anybody?"

"Is it really that dire?"

We sit staring at the bumpers in front of us.

He calls me from the forest. He says he's going to New Mexico for work and doesn't know when he'll return.

"That's fine. We'll work it out. Don't worry."

I hear him breathing, just breath.

I can hear the songbirds.

"Will you be back tonight?"

"I don't know."

I lick my arm. It is devoid of cuts or sweat.

• • •

There is a forest of basketball hoops. I saw them down and a man walks behind me to collect them as they fall. His court is loaded with decapitated basketball hoops. The wheels squeak and I walk in front of him.

He was once a forest fire fighter dropped into fiery wastelands to save the land. He told me that nothing was so exhilarating as this. It cleared his head.

He is not afraid of commitment. He is not afraid of companionship. He's afraid of these moments of wildness.

• • •

He calls from New Mexico to inform me he's staying there.

"I'm my own man really. You know."

I want to tell him I'm pregnant. My trapping instinct runs high.

I listen to the background noise. It sounds like traffic congestion—honking and whirring truck wheels.

"Where are you?"

He doesn't pause.

"Down the street."

"Why did you tell me New Mexico?"

"I'd *like* to go back."

"So go then."

"Someday."

· · ·

People drift. There's no tragedy here. Our wants often collide with the brick wall of reality. New wants emerge.

I close my eyes and the tree sprouts. The hermit living in it has his head buried between his knees. In his mouth a seed grows. I watch it emerge and bristle with leaves. And I know this sprout will become a tree and on this tree another man will live and then someday a tree with sprout from his mouth and so on and so on and so on.

I am light. This is the upside of wreckage. So light a brisk wind could carry me over the sea.

The Caretaker

I am a volunteer at the county park. Once a week I drive fifteen minutes to the wooded, twenty-five point seven acre lot
which features tennis courts, a soccer field, a basketball court,
a skateboarding "zone" and trailheads for hiking and biking,
which lead cross-county, Northwest, roughly along the path
already carved out by the power lines.

I enjoy the caretaker gig. It distracts me from my rather
mundane day job (I am an appraiser). It's not a job I dislike.
It's not, however, a job which inspires me. I was, in a previous
incarnation, a kind of local celebrity. I once was the traffic
reporter for the local go-to radio station. As a result, every
ten minutes I was in the public ear—a kind of human gnat
(though with a helpful bent).

But back to the enjoyment facet for a moment.

I enjoy volunteering as a result of its purity and utterly nil
expectations.

--Purity: since I don't receive compensation for my services, I am highly appreciated no matter how little I accom-
plish. I feel "good" about myself before, during and after. I
find it cleansing.

--Low expectations: I "check in" to the rec center and
they inform me what needs to be done vis-a-vis the physical grounds—sweeping debris, picking up leaves or garbage,
painting over graffiti. They are grateful for whatever I do. If I
don't finish, they shrug and thank me anyway for helping. It is
a demonetized experience.

When I die I want my ashes sprinkled over the grounds of this park.

• • •

One day I am at the park shoveling snow. The tennis courts are covered with about four inches of heavy, slushy stuff. It's moderately cold, but I'm working up a sweat, as one does. It's bright and sunny.

I was so focused on the job at hand I didn't bother to notice my surroundings (unlike me—I'm usually hyper-aware). I look up; there's a man on the sidewalk which connects the courts to the parking lot and other park facilities. He's outside the tennis court fence. I'm inside it (obviously). He has his thumbs hooked in his jeans belt loops. His legs are spread far apart and he wears a red and grey flannel shirt. He wears light tan work boots—the generic kind you might find at Wal-Mart. He wears sunglasses. No hat or gloves or coat. He manipulates his mouth slowly, as if he's chewing on a toothpick (I don't see one).

It's creepy as hell.

I am surprised by his presence. There's nobody else out here and the guy is just standing there watching me.

I lower my head just a bit and stick up my hand in a peaceful, howdy-pardner manner. I smile.

"Hey there," I say. "Nice day, isn't it? A bit warmer than yesterday." I sound idiotic.

The guy just stares at me. He doesn't register this one iota. He continues staring at me, chewing his toothpick or Chiclet or cud, or whatever psychotics chew. Sticks and bark.

• • •

I used to be a male babysitter. I didn't think of this as

peculiar at all. At the time it was just another means by which a fifteen year old kid could make money—one of the only ways aside from lawn mowing, snow shoveling and other odd yard work gigs. In retrospect, however, it seems truly bizarre. What parent in their right mind would leave little six-year-old Joey alone with a pimply fifteen-year-old *dude*? It was a more innocent time. Or they were just, for some reason, fond of me, for reasons unknown.

Around fifteen I began to discover my affinity for electric fans. I'm talking window or oscillating, not ceiling fans. Ceiling fans don't properly disperse the air flow; they just churn meaninglessly, circulating the air without truly refreshing anyone. I discovered that if I turned my window box fan on while I slept, I never woke up. I slept peacefully as if nurtured inside a shimmying womb of slightly rattling white noise.

I always sleep with a fan now. If I travel, I bring a fan with.

• • •

So I go back to shoveling the snow. My thinking is that if I ignore the psychotic, he will either freeze from inactivity or from boredom—either way I will thusly find myself again with only the woodpeckers and grackles watching. I can deal with them. I tell myself not to freak out. I focus on my methodology, in some kind of Zen reenactment exercise. On such a large flat plain I find it generally more effective to "plow" with the snow shovel than scoop and toss. Also, though the scoop and toss method is more rewarding—as a result of the expanse—I must toss the snow for some considerable distance. This is neither good for my shoulder nor is it efficient. The "plow" method is energy conserving, and it also has the added benefit of reducing perspiration—always useful on a cold day.

I glance up and psycho lumberjack is still eyeing me like

there is no tomorrow. My mind goes all whirligig:

--Is this a house owner who has hunted me down over a low appraisal? I heard the Prince of Qatar lives somewhere in Shady Woods. One of his henchmen?

--Does this guy envy my caretaker position and secretly want in on the shoveling? If so, he can spell me. I have no ego at stake in this.

--Is he on a rape and pillage mission? If so, can I outrun him? He looks a bit chunky in the middle. But I have ridiculously clunky snow boots, which would hamper me.

--Why didn't I listen to Katrina when she told me to purchase a damn smart phone? This was her parting shot, as a matter of fact. This absurd scenario could certainly be an ad for Verizon or whatnot.

--Do I remember any Tai Kwan Do? I made it to…was it the green belt? I think it was the green belt. Maybe it was the yellow belt. That was still pretty good for somebody who didn't care much about self-defense.

--If so, how do I go about dislodging the chainsaw or switch blade or ball-peen?

• • •

Recently I've been losing things. I don't mean forgetting things—my memory is clean. I mean misplacing them.

--The keys.

--My wallet.

--The latest issue of *Harper's Monthly*.

--The chicken I bought for dinner.

--My glasses.

--My car. Where *did* I park it?

--My boat (canoe). Where did I leave it?

--My house (e.g., vacation cabin).

Over the years I've always been ultra-reliable. Perhaps I've exposed myself to too much sun. Perhaps I'm simply growing distracted and flaky, though I don't think of myself as such.

Someone told me recently that he only in all probability has eighty dental appointments left in his life. He explained that this is assuming he goes for a biannual checkup and that he lives an additional forty more years—which is to say, he could be *overestimating*. As he admitted, it's a terrifying, macabre thought. It shook me.

I linger on these insights too much. My mind floats. This is why I lose things.

As a side note, I'm thinking of patenting an invention: a digitalized "sticker" which can be affixed to any household object linked to a central sensor. As with a car or a cordless landline, you press a button and the item beeps—you find it that way when you lose it. It's not an altogether bad idea.

• • •

I'm even about to blurt out my sensor invention idea to Red Flannel Shirt when something happens: another caretaker walks down the path. It's Ratty, or so he likes to be called. Ratty is a chain-smoking thirty year-old Korean guy who lives with his parents and spends most of his time out at the tennis courts. We're friendly.

"What's going on, Fred?"

He's trudging laconically, almost *digesting* his unfiltered Camel. He makes small slurping sounds. Ratty has two red shovels. He brushes past the psycho and onto the half-shoveled court.

I wish he hadn't used my name.

"I'm glad you came out," I say, pointing at the starer with my eyes.

Ratty exhales smoke from the side of his mouth and smiles. "Yeah, *that* guy."

Our voices are down to a whisper. Ratty is usually a shout or upwards.

"Do you know him?"

"I tried to talk to him," Ratty says. "But nothing doing. That's just the way he is."

"What does he want?"

Ratty shrugs and does his Ratty sardonic laugh. As if to say, Fool, what do any of us *want*?

• • •

I've never liked being watched. It's the pressure of eyes. I can feel them crawling up my skin. It's why I'm pee shy. Can't use a urinal unless I'm guaranteed a pee in solitude. Usually it's not worth taking a chance—someone will walk in. Concerts and plays are a nightmare. I just hope I get lucky and find an open stall.

This is another reason I like the caretaker gig. The moss and lichen don't have eyes (I'm fascinated by moss and lichen). Even animals with eyes are fine by me. Sometime I'd like to dabble in beekeeping. Those eyes wouldn't bother me. This, by the way, is despite being stung many times—most notably dozens of times by yellow jackets in 1979. I'd imagine bees would calm me—the animal equivalent of fans.

• • •

Ratty brings food. Sometimes Kim-Chi, other times cold lasagna in a sandwich bag. Oranges. Grilled potatoes. Whatever he can snag from his mother's fridge.

He hands me a hardboiled egg. He has one, also. He says his mother gave him the eggs in lieu of a sandwich. He doesn't use the word "lieu."

We don't know where to crack them. Maybe the back of the shovel, but given the dirt, I reconsider. I opt for my head. So I tap the egg against my skull, then peel the shells off into the snow.

If Charles Manson didn't have much to watch before, the sight of two men cracking eggs on their heads might capture his interest.

Ratty sprinkles some salt and pepper on his from little packets he swiped from Burger King. I decline. Good eggs, though just a tad dry (I prefer mine with a dab of mayo).

The guy hasn't changed position. Still staring holes through us. Perhaps he's a mime, I realize. A living statue. A performance artist. It's a real possibility.

Ratty and I shovel. He gets one side of the court, I get the other. I'm plowing. He's scooping and tossing. It's easier with Ratty there; I disappear into my labor.

When I look up the starer is gone. Poof.

• • •

When the weather warms-up the starer reappears every so often, freaking out the ladies in particular. Several threaten to call the rec center desk, call the police. Several do. The starer doesn't negotiate; he refuses to react to what others say.

He unnerves the park patrons as they go about their daily activities. Nobody knows if someone who may or may not mean them harm is watching. He's a specter.

I'm out there one afternoon in April when couple of tennis players confront him. "Get lost, freak! Go back to your freak nuthouse where you belong. Stop bothering us."

He doesn't move. He doesn't speak or protest. I almost feel

bad for him. He's the Gandhi of stalkers.

But something somebody said must have stuck because by May he's gone completely. I ask around and nobody has seen him. I haven't, in my limited time at the park.

By August I almost miss him. It's hot and humid and a little oddity might keep me alert, I think. I wonder if I almost needed the threat of him.

In September I stop by the main rec center and on a whim ask about the starer at the front desk—ask if anybody has heard about his whereabouts. One woman shakes her head and says she has no idea. The beefy guy at the computer lifts his head.

"No, didn't you hear? He was killed by a train some point in the summer. He apparently was standing on the tracks and didn't move out of the way. He wouldn't get off the tracks. The train ran right over him. At least this is what I heard."

The Lone Caucasian male

Nest Egg

At forty-eight Elliott Gurney had accumulated $953,608. As a younger man he was frugal, never spent much on cars or vacations or electronics. He used to run contests with friends to see who could spend the least amount of money on food. He knew he could afford to retire, at least test the waters of retirement. Live off his pension and investments. This is what he worked twenty-five years for—EPA. He did well; he considered himself fortunate.

On June 1, Elliott submitted the retirement papers, put forth his notice. Two weeks later Elliott considered himself unshackled, a free man. He bought an inexpensive bottle of Chilean wine (he didn't like champagne), ordered pizza, and watched a PBS documentary. He fell asleep by 10:37, reading the latest issue of *National Geographic*—as if asleep in a chaise lounge by a pristine azure pool.

Chaise Lounge

For decades Elliott listened to the sounds of the Thistle Bush, the neighborhood pool. Saturday mornings he could hear the bullhorns, the screaming parents, the cheers. On hot summer afternoons he could hear the sounds of teenagers playing thumping volleyballs, goofing around. The pool was located on the other side of a stand of the county park which ran through the neighborhood.

For all these years, however, Elliott had never set foot in the pool—never even walked into the entrance. As a bachelor (sans children, of course), there was no reason to join. Elliott considered pools to be for families and children.

As a new retiree, Elliott decided he'd like to spend some afternoons at the pool swimming and reading. It would get him out of the house for a few hours. It would be something different. The next day he paid his $450 membership fee and positioned himself in a yellow and green chaise lounge—wiping down the dewy seat first. He bought a can of iced tea and read an issue of *The Economist*. His thighs stuck to the rubbery plastic. The can sweated. Elliott felt fifteen again. His eyes skirted; it was a wonder.

Eyes

When he lifted his gaze from his article on traveling in Sumatra (he adores travel articles, though he hates traveling himself), he noticed the eyes. In the pool were women and children. In the adjacent baby pool—women and children. The lifeguards were college girls. Aside from the kid at the snack bar he was the lone male representative. Returning to his article, Elliott was aware of a presence in front of him, on the other side of the magazine.

"Excuse me, sir," a female voice uttered.

Elliott drooped the pages of the magazine. A young woman—early thirties, most likely—stood in front of him, shielding her eyes from the sun with a plastic shovel. She was wearing a lime green t-shirt over her blue one-piece. She was eager-looking, on edge.

"Hey," Elliott said.

"Is that your son over there?" She pointed to a boy spasmodically doing jumping jacks by the diving board.

"Um, no," Elliott said. "I actually don't have children."

The woman froze in place, the yellow shovel ledge-like over her eyes.

"Oh," she said. Then she walked away.

Elliott returned to his magazine. He enjoyed magazines. One needn't expend too much time and energy reading a magazine. One could put it down at any time. To Elliott magazines represented an American virtue—streamlined, basic information in an easily consumable package.

But Elliott was aware of the eyes. The women whispered, diverted their children away from him. This single man reading a magazine.

White Bread

As a child he ate white bread every day. His mother would pack his lunch—invariably tuna on white bread or PBJ on white bread. Occasionally, if his mother ran out of tuna and/or Jelly or peanut butter, Elliott would eat a butter sandwich. The mere sight of a Wonder Bread package filled Elliott with aching nostalgia.

Now Elliott knew most schools banned PBJ (allergies) and white bread was deemed toxic by Whole Foods yuppies.

Elliott typically did his weekly shopping on Saturday evenings. Though he had to put-up with college kids going on a beer run, the checkout lines were otherwise free and the aisles easy to maneuver. Usually he would pull his cart into checkout lane five where Arika, a Muslim immigrant from Bangladesh would kindly process his purchases. He often wondered what Arika thought about the many bottles of beer and wine she had to handle on a Saturday night. He often watched her check out the parade of frat boys and their twelve packs from the local college. Someday Elliott would ask her.

Saturday nights at the local grocery store were also relatively scowl-free. It was an acceptable time for single men to shop for their food, without accompanying judgments. Yes, the mushrooms would be covered with black tarps. Yes, the pickles would be slim in the bakery department. These were a small price to pay.

Among other things Elliott bought a loaf of white bread, five cans of tuna fish. He bought celery sticks and cream cheese. At home he sliced the celery and filled it with cream cheese. It had been decades since he ate celery and cream cheese. He fell asleep at 10:37 p.m., listening to the crickets and the sound of the oscillating fan.

Oscillation

Elliott saw the woman who accosted him at the pool the next day, her head oscillating toward him. Elliott was reclining on the same chaise lounge, eating celery and cream cheese and his tuna fish sandwich. He leafed through the latest issue of *The Economist*. Elliot wasn't a pure man of habit, but he also did tend to gravitate to the habitual.

"I didn't really introduce myself last time," she said. Her hand was already jutting towards his. She took it.

"My name is Minny, like Minnie Mouse but with a Y instead of an "IE.""

"Nice to meet you."

"Likewise. The girls and I have been talking. Did you say you don't have children of your own?"

"That's correct," Elliott said.

"Do your wife and you have a membership? Or are you guests?"

"Just joined," Elliott said, hoping he could return to his article on Eastern European debt cycles. "Just me though. Not married."

By the expression on Minny's face Elliott could tell where this was headed, or at least he saw several possible scenarios, neither of which he liked.

"We don't really, you know, usually see too many single men out here with all of these children."

He knew then which scenario it would be.

"So are you saying my presence makes you uncomfortable? I'm just sitting here reading a magazine."

"Are you?" she said, inspecting Elliott. Her brow furrowed. Her thumb retreated into her palm. She was forming a knotted first, clenching it to her side.

Clenching

His stomach muscles, Elliott sat at the diner reading his *Economist*. It was 3:57 p.m. The jukebox was playing Supertramp. The only other customers were an ancient man in a yellow pin-striped suit and a young woman sitting next to him—his granddaughter?—drinking orange juice. In the booth behind Elliott a couple argued about money. Elliott could tell by the tone and bristly nature of their conversation they would never make it.

He was hiding out.

Elliott didn't like feeling the suspicions: pervert, child molester. He just wanted to be a lone Caucasian male in public, relaxing; he just wanted to be left alone. He didn't watch porn. He drove a rusted-out 1998 Sentra rather than a Benz (which he could afford). His face was scruffy (two days); his jeans had a small rip: however, he was not in-your-face sloppy or unclean.

Elliott drank a V-8. He liked this diner. This is good, he thought. This could be a safe haven of sorts.

Haven

For the Minnies of the world, Elliott shouldn't get a haven—not in *their* habitat at least.

After several days of hunkering down at the diner Elliott decided to test this theory. He found himself a chaise lounge at the pool and parked himself on it. Sure enough, Minny was sitting—legs speared into the pool, sunglasses, hand over eyes. She saw him and shook her head. She probably didn't realize he saw her, also. When she waved over to him this time, he had something for her.

"So, are you married?"

"What kind of question is that? You see my kids over there."

"And what does that mean? You could be a single mother."

"Do I look like a single mother, you unemployed prick?"

"Yes. Yes, you do."

Minny threatened to fetch the pool authorities, to kick him out of the vicinity. She threatened to call the police.

"And what have I done exactly?"

"Disturbing the peace. There have been complaints."

"By you! Lady, I'm just a guy sitting here reading a magazine."

This is what it has come to, Elliott thought. He snapped the pages of his magazine open in a huff. People and their silly hang-ups.

Magazine

The article discussed retirees who become aimless and decide to return to the workplace. Not desirable, he thought. But Elliott could understand the impulse. He could understand the instinct. Not him though; no way. He'd never call his boss and beg for his old job back just to save himself embarrassment.

He stretched his legs on the chaise lounge.

The sun felt good on his skin.

He was in the prime of his life. He wouldn't budge. They'll have to carry him away.

Which is what they do.

The Looser

Not much in life is more dispiriting to Adam Faslet than a Styrofoam cup. Inevitably the cup becomes pock-marked with teeth marks, then knocked over by a slight breeze (a person simply walking by can do the trick). He's staring at a lone Styrofoam cup on the counter in the faculty break room. It's just sitting there, stained with rotgut coffee, half-empty.

He doesn't want to go back. Two more hours of torture—it's too much. In Adam's notebook he has a count-down: thirty-two more days of teaching, and then a small, small break, then summer school. He wishes he could truly afford a summer off. His salaried friends who teach full-time can swing it; Adam doesn't have health benefits, or a pension, or any job security at all. As usual, he has to work. And he has to smile and pretend to like it.

He's staring at the Styrofoam cup as if it might offer him an answer, as if it might act as a kind of talisman, a pedagogical guide. It's 7:55, rainy and dark outside. He has a stack of research papers at home stacked ominously by his bookshelf of classics he never has time or energy to read. His weekends consist of making basic grammatical changes to essays, grading worksheets on commas and passive voice. Worst of all, he teaches mandatory night school. There his students consist of all the expelled and suspended students in the county—the violent offenders, the druggies, the bullies. A county bylaw passed five years ago required such students to continue to attend school regardless of their status at their home school.

This is Adam's second year.

The students have regular class sessions of fifty-five minutes each. They receive grades. Class sizes are small, depending—five or six students. However, each student comes with so many issues that they occupy the energy of six or seven "normal" students. They *are* the Styrofoam cup, Adam thinks. "Disadvantaged" is the word of the day. "Fucked up" is his own phrasing. Luckily, work is only four periods with a fifteen minute break in between. If he had to deal with the sociopaths for more than that, he'd lose it.

The break room door opens—Ken Cohen, the "principal" of the high school, an up-and-coming administrator with a brass knuckle mentality. The wind from the door wobbles the Styrofoam cup and it spills and coffee oozes onto the grimy counter.

The bell rings.

"Crap, I'll get that," Ken says. "You can go on."

Back to the salt mines. In his mind Adam hears the crack of the whip. The crack echoes and reverberates.

• • •

Adam loves sports. His intellectual/hipster friends don't understand, but he doesn't care. When he's grading he always has a game on. It relaxes him. He likes the sound of the cheering crowd. He likes the background adrenaline buzz. Yet Adam has a problem with competition. He thinks of himself as competitive, but when he plays tennis he usually loses. Perhaps he's not as athletic as he thinks he is. Perhaps he just can't concentrate. Maybe he has the wrong sport.

Whatever the case might be, Adam hates losing. However, it may be his only real talent. Adam is a skilled loser. If he's up 6-1, 5-0 he'll find a way to drop the second set and lose the third.

Everyone loves a loser, Adam thinks. The loveable loser. When you lose, people think you're more human. So perhaps Adam loses to gain acceptance: Adam likes being liked. Nobody really *likes* a winner, Adam thinks. They admire a winner, but only for a short while. Then they envy the winner. If the winner continues winning, he will inevitably find himself hated—usually in a backstabbing manner.

Adam likes to pontificate about intangibles, about the inevitable human quality of sports. This is what he finds so appealing in sports, in games. In a competitive society, what is more brazenly unapologetically competitive?

• • •

He has the C group diagramming sentences. They're on simple and compound sentences. Subject, verb and adjective, coordinating conjunction, direct object. Adam stands on the white board, rubbing the last sentence out, throwing up a new one. Cody seems to like it—visual learner. Amanda goes along with whatever Cody says, she's fine. Yukio has shut down and reads his comic book in the corner. Jermaine has livened-up. "I get it now, Dog." Woof, woof. Princess thinks it's stupid. She rolls her eyes and offers up delayed responses. "Whatever, this shit is gay."

Adam lets some things slide—he has to. Picks his battles. Ken tells him he needs to treat the night school students just as if they are "regular" students. Adam knows Ken doesn't mean this, however. This is just the party line—the hard line. Adam knows Ken knows that Adam does what he has to to get by. They all do. Nobody likes it or respects themselves.

"Don't take shit from them, Adam," Ken told him once. "That's why they're here in the first place."

Overall the C group is calmer than usual. No completely outlandish behavior, no bickering. They haven't called him Mr. Faglet today, much appreciated.

Adam tries to be generous and understanding. He knows they are still kids, trying to figure it all out. Some, however, are better than others. Princess is always going to be a psycho bitch (she's here for biting another girl on the cheek in the middle of a fight, Mike Tyson style—and she had a knife in her backpack). She'll do or say whatever first comes to her mind. Adam doesn't want to think her parents doomed the child by naming her "Princess," but it did not help.

Adam knows he's overly patient, to the point where he'll take more than he should. He's not sure he can help it. A month ago he found a crumpled note by the trash can which read, "Mr. Faglet is a looser." He should have the diagram that sentence, and spell "loser" correctly. Yet he knows this would be some kind of pedagogical cliché. The dumbasses can't even get their insults correct, he thinks.

Fuck it all.

Princess doesn't matter in the long game. The ones who do have a glimmer of respect and/or remorse—these are kids who made a bad choice or two and now they're (mostly) trying to right the ship. What Adam knows is that you have to discern between the dead wood and the promising—not always an easy task.

• • •

Group D is smaller, but tougher—a hard kernel at the end of his evening. All boys: Gus, Bradford, Kyle and Tyler. He gets along with Gus fine—they bond over football and Gus has an interest in playing music. He just should've never brought the pistol to school. He wasn't thinking.

The others are a difficult read. Bradford is sullen and detached—he won't cuss Adam out, but he does nothing, says *nothing*. Kyle and Tyler like to fuck his shit up. One of them, Adam is sure, started the Mr. Faglet moniker (he'd guess Tyler). They resist doing work, mock English as fagalicious and talk about pussy and pot while Adam is attempting to teach the class.

Last week Adam had to summon Mr. Cohen, who yanked Tyler out of class and gave him extra work personally in "detention" as it were, in the central pod. Didn't leave an impression on Tyler, clearly. Kyle is actually worse in some respects, throatier, harder, more vulgar. Yet Kyle follows Tyler's cue. If Tyler is at his worst, Kyle will be also. If Tyler plays nice, Kyle will as well.

"Mr. Faglet," Kyle says. "How can you diagram this bullshit? This is monkey work."

Kyle and Tyler make monkey noises and laugh. Adam knows he should stamp out the Faglet nickname once and for all, but how? And what will be the repercussions? How will they react?

"It's like put one word here, put another word there. This gay box, that gay box."

"Well, good observation there, Ty—"

"What's an obsertation?" Kyle asks. Laughing. Not only are they dumb, Adam thinks, but they play dumb on top of that.

"You know what it is."

"No, I don't know. Don't think I know anything. That's where you make a mistake. I don't know shit."

"They're just messing around," Gus says. He shoots Kyle and Tyler the evil eye. "C'mon, let's just do our work and go home."

"Oooh, you and Mr. Faglet must be having inappropriate relations? Don't you know what happens to teachers who molest?"

Adam claps his hands on the desk.

"That's it, I'm getting Mr. Cohen."

"Ooooh, he's getting Mr. Hoc-cn," Kyle says.

"I'm going to shit my britches," Tyler says in a fake southern accent of indeterminate origin.

Rough night.

By the end of it Adam is downing half a bottle of wine at the local pub and cursing his lack of professional drive. I should've been a lawyer, Adam thinks. My mother was right. The hockey game is on. Maybe there's still time.

• • •

When Adam gets home Carly is on the laptop, as usual. She's on the floor on her stomach, slowly humping a pillow, typing quickly. She has headphones on.

"Hey," she says. She doesn't look up. "Give me a minute, okay?"

Adam stands at the threshold of his bedroom watching. Carly doesn't care.

"Oh, shit—it's huge," Carly says. "Hell yeah, I want that shit in my mouth. Mmmmm. First I take the tip and I swirl my tongue around…"

Adam pivots, goes downstairs, turns on the basketball game. The buzz he has feels good, but nothing else does. A year after he and Carly got married she asked for an "open" relationship. She said that she had room still to grow, as a person, as a woman, and that she always felt as if monogamy was just a word people used for imprisonment.

"I love you, hun," she said. "But I need to strike my own balance, also."

Adam is still not sure what that means.

This was take it or leave it terrain, he thought at the time. If he said no, she'd leave him. He could feel it coming. So he took it. He never truly felt worthy of a goddess like Carly in the first place. She was so physically striking it was impossible not to feel somewhat inferior in her presence. Aside from her model-like physique—tall, elegant, Audrey Hepburn neck, gorgeous figure—she had these Caribbean blue eyes that just seemed to stare right through him.

Adam snags a beer from the mini-fridge and turns up the sound on the television to drown out Carly. He can hear her pounding the floor, almost shouting. He downs half the beer in a few gulps. A few minutes later Carly slumps down the steps in a half-sweat. Bathrobe.

"Hey, hun. How was work?"

She kisses his cheek.

"Fine," he says.

"Good day?"

She's so casual, nonchalant.

"It was okay," Adam says.

"Sorry, Phil was on a tear just now."

"I'm just watching the game," Adam says.

"That's good. I'm going to go take a shower. I'm all hot and bothered. All sticky. Don't you hate that?"

Nothing goes unstated, Adam thinks. She is like a child. And this is the life he chose.

• • •

Adam plays tennis in the mornings. He has a regular crew of guys. His Thursday morning partner usually beats Adam

6-1, 6-2 or something close. Adam has gotten the vibe from Doug recently that his partner would be better off without him, practicing with someone else.

Adam doesn't struggle with court rage like some of the other guys he knows. What frustrates him is his inability to care whether he wins or loses. Doug calls him a "good sport," but Adam thinks this is code for being a "good loser." There are moments when the ball is just sitting there and Adam hits it long. He can't concentrate. He can't see through the omnipresent fog in his mind.

Why must he always be so nice? Such a pushover. Adam knows his greatest weakness is emotional kindness, a kind of laxity which he'd loathe in others (if it became apparent), but which he himself feels predisposed to cultivate in his own behavior.

After the match, Adam says, "I think I'm going to take a break from tennis right now."

"Why? I mean, your game is coming along so nicely."

"I don't know, I just have so much else going on right now. I'm finding it...I don't know. I'm just burned out."

"It's okay, dude," Doug says. They're old friends. This has happened before. Adam knows, that on some level, Doug is likely relieved. Adam will call Doug in a month, after he straightens out.

That evening Adam goes through his boxes of old letters, re-reading ones from his childhood friends, his cousin, his sister, old birthday cards. He settles on a letter from his grandfather. It's a two page note, front and back on a piece of spiral notebook paper—the raggedy edges still cling to the sheet of paper proper. As a product of the Great Depression, his grandfather used whatever was available.

"You make sure to respect yourself too, Adam. You're the kind who can ignore your own well-being. It's important to think of others. Think of yourself, also."

This passage was buried in a larger discussion of Adam's parents and their struggles. His grandfather usually shied away from direct unsolicited advice, most likely viewing it as overly nosy. He wasn't one to stick his foot in his mouth. Adam reread the passage.

• • •

Group A is in rare form. In this case, a class of four was about all Adam could handle. The most difficult student was Andre, a head case who liked to walk around the room, spouting anything and all that crossed his mind. Not only did he refuse to do his work, but he was a direct obstacle to the achievement of others. About half the time Adam became so fed up with Andre that he summoned Mr. Cohen, who frequently had Andre in the central pod twitching to get up.

Cherelle was, in Adam's view, a nice girl underneath, but she became immediately defensive when Andre went on one of his rages. She would frequently clap her hands over her ears and mutter to herself to block out Andre. Gary and Lawrence were twins who were more interested in bickering with each other than anything else. Adam asked if Mr. Cohen couldn't separate them into different classes, but Ken wanted the twins to learn how to work together.

Andre is strutting around the room talking titties. "Your aunt has huge titties," he's saying. "Her titties are like basketballs. Huge watermelons. They're bigger than my head. I'm not that smart. Smart people got big heads. Smart people know what to do in a situation because their big head tells them. I wish I could have a big head and big titties. I'd smack my big titties all day long."

"Mr. Faglet!" Cherelle says.

Adam has had it. He picks up the large dictionary. Then he lets it go. It makes a loud clap as it hits the desk.

"Andre! Sit your ass down and *shut* the fuck up!"

The twins look at each other. Bug-eyed.

"Good for you," Cherelle says. "You tell him."

Andre freezes and looks as if he's not sure what to do. For ten second he just stands there staring at Adam. Adam stares at Andre.

Then Andre sits.

"I don't know what we're doing," he mutters.

"This worksheet," Adam says, handing it to him. "And get to work."

• • •

When Adam drives home he turns up the sound on the radio. He takes the long way home, the stands of pine trees whizzing by. Even though it's cold outside he rolls the window down and breathes the air deep into his lungs. He pulls over onto the shoulder and sits there for a bit.

At home he takes a shower. He logs onto the computer and clicks on the classifieds. There is a better way, he thinks.

He spends the evening working on his resume and crafting cover letters. He doesn't have to have the dream job, but at least something that doesn't make him miserable.

"Good for you, hun," Carly says. "Get out of that bullshit job."

He can see a simultaneous disappointment in her eyes, however. He knows she revels in his evening job, which allows her time to play. She doesn't necessarily want him there.

Even more a reason, Adam thinks.

He finds several jobs which seem up his alley—mostly editorial (boring, but at least he won't have a sixteen-year-old berating him), and he applies right away.

• • •

Three weeks later Adam still hasn't heard back from any of the jobs he applied to. After a particularly dispiriting evening of teaching, he drives to 7-11 and purchases a six-pack of beer. Rather than driving home, he drives to a local park and sits on a swing, the six-pack in the bed of mulch. It is dark and quiet, with the exception of barking dogs and crying babies. The artificial lake water laps against the grassy shore. It's not a bad place to be.

Adam tightens his jacket around his waist. It's a cool evening and the wind smacks his face and ruffles the hood of his jacket. He stares up at the hill of grass and reeds in front of him that leads up into the woods that go around the lake. When Adam hurt his shoulder, he resorted to early morning runs around the lake. Those were some of the most peaceful moments of his recent life—startling the herons and ducks in the frosty morning. Just the birds and him.

Adam has been fantasizing about hiding out in a cheap motel, just getting a break from everything. Leaving his job, leaving Carly, leaving everything. It sounds blissful—the notion of solitude and escape from obligation and pain.

He opens another can of beer and drinks from it.

Adam just wishes he had the cojones to do it, to fully break from his life.

His mother left his father when he was in college; he wonders if she had a similar thought—the need to escape. In her case though, she left his father for someone else. She had a goal. Adam knows that he would chicken-out after a few days, return to Carly and the grind of his miserable job. However, maybe not—maybe he would discover some inner strength, something to get him through. There's only one way to find out.

He wishes he wasn't so risk-averse, so tentative to embrace what he actually wants.

He finishes the beer and swings himself, using his feet to push off.

He thinks of Route 29, with all those seedy motels. There's the one which is shaped like a (moldering) ship, with a fake prow and fake mast. That's the one he would go to, if he could. He'd sail away there to a destination unknown.

• • •

He drives home, kisses Carly, who asks why he is so late. He shrugs and goes up to bed.

In the morning Adam makes coffee, reads the paper and Carly asks him what happened last night.

"I don't know," he says. "I just took a walk."

He doesn't say anything else.

When she leaves, Adam packs.

He grabs a few water bottles, some bananas, cheese and potato chips and his pillow. He drives toward Route 29, going the scenic route. He's not in a hurry. He hopes he won't be for a long time.

The Room of Sun

It was something he wanted to share with me, and he did so on a persistent basis. He insisted I spend quality time with him.

"While I have quality time to spend," he said. "I'm not going to live forever."

We lived near the elementary school at—now an arts center. In back the school had a field up a hill beyond the playground. My father would load up a large handcart with the set—the bow and arrows and target, and we'd get to work.

One day we were there. The target lay in a rectangle of sunlight but we were in shade shooting into it. I shot straight and true, or tried to. My father watched and occasionally shot an arrow or two of his own.

We walked into the sunlight to retrieve the arrows, the target, and beyond.

"I'm dying, Mitch," he said. He didn't look at me. He looked through the gnats and dandelion spores into the cool dark of the woods.

"It will only be another year or two, probably closer to one. Maybe less."

I didn't know what to say. We were never a sentimental family, and I didn't have the language to provide a salve to him. I don't think he needed or wanted that anyway.

"I'm just telling you now so you know," he said. "Things might change quickly. You should be prepared."

"Thank you," I said.

He told me the cause and I didn't say anything after that.

He said it would be painful, but that he didn't have a choice—
and he didn't.

I watched a cloud of gnats lazily follow him. He refrained
from swiping at them, though I would've.

"I need to tell you something, Mitch." Sunlight shot
through his hair.

"Yes," I said.

"I have a friend you need to see—once I'm gone. His name
was Eric, and he was a good friend to me for many years. It's
important."

My father told me that Eric won't be at the funeral, but he
didn't explain why. He said Erick would explain it all to me.

We continued shooting. I aimed my arrows harder and
straighter than before, but they all missed the target.

• • •

My father did die the next year—about sixteen months
after he told me. He died with his own measure of calm, rarely
complaining despite the pain.

My mother suffered.

There was a day when I played cards with my father. We
liked to play gin rummy together and it worked fairly well as a
game for two. During my father's waning days I let him win—
blowing hands on purpose. I don't think he could tell. When
the game was over my father handed me an index card. It had
Eric's name and address scrawled on the unlined side.

I didn't know what to say. I touched the back of his hand
as I took the card.

• • •

We sat face to face. The room was leafy, jungle-like. It
was a sort of sunroom, he said. It was filled with them. Spider

ferns. Calla lily. Begonias. Bougainvillea. He had a thin, angular face, peppered with pale freckles. His forehead was smooth and unwrinkled. His hair was thinning, but only slightly given his likely age. At least I thought he was about my father's age. His mouth and eyes bore no trace of malice or frustration. It was calm and clean; I could see the remnants of his infancy. Right down to the core.

"Your father was a rare man," Eric said. "I'm sure you know that."

He smoked a thin cigar. I usually found smoke and smokers aggravating, but Eric's smoke smelled sweet. Welcoming somehow.

"I guess I do," I said.

We drank lemon water.

"Well, he was." He paused and took a deep breath. "I don't know what your father told you, but it's fair to say that he and I were close friends for many years. This was despite everything else in his life—despite his marriage."

I didn't ask what that meant. His facial expression was neutral, shaded slightly to the downturned.

I told Eric I had something to give him, handing him an envelope from my father. I know it was money only because my mother let me see the will. She wondered who this Eric was. Eric let the envelope sit in his hands, but he didn't open it. His fingers shook slightly or perhaps it was a vent, a passing breeze from the window. The envelope sat there on his palm, as if it were a raft.

"Excuse me for a moment," Eric said. He lifted himself from the table. I could hear the whoosh of plumbing.

When he returned Eric told me. He said he and my father met when they were much younger—in their thirties. My father invested in real estate and Eric was an agent in one of the areas in which my father was interested, down in the valley. They struck up a friendship based on conversation. A good foundation. I knew some of these things, but not all.

"Your father was a great story-teller," Eric said—a fact unknown to me. In my experience my father *withheld*.

Eric said he missed my father on a deep level. A profound ache.

He selected his words carefully.

"Growing up I never...I thought maybe I would've met you," I said.

"Yes," Eric said. "I can see that. Our friendship wasn't based on the home."

Eric asked me if I would come over from time to time, to reminisce. He wanted to keep the memory of my father alive in him.

I told him I didn't mind. I enjoyed hearing about my father as well.

• • •

Over a series of meetings Eric and I developed somewhat of a symbiotic relationship of sorts.

I kept my father's word and didn't share Eric's existence with my mother.

I would drive over to Eric's house every Friday for lunch. This, Eric said, was the day he'd spend with my father also. Eric would fix lunch and we'd listen to jazz—Kenny Burrell or Dave Brubeck or Earl Hines—and eat and talk. My father loved jazz, also. I didn't find Eric's gesture sentimental, though I can see how some might. At first Eric would speak of my father, telling stories about their outings, but then he'd be more interested in listening to my stories. We'd drink wine. We'd talk like this.

"I never married," Eric offered. "Not for want of trying."

"I go through girlfriends quickly. I know."

"That's the way it is sometimes. Friends are more important," Eric said. "Longer lasting." Many cultures revered friends over lovers. I know why.

I clicked a small wedge of ice into my mouth. I sucked on it and watched a palm frond jostle.

"Friends," I said. "It's true."

● ● ●

I didn't mean to. When I saw the box I thought it contained shoes. I was housesitting for him. By this point Eric and I had become close. In some ways perhaps he was a kind of surrogate. I felt obligated to my father, but I also enjoyed Eric's company. The conversations. The memories. I realized my life was previously fairly empty without him.

The photos were intimate enough that I knew what I already suspected. I didn't need to examine them to know. What *friend* has pictures of this sort of another friend?

When Eric called the next day I let it ring through. I wasn't angry or annoyed. I was simply perplexed. However, the more I pondered my father the more sense it made. "Every man contains hidden reservoirs," the quote on his desk read. Jesus, I thought.

When Eric returned I wondered what would happen if I embraced him rather than shook his hand goodbye; if my lips grazed against his shirt what would happen? I wasn't angling, just considering. I wasn't sure I could avoid them even if I wanted to. Or that I particularly wanted to.

The leaves jostled in the sunroom. The Camellias. Fiddlewood.

"Where do these breezes come from?" I asked.

"I'm not sure myself," Eric said. He watched me watching. He watched me watching him. The sun angled through the window, blanketing the upholstery of the couch. The rest of the room was in shadow. We moved out of it.

One Toe In

Tucker is one of those guys. Workmanlike, steady but dull. He's a backslapper. He's a beer hall guy with a squishy gut— Cheez-Its, cashews and Miller. He doesn't have a particular talent or interest and he usually tries to get by on a half-assed effort. Tucker thinks of himself as "fun loving," which is often a goal as much as an effect. He wants fun. He wants a fun lady to spend time with in a fun life. Tucker is not particularly smart. He's not charismatic. Sloe-eyed and shovel-nosed—he's not making anyone's "most handsome list." It's okay. He is who he is.

Post-2008, Tucker finds himself jobless. The firm for which he put forth a half-assed effort consolidates and cuts a third of the work force. Tucker is one of the first to go.

In the beginning Tucker views his layoff as an opportunity to "find himself." Tucker goes on several small local trips. He sits on the ledge overlooking Kitterstone Falls and kicks shards of bark into the torrent. This gives Tucker some amount of small pleasure. He revisits Echo Chamber Park—a favorite of local spelunkers. He used to go there once a year or so with his buddies. He hadn't been for years. Too chunky now to navigate through tight passages, Tucker peers about the mouth of the cave and listens to woodpeckers pock the rotting elms.

The surrounding woods are patchy and desiccated from the drought. Still, he thinks, nice spot. It's relaxing to be out in the elements. Something different, he tells himself. I need to step forward with a whole new attitude.

・ ・ ・

Tucker was raised to look askance at the products of counter-cultural "transcendence"—the crystal shops and yoga classes and organic health food stores. Who needs all that crunchy bullshit? It doesn't add up to anything. It's a crock, or so he was told.

So when Tucker's friend Selim approaches him with an idea—investing in a nail fungus laser nail center—Tucker is skeptical at best.

"What are you talking about, man? There's no money in that."

Selim shifts the ladder and clambers up it to reach the next stretch of gutter.

"Watch your head, Tuck," Selim says.

Clumps of wet leaves thump around him. Tucker stares at the back of Selim's legs.

"Did you hear what I said?"

"Trust me. This is the single fastest growing component of the personal hygiene industry. Bar none. Women schedule a year out for this shit."

Selim climbs back down the ladder.

"Nail fungus?"

"Nail fungus. I know, I know. It sounds stupid."

"Weird, man. It sounds *weird*."

"Admittedly, but this is something people care about now. Women go to get a pedicure and they find out they have nail fungus. And eeek! Who wants fungus on their extremities? So they are directed to us. We'd be like a sidebar to glamour. Glamour's ugly cousin."

"So it's a scam?"

"No, it's a solid niche. It's a niche, but not *too* nichey, know

242

what I mean? It's where funky toes go to get back on the right track. It's a fear-based model, I guess. But nail fungus is a real thing. Shit, you and I probably both have it. We could use a scrub."

"But I don't *care* if I have nail fungus," Tucker says.

"But *they* do. They care a whole lot. And they're the customers, not us."

Selim has Tucker peruse the literature in the kitchen. The folder for Nail Fungus removal systems is encased within an orange and purple swirled folder, each page laminated and featuring an array of statistics and images of removal and burnishing techniques. Tucker tries to read the fine print, but he can't bring himself to concentrate. Tucker wishes Selim could just provide him with a SparkNotes version of the nail fungus literature. Simplify. Streamline—tell him what it is and what's important to think about. Life is difficult enough as it is. He wants a sandwich. A big roast beef and provolone sub, hold the lettuce and mayo. No tomatoes either.

"How much of this do I really need to know?" Tucker flicks his emerging nose hair. "Break it down for me."

Selim tries to explain that if Tucker is interested in investing in the franchise, he should at least know what he's investing in.

"I trust you, man," Tucker says. "It's good. Just tell me what's important."

Selim explains that it's a business that essentially sells itself. A friend of his is running a nail fungus center in New York, he says, and making a killing.

"All you need is a D.P.M., an assistant or two max and an admin assistant."

Selim explains that the process penetrates the nail plate

and people are absolutely desperate to have normal-looking nails again. They've tried oral supplements tea-tree oil and other topical meds. They have to do something new.

"You've seen the pictures. Who wants gnarly-looking yellow nails? It's nauseating."

"So it's a vanity thing, then?"

Selim's face erupts into a caustic smile, and he leans forward. He taps on the counter as he talks.

"*Of course* it is. On some level most medical treatments are vanity things. But also, with all the money in this area, nobody's going to walk around with yellow nails if they can help it."

Tucker feels the pull of hesitation. But he believes this is potentially just his own cautious nature.

"What's a D.P.M.?"

"A podiatrist, man. Foot guy."

"So I'd be in the foot business."

Selim nods. Putting it like that makes the enterprise seem somehow unsavory or unclean or overly minor and inconsequential. It seems like entering into a garbage collection business focused on one particular type of garbage. Tucker tells himself not to over-think it. It is what it is.

"Sure. What the hell. Let's do it." He'll dip a toe in, why not?

• • •

Tucker never considered himself a businessman before, but NFRS has thrust him into board meetings and e-mail listserves with subject lines like: "Distal subungual onychomycosis—basic facts!" and "Beneath the nail matrix?"

In a few months Tucker goes from weapon systems to toenails. He's not sure if he can ever get a date again. What available woman—aside from marathon runners or old narcissistic biddies—want to hear about deformed toenails? He will have to construct a fictional job, that's for sure.

After several weeks Tucker realizes that it's better for all involved if he stays away from the center (Selim calls it The Fungus Stool) and simply lets his investment do the work for him. Anyway, he feels queasy looking at the images. All those yellow toenails look deathly.

Selim doesn't push him. He says he'll keep Tucker "in the loop." Tucker trusts Selim—he was always the smartest guy in the fraternity, or one of.

In the meantime Tucker knows he needs to find a way to generate more income. A thirty grand investment in toenail fungus removal won't pay the cable bill. Plus, this venture taps his savings—only leaving him with an additional five grand to cover monthly bills and incidentals.

Tucker needs a damn job. He can't *live off* The Fungus Stool—no way, no how.

The problem: zero jobs listed for his background. Zilch.

After pushing off his resume, Tucker applies everywhere—flower shop delivery guy, KFC cashier, RadioShack, barista at the local coffee shop. Good thing I'm not a snob, Tucker thinks: thin pickings. After weeks of applying, nary a nibble. Tucker even strikes out with the mattress store, and who in their right mind would want to sell mattresses all day? Finally, Tucker receives a call from Ed.

"Mr. Tucker Harris? The baritone voice exclaims, seemingly almost surprised by its own declaration.

"Yes?"

"This is Ed. Ed from Too Tall Tires. You applied for a job as sales rep."

At the interview Ed never moves from his black metal folding chair. Ed sits in front of the large matching metal desk, which, to Tucker's eyes, looks to weigh two and a half tons. Ed is dressed in a powder blue suit with matching shoes. His rust orange bolo tie is too long, reminding Tucker of a rat tail dangling from his chin. Otherwise, Ed is a spitting image of Frank Zappa with a salt and pepper goatee.

"Welcome to TTT," Ed says. "I sincerely apologize for the informality. There was a minor mishap behind my desk, making it temporarily unfit for business."

"No problem," Tucker says.

"As you may know we have what you might call a slot business. We only sell tires to monster trucks. Hence the name."

"That's fine."

Tucker shifts in his chair. The folding chairs make the business seem somehow makeshift.

"It's a tough business environment, to be frank. We're operating at a net loss right now. The lady who held your position previously—well, she got arrested. I can't tell you any more details about her at this time. But needless to say, she did some bad stuff."

"If you want the job, you're hired. It might be a lot of finger drumming, but I need someone to man the store and answer the damn phone. That's pretty much it. Nine to six every day. I have a weekend guy."

"Sure," Tucker says. "What the hell."

Tucker doesn't have anything else to do. And he needs the cash—that's for damn sure.

"No cursing in the store, though," Ed says. "No, 'damn,' no 'hell,' no 'jeez.'"

"'Jeez' is a curse word?"

"Affirmative. What do you think it's short for?"

Tucker shrugs.

"I thought it was a 'gee-whiz' kinda thing."

"No, it's short for 'Jesus.'"

He goes home and celebrates with two glasses of Miller from his fridge.

• • •

Working at TTT gives Tucker the chance to catch up on his reading. At home he has a pile of five books he's been meaning to read for the last few years. Best-sellers. Tucker thinks Dan Brown is genius. Most days he sits at the storefront booth surrounded by massive tires and reads. Nobody calls. Nobody comes in. Nobody e-mails. Nobody inquires.

Ed has Tucker update the TTT Twitter feed to enhance the effect that they are busy with customers, but Tucker ultimately just types something general and uninspired (like "it's a bright and shiny new day at TTT!") and hopes it meets with Ed's approval. Most days he doesn't speak to Ed or see him at all, though Ed sends a quick e-mail stating that he's "out canvassing!" Ed likes to always include a winking emoticon. To Tucker this seems at odds with Ed's casual retro demeanor. Who knows?

Ed was right: Tucker is bored out of his mind. Aside from reading the entire Dan Brown oeuvre he has nothing else better to do than walk around the store running his hands over the immense treads. He texts Selim twenty-five times a day every day about The Fungus Stool.

Tucker doesn't see great things coming out of this job.

• • •

Two months later: "Emergency meeting re: fiscal

situation," the subject line of the e-mail reads. This comes accompanied by a red exclamation mark signifying importance. "Shit," Tucker mutters. Selim is not one to send careless red exclamation marks.

Tucker goes to the meeting—arranging for Ed to cover at TTT by using the excuse of a "family emergency." It always worked at the third rate party school he went to downstate. In fact, Tucker is the first person sitting in the conference room. He pours himself a glass of water and enjoys the plushness of the upholstered seats—nothing so nice at TTT.

"We've hit a snag," Selim explains. "I don't know if it's the recession or what but we're just not getting clients so far. It's all marketing though, don't worry. You all know the bad news already, most likely. It's not what we thought. Vanity, apparently, is on a downswing. The fucking economy. We're taking a hit. Big. I guess nobody cares about their toes right now."

"So what does this mean for me?"

"Just hang on. Things will pick up," Selim says. "We just need to get the word out. More social media. More word of mouth. Can you help out?"

• • •

Tucker has a thinking place he has been going to since high school. He drives down the access road, past the Halliton's farm and to the pond, where he parks, and then he walks around to the small cave behind the pine trees. He sits on a rock and cracks open a Miller. The cave is littered with bottles and cans and garbage. It's not exactly a secret to Edgemont proper—but he's never seen anyone there in person, just the remnants.

He fantasizes about running away to Belize, living in a grass hut by the beach. He knows a few guys who now live in

South America or Central America (he gets them confused) and he sees their Facebook posts. Their overhead is low and they live well. The only downside is living away from his friends and family. Could he hack that?

His mother is getting older every year, and as the only child he just can't imagine abandoning her.

Tucker kicks the empty Miller can across the cave and opens another one.

He drinks the six pack and then does thirty pushups and thirty sit ups on the floor of the cave.

Feeling woozy, he drives off slowly, his arms stiff on the wheel.

● ● ●

Feeling pressured by Selim's desperate texts, Tucker takes off several days the next week to help. He takes two bags filled with fliers and begins canvasing the neighborhoods within a mile of The Fungus Stool. He slips the fliers on car windshields, slides them under doors. Tucker is not convinced this is the most effective strategy, but this is what Selim wants and Tucker is technically only a minority investor.

Tucker even does some cold-calling from back at The Fungus Stool. He doesn't like the click of someone hanging up on him. He gives up and marches into the back room where he does pushups and sit ups as fast as he can. There's a reason he never liked sales. He sneaks out the back door and heads to the corner bar.

● ● ●

"We need to talk," Ed says. "You're missing way too much time and you're making too many mistakes."

"I apologize," Tucker says. "I'm just distracted for some

reason. I'm not sure why."

"You're drinking too much, that's why."

Tucker sits there and takes it. It's not the first time and it won't be the last.

"I'll do better," he says. "I promise to."

Ed raises his eyebrows.

"I will," Tucker says.

• • •

At the meeting Selim breaks the bad news. The center would have to shut down at the end of the month—little revenue with not much uptick. Selim states that he and the other investors were "bleeding money." It is tough but he'd have to pull the plug on The Fungus Stool.

"At least we gave it a shot," Selim says. "Gave it the good old college try."

Tucker wishes Selim wouldn't phrase it like that. Tucker never finished college—that's part of the problem.

"What does this mean for me? Did I lose everything or what?"

"I'll have to crunch the numbers to give you a break-down, Tuck."

"Did I lose everything?"

Selim shrugs. That says it all. Tucker is the only one not wearing a tie.

From the car Tucker calls TTT and leaves a message resigning immediately, says his girlfriend is in the hospital and he will be wrapped up in this personal tragedy for the subsequent time.

Tucker just wants to drink and exercise and forget the rest. He can collect unemployment for the time being—that's what it's for, right? Everything else can just blur to background noise. He will achieve something, sometime, but for now he wants to be considered "retired." Let other people do the work until he figures out what he is able to handle.

Tucker drives toward the cave, a six pack of Busch in the front seat next to him. He parks in his usual spot and walks around. But when he gets there, he finds two scruffy looking men already there, smoking cigarettes on the floor. They both shoot him a nasty stare.

Tucker heads back to the car, locks himself in and pops open a can right there in it. He'll drink four more after that. The pushups and sit ups will have to wait.

Go Ahead

The sunlight through the canopy formed a pattern. The pattern reminded her of pa, the canoe, the muck beneath. The smell of river mud, pregnant with rot.

Her watch was broken; she noticed the second hand perched on the precipice of eleven. Time frozen on her wrist.

She had somewhere important to be. She had forgotten where.

She sat in clover, under the poplars.

Did she turn off the oven? The coffee maker? Sometimes she had to check three or four times, often more than this. A buzzing in her mind, always a buzzing.

Pa would take her on the canoe, on the river. They would fish for eels. She would drag chicken necks from the canoe hoping to snag blue crabs. She loved the way they scrabbled in the cast iron pot.

They would listen to the sounds of water slapping the canoe. She would daydream of boys.

Her father warned her about them. She didn't know what else to do.

"Look at the fat on your face," her mother would say. "You're *collecting* fat cells, aren't you? All that chocolate crap you eat."

She'd protest. She didn't. She just. It wasn't. Fifteen.

"You're going to look like a sow, and then what? Who's going to want to even touch a sow? Men don't like sows."

Her father, however, told her looks weren't everything, not

to get so hung-up on superficialities. She had a head on her shoulders, he said. That counts for something. Worst-case scenario, she could be a working girl.

Her father offered positive uplift. Her mother offered something different.

Then the boys.

She couldn't lay off.

Jacob and Mike and Gabriel and Ted and Chad and Gary and Edward and Fred and Bill. They made her feel so…They gave her that…They let her into…

It was a different way of being, something she didn't expect.

Intoxicating.

It was something. The sunlight in the canopy. Speckled and swayed with the wind. Her mouth was dry and yet she felt ripe with summer. She *wanted*.

Her father told her she was beautiful, just the way she was. Nothing needed changing inside or out. She didn't tell him what his wife said. He might not *want* to know. More likely— he knew and was providing counterpoint.

Everyone said how "different" her parents seemed. "Different"—what does that mean?

Now there was the man she met at the store—Brendon. He was a large guy, at the foundation. His legs were thick and substantial. Yet he was gentle, an introspective type.

When she fucked him it was as if she were on top of a butte in the midst of a vast plain. She watched for miles around from up there. Looking down onto Brendon she could see his face withdraw into a reservoir of pleasure. He let his concentration dissipate as she rose and fell. She enjoyed feeling as if she had something to *give*. This feeling was rare.

"I just like watching you," he said. Her lingerie. The sway of her body. Her movement around the room in the flickering light. "I could watch you all night. I wouldn't even have to…"

The canopy light above her. Almost phosphorescent green. The sounds of birds within it. The grass bristeled against her thighs.

She wouldn't answer when her husband called. Nick had to learn. Boundaries. The concept of autonomy. She is her own maker, she told herself. She is not beholden to him, she told herself. When she did call him back—an hour or more later—she wouldn't explain. She would just say "errands—the usual." She would sigh, as if she was put upon.

Anything but usual.

"I can't believe it," Brendon said.

She knew what he meant.

He said a woman like her—so gorgeous and sensual and everything—shouldn't even consider someone like *him*: a sack of lard, a puddle of mush.

There was no revenge in the works. This wasn't about retribution for her. She loved her husband.

But.

She couldn't resist the touch of a man who found her so intoxicating. She fed on the devotion. She wanted to feel chosen.

Look at me. Look at me, she thought. She almost said it.

She put him inside her again. His eyes were far away. Hers rolled into themselves.

"I'm home," she said. "I feel that way."

Brendon embraced her. He pulled her close. He smelled sweet—of burning cherry and honeycombs and the slightest tinge of smoke.

If he doubted her he never said. He never would.

The canopy above her filtered the light. It wasn't diffuse. It was thinned-out, watery.

Her watch didn't move. She remembered.

Brendon touched her face, held it between both palms. She could smell Brendon in her and on her still. It was a mustardy odor. She wanted only to bathe, but not yet. At first she wanted the odors to linger, to sully her. But then she wanted them to disappear down the drain.

• • •

"I've made dinner, a candlelight dinner," Nick said. She dropped her keys into the basket by the door. He did this all the time. Nick wasn't a bad husband. He was sweet and he doted. She just found him uninspiring. He seemed to do just what was expected, but no more.

"What would you like for me to say?" She knew it was wrong as soon as she said it.

"Not sure what you mean. I'm…"

"It sounds good, Nick. Let me just shower," she said. "I feel a bit…gummy."

She knew he would never guess at it. His imagination didn't carry him into that terrain. Or if it did, he would never verbalize it.

"Okay," he said. "Go ahead."

He always said that. He was laissez-faire about everything. Somewhere within her she almost wished he provided more resistance, more suspicion. It was too easy, all of it.

She also wished she could feel *some* guilt. At least the residue of guilt. She didn't. The pleasure of being watched was too strong.

Her father would disapprove, she knew. He would scold

her in the canoe, water lapping against the bow. He wouldn't lecture her but he wouldn't have to. She would receive the silent glower.

After the shower she lolled on the grass. The light grew faint. She would need to go inside eventually. She knew that. But first she would call Brendon, then Carl, then Bryan. Maybe others. Nick, he could wait.

Much later, when her mind was numbed by alcohol and exhausted, she would let Nick embrace her. They would fall asleep early, as usual. There was something comforting about this, she thought. She could listen to the cicadas as she slept. Sleep would come easy after it all, she knew that.

A Sordid Boon

The grass wafts on the median. If Annie could just ignore everything else around her—the asphalt, the gum wrappers and crunched water bottles—the filthy grass would almost seem almost beautiful, wind gently ticking through the vertical strands. Something out of an Edward Weston photograph, perhaps. The wind picks up slightly and the grass flops back and forth. Annie is so tired she almost wants to step out of her car and collapse right there in the median—broken glass and Gatorade bottles half filled with urine be damned. She wants to sleep right there, her head in the crook of her arm. What wasted beauty. Annie is so exhausted her mind drifts toward wondering what species of plants actually grows on the median. They must be a hardy sort, adapted to carbon monoxide and the detritus of humanity.

She turns off the ignition: What's the point? Traffic hasn't budged in ten minutes. This is not the ordinary tug-and-pull accordion traffic—something else entirely is going on. Annie flips the station to WTOP to suss out the problem, if she can. For three minutes the nasally traffic woman rattles off the problems encountered at one accident and construction zone after another, hundreds of stretches of barely moving cars and trucks, millions of hours of demolished time. If the station could only find a more soothing voice, one that doesn't *sound* like traffic congestion.

Time, she thinks of time. All the time.

Annie is so overworked she can't remember the last

moment she set foot outside other than to walk to and from her car. Even then it's dark. When was the last time she truly lingered outside in nature, walking around, observing the wind through the leaves? Back in May there was that company picnic—that was outside. But aside from that…? She has no idea.

Annie feels light-headed, the late summer heat already getting to her. Perhaps mild malnutrition. Dehydration. Low blood sugar. It's barely seven in the morning. She digs into her lunch bag and eats a bite of her butter sandwich. She knows she eats in her car far too often. She can't help it. The ninety minute (without traffic) commute makes it difficult to avoid.

Finally the traffic starts up again. Annie is already running late and she has 125+ e-mails to respond to, the presentation for tomorrow to complete, the Glitter Page to update ASAP before Max Snyder sees it's the same shit as last week, plus three meetings to attend, all to "maximize efficiency." How can she *be* "efficient," Annie wonders, if she's always *listening to* how efficient she should be? At some point "efficiency" becomes inefficient. She'll be lucky to get home by 10:00 p.m. and then she'll have to wake up at five tomorrow to turn around and do it all over again. Brutal.

In this traffic Annie has to turn off her audiobook before it lulls her to sleep. She could use another coffee—her fourth cup before 8 a.m. This does not bode well.

Annie makes a quick call at the next light, a hello to her mother—she meant to call her back three or four nights ago but was already zonked and the days since then have been a blur of shit. And then she checks her voice mail, which is jammed with messages from various male suitors (all for her roommate Britney—her and "Calvin" sprawled on the living room floor in their underwear on Tuesday night in pre or post-coital convolutions).

"What do you *do* exactly?" the girl at the CITA happy hour asked last night.

"You know those rodeo clowns?" The ones who steer the bulls away from where they want to run—which is right at someone? That's me."

"Do you find that humor helps you to succeed at this?"

"You are missing the point," Annie said, and then snapped off to mix another gin and tonic. When she returned to her space at the bar, the girl was gone. Annie knew her friend-making skills were surely lacking. She needed to work on this.

The girl had no idea what it was to be an adult—maybe twenty-three, some intern or Mastis ass-kissing lackey.

"*Run!*" Annie wanted to squawk. But the girl had dissipated. Snap—like that.

By "rodeo clown" Annie meant a Jackie of all trades, master of none—"a kissing cousin to an administrative assistant," Steve Phillips said once, "but not exactly." "You're the store front," George Blighton pronounced, as if shouting "Eureka!" The "big five" as the underlings (like Annie) called them—they were a confident lot. They loved their ideas and they loved themselves and they loved CITA. They marinated in devotion.

Or was it all a masquerade and any day the entire kit-and-caboodle would burst into flames?

These days Annie finds herself hoping for the latter—not that she didn't do her job and put up a good fight. She just cannot *care* any longer, on a deep cellular level. She is thirty-five years old, has worked for CITA for ten years and hasn't taken a vacation in five. She attended graduate school for art history and hasn't looked at a painting since the Bush administration. When she has a spare five minutes, she might do a

Google-image search for the Uffizi or the Met and sigh at the digital imagery. Then back to reading her e-mail. But Annie finds it easier, usually, to just ignore art and life and nature and everything altogether—pretend it no longer exists. Because, in reality—her reality—it doesn't.

CITA needs her. They always need her.

Incoming text—Lauren.

"Fucking Hammer will be there."

Shit, Annie thinks.

The Hammer is Jack Fizer, the bigwig even above the Big Five. There=the ten o'clock: the first and worst. Everyone called him "The Hammer" because he was the one to dispense the layoffs. "Lean and mean," Fizer said once. "No fat on this beast." CITA, he meant. "We want CITA to be like a fucking marathon runner. Not an ounce of intolerable blubber. Everything and everyone on board absolutely essential. It's the only way we can compete." Meaning, it's the only way he can answer to the investors and rake in his seven figure salary. CITA only has fifty- one employees, Annie discovered recently, which at $537 million up puts each employee at ten mil a piece. Not that she is seeing one-one hundredth of that.

"GR8!" Annie replies.

For the past several weeks Annie has fantasized about quitting, buying a little cheese shop in Maine or going in with her cousin on a vending machine business or selling vintage ceramic dolls online. Moving to the beach and waitressing. Barista in West Virginia. Something else. Anything.

She has a beautiful condo in the middle of the woods. She's never in it. She has a cat—Kleenex—who she never sees (Kleenex turns his tail and hides when she walks into the room). She eats standing over the sink, the disposal clogged with food from the past week. Annie doesn't read books, attend concerts on Saturday nights. No dates since April. When she is not working Annie sleeps. Even watching television takes up too much energy.

The traffic is a slog—Annie drives three miles an hour, stuck in first gear (why did she buy that stick shift again?). Hipster posing? In twenty minutes she'll hit a breakaway—in the normal spot—and she'll be able to shift into second gear. Her glutes are killing her from the sitting—a serious bout of sciatica is not long off it this keeps up. She knows the stretches—she watches them on Youtube to remind herself—but she's always driving to work or sitting at work. When can she actually *do* them? That's the problem. At midnight, when she finishes her dinner? Recently Annie has been parking at the far end of the lot on purpose, so she can at least get two minutes of extra exercise and savor a few minutes to herself.

But as Annie wastes her life creating meaningless PowerPoint slides and attending idiotic meetings where she will be chastised for not being as mindful of her client's concerns as possible, what she mostly fantasizes about is going back to that novel she started many years ago. She's two thirds of the way through it. *Leaves of Winter.* She likes the irony in the title—a story of a mother who gives up her two young children for adoption and then fifteen years later attempts to reestablish roots, if she can. Annie never wanted children of her own—she loves being an aunt, when she can—but she felt as if she really captured the character, Willa Nieve. She knows it's an obvious name, but Annie likes it regardless.

When Annie was deep in writing mode she found herself dreaming of Willa. What Willa must feel, think, her memories. She—Annie—felt alive. She had never felt more alive.

It's a lark, Annie knows—there's no money in writing. She knows. She'd be lucky to land the book at a tiny indie press somewhere, sell fifty copies. Still, a hope. Something beyond the scraps of shit she currently clutches to her breast. Annie wishes she could be Willa constantly. Now she understands the deep appeal of writing—shedding her skin, trading it in for another's.

Annie still has to cross the dreaded 212 and 186 intersection—the intersection from the depths of Hell. Annie has calculated that she spends 156 hours a year—almost a month of work—at the asinine 212-186 intersection. It gums up with sheer volume, trapped as a result of the timing of two closely tethered lights and the narrow right hand turn lane. Talk about inefficient. She sometimes feels as though she might actually *die* at the 212-186 intersection—expire right there in her car, waiting for the light to turn green, finally, so that the queue of cars in front of her can nudge forward twenty feet to wait for the next cycle. Sometimes Annie screams. Sometimes she cries. Sometimes she just sits there in muffled misery, bleary-eyed.

This morning is no different. It takes Annie twenty-five minutes to drive half a mile. She tries to explain the insanity to her rural friends—they don't believe her ("why do you live there?"). By the time Annie finally pulls into the CITA parking lot at 8:56 p.m. she is already whipped and sweaty and ready for a vacation. She has two hundred and eighteen e-mails waiting for her. She most likely receives three e-mails a minute each morning.

When she turns on her computer it takes twenty minutes to upload Microsoft updates.

● ● ●

As Annie slumps in the mundane beige wheelie chair in

conference room twenty-eight, she wonders what percentage of her brain is she actually utilizing at her current job? Five percent? Seven percent? Can't be more than ten percent for sure. She gulps the water, which tastes of warm plastic. Fantastic, now I have stomach cancer, Annie thinks.

EFFICIENCY is on the white board in The Hammer's precise, red lettering. The Hammer stands at the head of the table, twirling the magic marker between his fingers, smiling. His tie is a silk micro thread print of geometric shapes and squiggles. His tie probably cost more than Annie's entire ensemble. The Hammer's tie is likely the equivalent of an entire week's wages.

"Come on in!" The Hammer encourages, toothy smile. The Big Five sit near the head of the table, the power garland. Ten other key players sit partially or mostly slumped in their ties and power suits, trying to put a shine on this turd-to-be. Annie feels trapped in some kind of bad Baldwin Bros sausage-fest.

Still, with the efficiency mandate, Anne thinks. Like we're a cast of refrigerators and washing machines. Cut the waste!

The Hammer cracks his knuckles and underscores "EFFICIENCY" again, as if the ALL-CAPS and red somehow didn't already garner the attention of the underlings.

"Greetings CITA folk." He loves "folk." Helps him "connect" to the commoners. Annie thinks of paisley shirts, harmonicas and slowly strummed obsessive stringed instruments. "I hope you are healthy, wealthy, and I know you are wise. Otherwise (hahahaha) we wouldn't have hired you. However, we are gathered here today to talk about improvements. Which must, always, be made, folk. Still lagging in the old efficiency area, as indicated in last week's report. Folk, we can do better."

Folk.

The Hammer taps the white board with the tip of his finger.

"Let me be a bit more direct in my definition and explication of this concept, sound good? Mr. Williams? Do we have a Mr. Williams here?"

Annie couldn't believe he wouldn't know his own employees (only fifty odd).

Greg Williams raises his hand tentatively.

"Good, good, good. I'm sorry to report, Mr. Williams, today will be your last official day here at CITA. I mean, sure you are more than welcome to come in over the next few days for the various knick-knacks and picture frames and do-dads you might need to collect, but otherwise our partnership is kaput. Over. Finis, see. My apologies."

Greg sits ram-rod straight, nodding twice. He pushes his glasses up to the brim of his nose. Stoic.

"Is there something I didn't do right? Is that it? I've devoted…"

"Yeah, yeah, yeah. You've 'devoted.' 'Devoted.' Let's massage that 'devoted' idea, folk. Yes, as a matter of cause, there is something not right. Something amiss. Too much social networking on our dime. Several games of solitaire a day—again, our dime. Personal e-mail checking, browsing the Internet. You get the idea. Lack. Of. What? Efficiency," he points to the white board again. "Same work—a lot of bullshit to bide the time. If you think we aren't watching, you would be wrong. 'Devotion' is just the beginning of the equation."

"If this sounds like you, you may be next. We are not *impressed*. When at work, folk. W. O. R. K. 100% of the time, not 60% of the time. Not 80% of the time. 100% of the time.

Absolute concentration. Now *that's* devotion. Remember the clause in your contract about the use of personal gadgets and electronic devices. Same thing. You can diddle around on your time, on your dime, folk."

Annie's heard it all before—the patronizing speeches, the assumption she and her colleagues are guilty until proven innocent, the assumption that sitting in a meeting listening to reminders they've heard before a hundred times before helps anything. She simultaneously feels fifteen years older than she actually is—worn to a nub—though she is treated as twenty years younger than she actually is, a little girl who ate one too many Oreo cookies before dinner and now must belly up to the broccoli and bitter herb trough.

Poor Greg Williams though. And yet at least he's out—he's *free*. He doesn't have to answer e-mails on Saturday night any longer. She's almost envious. Annie thinks back to the time several years ago when she had a chance to buy a woman's entire room stacked with collectibles. CITA makes nothing tangible, yet here was a woman selling old books and records and Match Box Cars and autographed hockey pucks and vintage clothes and etchings. She was moving and everything had to go.

"Tell you what, buy out my room for a grand. You'll be able to make ten times that, no problem. Sell things one at a time." The woman was trying to help her.

But Annie hemmed and hawed—she'd have to rent a truck and a storage space and she wasn't 100% sure on the value of what she would be buying. It was a leap and she decided to pass. Annie still checks Craigslist from time to time—hoping for a deal, something she can flip. But she's too continuously busy to get a consistent read.

The Hammer prattled on—no more printing, no copies, no more free coffee, no more CITA-sponsored holiday party, unless 100% employee funded, and even then it would have to take place after hours and off-campus.

"We're in a new paradigm."

He loves to use "paradigm," Annie thinks. Also "interface," "the cloud," "community values"—often all at once. The new paradigm=interface with the community values cloud.

Annie feels sweaty and fat and wants a shower. And the last time she took one at work a male employee "accidentally" popped into the ladies locker room. She had to cover up with her hands, barking at the door.

• • •

The meeting finally over, Annie returns to her "work station" (God she loathes that term). The first thing she sees is an e-mail from Craig Oates:

"No need to finish the presentation—it's canceled, something about the need for more symbolic awareness on their end."

Annie stops right there, deletes the e-mail and logs off her computer.

She had spent twenty-five plus hours constructing the two hundred odd PowerPoint "slides." And now—poof—all that for nothing. She wants to heave her computer into the stupid, fake man-made lake, plug up the idiotic fountain with this waste of space.

She texts Lauren and tells Shirley, the admin assistant proper, she's had a "family emergency" and will return in a few hours.

Shirley nods—she's heard it all before, very worldly-wise, coffee klatch with a throaty smoker's voice. In her nod is an acknowledgement that she's been there, too. She *knows*, oh does she ever.

Annie sweats bullets in her boiling car, blasts the A/C and just drives. She has no real destination, nor does she really know the area around Corporate Campus 3 (another name she detests). For ten minutes Annie circles around an anonymous, bland road with little anonymous saplings from last year and sleek, anonymous corporate buildings—no shops, no parks, not even a gas station. Eventually she finds an elementary school—that'll do, she thinks. She pulls into the main entrance, circles around back near the playground, finds a barely shady spot near the largest sapling there and parks. Thankfully school is not in session.

Annie rolls the windows down a crack—all of them—and leans her seat back and closes her eyes. Sleep comes quickly.

But in the deepest throes of sleep a hard rap on the hood of her car.

"Ma'am! Ma'am! Excuse me."

She is now fully awake, if disoriented.

"Huh?"

"Are you okay?" The officer stands on the driver's side, head tilted sideways. The image is almost surreal, at least in her current state.

"Huh?"

"I saw your vehicle, ma'am, and you were asleep inside of it at the wheel. I am just making sure everything is okay."

Yes, Annie tells him—it's been a long day. She shakes her head and slaps her face. She probably shouldn't be there sleeping on school property, she admits. But exhaustion hit her, she explains, and they always say if you are too sleepy to drive….

But why did he have to wake her up at all? Couldn't he

use his common sense and see that she wasn't a meth addict or a homeless person? Everyone is constantly *on* her; she can't *breathe*. Can't people think things through before they act? The world can't even let Annie take a nap.

"Thank you, I'm fine."

She starts her engine and drives toward the entrance, buckling her seat belt as she goes. The cop watches her from his patrol car.

It's 12:30.

She knows she should drive back to Corporate Campus Three, return to the e-mails, the synergy session, the CITA bulletin and so forth. But she can't. There is no way. Her body won't do it.

She'd rather flip burgers for minimum wage.

Actually, she doesn't know exactly what she will do, but she knows what she can *no longer* do.

Annie turns right toward the interstate. She'll head North and drive until she finds a wide green space. She will find a store on the way and buy a change of clothes or two. She'll find an inexpensive motel. Nobody will know where she is and for once and her phone will be off and she won't turn it back on. She'll throw it in a Dumpster if she has to. She'll be able to breathe. She'll be able to inhale and exhale. The next morning, she'll look out over the green. When she builds the courage Annie will walk out into it. Soon enough she will let gravity do the rest. Then Annie will be where she needs to be.

Acknowledgments

any thanks to add here?

About the Author

Nathan Leslie won the 2019 Washington Writers' Publishing House prize for fiction for his satirical collection of short stories, *Hurry Up and Relax*. Nathan's eleven previous books of fiction include *Three Men*, *Root and Shoot*, *Sibs*, and *The Tall Tale of Tommy Twice*. His collection of stories, *The Invisible Hand*, was published in 2022. He is also the author of a collection of poems, *Night Sweat*. Nathan's fiction and poetry has been published in hundreds of literary magazines such as *Shenandoah*, *North American Review*, *Boulevard*, *Hotel Amerika*, and *Cimarron Review*. Nathan's nonfiction has been published in *The Washington Post*, *Kansas City Star*, and *Orlando Sentinel*. He is the series editor of *Best Small Fictions* and the editor of *Maryland Literary Review* as well as the organizer of the Reston Readings Series. Nathan lives in Northern Virginia.

Apprentice House Press is the country's only campus-based, student-staffed book publishing company. Directed by professors and industry professionals, it is a nonprofit activity of the Communication Department at Loyola University Maryland.

Using state-of-the-art technology and an experiential learning model of education, Apprentice House publishes books in untraditional ways. This dual responsibility as publishers and educators creates an unprecedented collaborative environment among faculty and students, while teaching tomorrow's editors, designers, and marketers.

Eclectic and provocative, Apprentice House titles intend to entertain as well as spark dialogue on a variety of topics. Financial contributions to sustain the press's work are welcomed. Contributions are tax deductible to the fullest extent allowed by the IRS.

To learn more about Apprentice House books or to obtain submission guidelines, please visit www.apprenticehouse.com.

Apprentice House Press
Communication Department
Loyola University Maryland
4501 N. Charles Street
Baltimore, MD 21210
Ph: 410-617-5265
info@apprenticehouse.com•www.apprenticehouse.com